NEW BEGINNINGS

ar' Ama Gedeon

by

T. D. Ree

ISBN 13-978-0-9912864-1-6

Copyright (c) 2013

Quintillion, LLC
Panama City Beach, FL 32413

Printed in the United States of America

$9.99
ISBN 978-0-9912864-1-6
50999>

9 780991 286416

This book is dedicated to my wife and daughters,
whose inspiration and love
have made all things possible.

Acknowledgments

I am forever grateful to Tammy, Marianne, Dan, Keith, Jo Dee, Amy, Mike, and Steve, for their open hearts, boundless energy, and eager assistance.

Special love and thanks to Doris and Bill, whose caring and inspiration helped start this journey so many years ago.

Contents

"History begins with the world's earliest memory. The world's memory begins at the time of first meeting with the Faeleriel. And when the first Faeleriel blooms from the Garden Tree, so begins time."

--Topper - Keeper, Caeltis Garden - 1268 C. E.

PROLOGUE

A wilderness now known as Northwest Florida - Many years ago

Duadine (the Age of Disbelief)

'The Others!'

Askuwheteauachachak Kitchi could not believe what was happening, as he ran excitedly along the coast, just within the forest treeline. His lean and tanned form moved within the shadows, nearly invisible to anyone in the open sunshine.

He looked from the forest, over the white sand, to the emerald sea beyond, amazed by what he saw.

'A ship. The Others!' he thought again.

He knew it must be a "ship", because grandfather's stories about The Others had talked of a giant canoe, which they had called "ship". It had come from the Sea of the Great Wind a generation earlier, and after it, everything had changed.

Though Ask, as everyone in the Hashakochi Iti tribe had called him since his sixth summer, ran energetically, he still ran more silently than any deer, hidden by the forest shadows, his bare feet making no sound that any man could hear.

As he ran, he looked toward the ocean inlet where the large ship had moored.

'This wooden structure floating on the water does not look much like a canoe, so it must be the Ship, and they must be the Others!' surmised Ask, confirming the possibility in his own mind.

Despite his running speed, he could see the people on board were men. Yet, they all wore drapings, garments covering nearly their entire body, even their feet!

'Strange! How can they run with such coverings and not snag on vine bristles?' thought Ask astonished.

For himself, he was pleased not to have to wear such heavy garments, since running, be it over sand, through the water, or through the forest, was one of his greatest joys. The small woven garment wrapped around his waist was all the clothing he needed.

Now Ask saw a much smaller boat was being lowered into the water. 'They are bringing a party to shore!'

'To me, Ask,' came grandfather's words into Ask's mind.

'Yes, Elu,' Ask responded. Without taking his eyes from the ship, Ask ran deeper into the forest, around trees and over obstacles, without a trip or a misstep.

He had performed The Rights and become a Man of the Hashakochi Iti earlier that summer, and at thirteen, had mastered quiet running, animal songs, flower whispers, sightless seeing, mind talking, and all the etiquette of the Gardens.

'The arrival of the Others must be an omen,' he thought. 'I have just become a man this summer. Can it be an omen for me?' This thought heightened his excitement, but it reminded him of the last time the Others had come to the Garden country. And that gave him pause.

A generation earlier, Eluwillusit Kowianu had listened to the forest and seen through the eyes of birds the arrival of the Others. The forest had been wary. None of the Others had been able to hear the song of the Earth, speak with the flowers, or see through eyes of animals. The leader of the Others had been open-minded to learning, but many of those who he had brought with him had been suspicious and refused to understand. The ways of the Hashakochi Iti had made them afraid, and the Others of that time had reacted harshly.

Eluwillusit had then decided to move the Garden, for its protection, though none of the Others had yet learned of its existence. It was because the leader of the Others was beginning to ask certain questions about the tribe which led some in the tribe to suspect the Others were planning something deceitful.

Often, the leader asked why there were no children in the tribe. There had been three children born in the last generation, and all three had been adults now for nearly sixty years, his own father one of them. The leader also noted no tribes people became ill, nor did the tribe appear to have anything in its village or its culture relating to health or care of the ill.

Though the Others had supposedly come to the Garden country from across the Sea of the Great Wind for riches of some kind, their leader soon believed that the tribe held a secret to long life and determined that this prize was more valuable than any other. The leader of the Others had announced that he was willing to take lives if needed to acquire this secret.

No one in the tribe revealed the Garden, nor would one... ever. As Eluwillusit mobilized the tribe to return to the Garden and move it to a safer location, the Others had overrun them with weapons of steel and fire. Their raid upon the village caused a great loss to the tribe.

All the tribes people were willing to accept the sacrifice knowing the Garden was safe. But that raid had been particularly costly to Ask, having lost his father that day. He was born just over six months later, the only child of his generation.

Ask focused back on the trail as he ran on, the sea all but disappearing behind trees and foliage as the ground began to rise. Ask turned his head now in the direction he was running. He could sense his grandfather's presence.

In his mind he called out, 'Elu Kowianu! There is a ship!'

No reply came back to him. Ask ran on, unafraid. He knew this was grandfather's way, always listening, always waiting.

In a moment, Ask had reached the top of the Putallah cliffs, the "Welcoming Hands", that rose over the beach and bay where the ship now rested. And there he saw his grandfather looking out over the cove.

Though his grandfather, Eluwillusit Kowianu, sat facing the sea, his eyelids were closed. Ask knew this allowed Elu, like all of the Hashakochi Iti, to see the world around them far better. To see in all dimensions, not just sight of the eyes, was perhaps the greatest gift he had received with manhood.

Ask stood behind Eluwillusit Kowianu, and having been a man for only a few moons, shifted his weight back and forth as he strained to look out at the ship.

'Sit down, Ask,' came the words from Kowianu into his mind. 'You will see farther when you calm yourself, close your eyes, and open your senses.'

Ask felt a moment of embarrassment, having been too excited to use his own skills. He did as his grandfather bid him, choosing to sit in the manner his grandfather always did, with legs crossed and hands resting on the knees, palms facing upward.

He sat and calmed himself, reached out with his senses, opened his heart and mind, and listened.

At first he heard only the wind, the bird song, and the music from the waves. Then the words from the Others came to him.

"Riches! Marquess Ponce de Leon," exclaimed the rough voice. "They say the rivers are lined with gold!"

"Who are 'They'?" scolded the second, more commanding voice. "We are the first men to step foot on these sands."

"Colombo, your Grace. A mate on one of his voyages told me himself..."

"Enough," chided the commander. "I seek something far more valuable than gold." And there was silence.

'Gold?' Ask pondered to Kowianu. 'What is gold?'

'Gold is the Other word for the Sun Stone.'

'Sun Stone?' puzzled Ask. 'Why would Others want Sun Stone? Do Others perform The Rights?' Ask was amazed that such a sacred ceremony could be shared with peoples he had never seen.

'Listen, Askuwheteauachachak Kitchi, and your questions will be answered.'

Ask knew this of course. As Holy Man and Keeper of the Garden, Eluwillusit Kowianu could see and hear better than any of the family. He was the Keeper. He had seen one hundred and sixty summers, it was said. And he could hear and talk, not just with this Garden and the Faeleriel who lived within it, but he could hear all the Gardens and talk with all the Faeleriel of the world.

'One day, I shall too,' thought Ask, proud at least that he could feel the other Gardens, even if he could not yet hear them.

But all the listening and focusing, thought Ask as he returned to the present, took time and energy. He simply wanted grandfather to tell him about these people. Why had they come? And what did they plan to do?

Reflexively, Ask opened his eyes and could see eight men in the smaller boat rowing toward the beach.

"What will happen?" Ask spoke aloud, a hint of apprehension in his words.

"You are concerned?" replied Kowianu, using his voice in return.

Ask gathered his thoughts, calmed his energy, opened his senses, and communicated fully with mind and heart, not voice.

'The Others, from the stories. They came to the Garden country but did not believe. Many of the Family and the Faeleriel passed on when they came.'

Kowianu nodded gently. 'Yes. The Others at that time did not believe, and some of the energy was lost. But no soul, no Thaen, is gone forever. Those who received the Calling are with Aelialtha now, as one day we shall all be.'

'Do you think energy will be lost again? That some will again receive the Calling?'

Kowianu paused in contemplation. 'That all depends,' he thought at last.

'Depends on what?' implored Ask.

'On what they believe.'

Kowianu opened his eyes and both peered over the waters toward the Others rowing in toward shore.

'Open your heart and your senses,' instructed Kowianu, 'and connect with all the Gardens. Let them see what we now see.'

Ask closed his eyes again and slowed his breathing. He tried to slow his heart, but the excitement of what he knew was about to happen made that nearly impossible.

'Taenoril sil,' Ask chimed to himself. He recited the Faeleriel words over and over, trying to control his mind, his heart, and his body. "Taenoril sil, da Luna Fael, Aelialtha mur, tul malia Hael."

Then, as his senses expanded outward, the coolness came, followed by the warmth, and in an instant, he felt not just his grandfather's presence, but the sensation of his energy leaving his body, soaring over the land, the oceans, and the world!

They were everywhere at once, seeing everything. Ask had only experienced this once before with his grandfather, the Eluwillusit, the Hashakochi Iti Holy

Man, during his Rights ceremony months earlier. That was when everything had been revealed to him, when he had received the sight, though he did not yet understand what it all meant.

Seeing now, on the other side of the Wide Ocean, the land far underneath them was dark. But lights sparkled from the enormous villages of Others. No Gardens existed near these.

Ask had learned that Others did not see. Elu had told him that Others had long ago chosen not to understand Taenoril sil, to stop believing, to stop seeing, and could no longer live among the Faeleriel. Ask could not imagine it, but the Others could not see the Gardens nor hear the song within them.

The Others had come to distrust anything of the Faeleriel or the Gardens. They called Taenoril sil "magic" and treated it with suspicion and hatred. For this reason, the Gardens had long ago begun hiding far from the passages of Others.

As the combined vision of Eluwillusit and Ask traveled in all directions at once, Ask counted the Gardens. Less than two dozen throughout the world existed now. All separate in physical form but connected through Taenoril sil.

In Ask's vision, the world was no longer a tapestry of light and dark, but that of color and grey. The several dozen Gardens lit small portions of the grey world with innumerable shades of iridescent yellow, orange, green and purple. He could feel each Garden's life energy like sunshine on his face. But he also felt that energy slipping away, like sand slowly trickling through his fingers.

'What is this, grandfather?' Ask implored.

'You are sensing the Duadine, the last stages of Belief that will one day lead to ar' Ama Gedeon.'

Ask opened his eyes, his energy now back in his body.

Watching his grandfather, the tribe's Eluwillusit, the most wise man he knew, take a long slow breath. Ask recognized that breath. He knew Eluwillusit Kowianu sensed danger.

'What is wrong, Elu Kowianu?'

'Each season is the end of the season before it and the foundation for that to follow. Such is the cycle of energy...the cycle of life.'

'What will happen if the Gardens diminish and belief is overcome by disbelief?'

'As so often occurred before, when the threshold is crossed between believers and nonbelievers, at a time when there is not enough belief to sustain any of the Trees, ar' Ama Gedeon will come.'

Ask's eyebrows furrowed with the realization. His words and emotion came out in verbal form. "You sense this is happening now?"

Kowianu did not reply in voice.

'History begins with our earliest memory,' recited Elu Kowianu. 'Our memories begin at the time we first meet the Faeleriel. And time begins when the first Faeleriel blooms from the Garden Tree. This is the life cycle of the world: Ar 'Ama Gedeon, the rise of belief, the spread of the Gardens, a world covered in Gardens and united in belief, then the initiation of Doubt, the spread of Disbelief, its diminishing of the Gardens, the eventual dominance of Disbelief, until ar' Ama Gedeon.'

"Duadine then. With the Others here, Disbelief will dominate?" Ask wondered.

Ask studied Eluwillusit Kowianu. Elu was now staring at the small boat which had nearly reached the shore. The Holy Man said nothing.

'Will it come soon?' Ask pondered, his emotion leaking into his thoughts.

'Settle yourself, young one. With the challenge of Duadine, you will one day take your place as Eluwillusit. When that day comes, the Garden will be yours to protect. Now...use the words. Tell me the story of Aelialtha. Tell me the story of all time.'

Ask knew what he was being asked to do. As he had done for his Rights ceremony, he would recite the history of the Aeleriel, the beings of light who came to this world countless seasons ago, and bonded with Aelialtha, the Earth spirit, to become Faeleriel, the bringers of life and energy. Ask knew that this story was the story of his tribe, kept alive by its members, and the responsibility of the Eluwillusit.

Elu Kowianu was preparing Ask to one day be
Eluwillusit Askuwheteauachachak Kitchi.

Ask's heart felt heavy with such a thought, but he
suppressed his sadness and began the story of time.

'Before time, there was lightness and dark. And the
light came from the Aeleriel...'

CHAPTER ONE

"We had not the understanding of the power of belief until the moment when we had lost it."

-- Ahliftalia, Keeper of the One Garden, during the First Age of Life, at the moment of the Garden's fall.

Three days until ar' Ama Gedeon

A gust of Autumn wind swept up the Montana plain and swirled over a small hilltop on which had been built a cabin. In front of that cabin, two men stood silently, eyes closed.

'...dominance of Disbelief, until ar' Ama Gedeon.' Ask breathed deeply and absorbed the sensation of the wind as he finished the story of time in his head once again.

'Over five hundred summers,' he thought, with some melancholy. Ask felt the wind sweep again up the foothill, through the forest, and across the weathered lines of his face, the face that had looked the same since its fortieth year, the year he became the Eluwillusit, but which felt now as hardened as any petrified tree matching his five centuries.

He inhaled the pine scent, tasted the dust that had been kicked up from a passing herd in a far off valley, and sensed...something else.

Ask searched through the eyes of his heart, expanded his energy outward, and sought the sensation of Taenoril sil throughout the world one more time. He had done this last night. But the result this time and that were the same. Something was happening to the other Gardens. He could not feel them.

Ask opened his tired eyes and turned to Martin standing next to him.

Martin Sinclair had not aged physically over the past three years. Since the day Ask had turned over the power of the Eluwillusit, Martin's face and skin held the form of its previous forty-nine years. He turned to face Ask.

"The other Keepers have stopped communicating," Martin said.

Ask nodded sadly.

The distant caws from a flock of birds flying northward rolled over the plain. Both men lifted their eyes to witness a near blanketing of the sky by massive numbers of migratory birds flying North. The mid day sun dimmed in their wake.

Martin blinked slowly. "North? Just before winter." He looked at Ask. "Ar' Ama Gedeon, then?"

Ask exhaled, "Duadine has overcome."

They watched the trailing edges of the flock pass over them, leaving no sound but the wind.

Martin broke the silence. "Susan is coming."

Ask's weathered face stretched into an expression of surprise. Martin's own slid into a grin, having seen so little expression from Ask over the years.

"How?..." Ask stuttered, then gathering his thoughts, he asked more calmly, "Is she bringing..?"

Martin nodded. "Susan will bring all of them. They leave the morning after next."

Ask said nothing, but looked outward to the horizon, his face steeled with concern.

Martin lifted his face toward the noon sun and inhaled deeply. "Yes, I am worried too. They may already be too late."

* * *

One hundred miles from the nearest human settlement, in the oldest growth of the Amazon rain forest, smoke belched from a pipe into a hot, humid, and foul air that was equally congested with the sounds of panic and terror.

Birds shrieked, monkeys howled, and anything that could run or fly did.

A bulldozer belched more acrid smoke into the air. The smoke rose into the jungle canopy, filled with fleeing birds, like a cave crammed with fluttering bats.

A dirty, gloved hand pushed a bull dozer control lever forward, and the rumbling pitch of the machine increased. The bulldozer blade elevated and tore into the foliage, releasing renewed shrieks of jungle pain and terror.

Benetio Negales had lived his entire life in the Brazilian rain forest and knew it was vast. In a thousand lifetimes of tearing it down, he was sure the Company could not destroy it all. At least that is what the Company had told him. Still, rain forest or not, the money was good.

He lived away from his family for a month at a time, working twelve hour days, tearing up the trees, and perhaps more often than he liked, tearing up the animals living in the trees. But the steady job supported his family and was more reliable work than the ceramics his father made or the construction work his brother was sometimes lucky to get.

He looked to his right and left at the other bulldozers in their long line, throttled his gears forward, and belched more smoke into the air.

High in the canopy, the smoke from the line of other bulldozers rose to meet that of the first machine until the sooty grey plume obscured a beautiful flower. A moment later, the smoke dissipated, and the flower and the canopy around it were ripped violently downward.

Animals of all kinds fled in panic, both predators and prey racing alongside oblivious to one another. In the midst of this, an orange and green sun conure bird flew daringly through the rain forest, skirting branches and dodging other birds in flight, not away from the carnage, but toward it!

A wall of rainforest was ripped apart by the flank of oily machines, as the conure raced between the dozers and circled a small clearing only a dozen yards beyond.

The daring bird landed on the roots of what looked to be a tiny willow tree, half the size of the bird and barren of any greenery.

Under its roots emanated a faint glow of pale green light. Protectively, as the grinding gears of the bulldozers clawed to just the other side of a drapery of vines, the bird spread a wing over the tiny tree.

Benetio Negales idled his machine for just a moment. There was something about the greenery in front of him that felt different than all the rest. He looked down the line of machines. The other drivers must have felt it too. They idled as he did.

'But these are just plants,' Benetio told himself. He could see no difference in the vines hanging in front of him than any other vines in the hundreds of acres he had already destroyed, nor, he imagined, the thousands of acres he had yet to destroy. 'Do your job,' he decided to himself, and throttled into gear.

The other drivers did the same, and the hum of machinery rose to destruction pitch once again.

Behind the curtain of vines, as the bulldozers renewed their destructive posture and ground closer, the tiny tree under the beautiful bird's wing folded and receded its branches, wilting from green to brown.

The glow from under the tree faded to darkness, and the bird hung its orange head.

The dozer engines roared now, about to strike.

Suddenly, a blackness spread from under the now tiny tree, covering the ground and spreading rapidly outward. From a distance, the blackness appeared to be a shadow. Up close, however, it looked like black ice crystals forming in, not just on, everything.

The black shadow covered the tiny tree's roots, as the bulldozer blades rose to demolition position. Then it traveled down the tree roots and struck the bird, causing the bird to shriek in pain and its back to arch violently.

The black shadow spread outward, across the roots, in all directions, like a wave, leaving everything a darker version of itself.

The bird had been changed most. Gone were its colors. Feathers of bright orange and yellow had turned grey and black, its eyes now pure white.

The high intensity pitch of bulldozer engines was suddenly interrupted by blades cutting through the foliage.

The bird gripped the remnant of the tree in one claw and spread its wings wide. Then with a great downward stroke, it rose into the air and flew out of the dozer's path. With a caw and a shriek, it made a wide turn through the jungle.

As the ground under the bulldozers turned black from the spreading shadow, the bird with white eyes raced toward the bulldozers.

It was then that the jungle, for the first time that morning, became quiet, except for the shrieks from the black bird and the screams of the men driving the machines.

* * *

Yakushima, the oldest forest in Japan, was suddenly filled with noise as the six young men left their car, and stumbled down the forest path.

'I'm not going to take any of Nikei's crap this time,' thought Osuki to himself as he crammed a piece of shrimp into his mouth from the bento box he held in front of his face. Osuki looked over and saw Nikei chewing a similar bite of rice and fish, licking his chop sticks.

'I'm the leader of this gang,' Osuki affirmed to himself, 'and my dad's got all the money that gets us what we want.'

Laughter from up ahead caught Osuki's attention.

Mako Neguchi and his twin brother, Daishi, were laughing at something Mako had said.

Mako continued, "In ten minutes nothing is going to matter." He mimed injecting something into his arm.

Daishi spread his arms like wings. "We'll be floating on air!"

The two broke into further laughter and turned up the faintly visible forest path.

Osuki listened, knowing that for all his hopes it was not he who was the real leader of the gang. It was Mako, even though he came from nothing and his family had no money. Mako was the leader because he was cool. He was tough. He could fight better than any of them, and he knew where to get all the things that Osuki's family money bought.

All six young men were dressed in dark leather, jeans, and acid punk T-shirts. They had walked nearly a mile from the car, where they had parked on the roadside. Along this deserted forest pathway, as they stammered down the trail laughing, they teased and pushed one another. The path held few signs of a trail, but they knew where they were going.

Suddenly, Nikei, having finished his food, and seeing that Osuki still had some, grabbed Osuki's bento box.

Osuki spit the food he was chewing at Nikei. Nikei then threw both bento boxes into the nearby woods, turned, and pounced on Osuki.

The other teenage boys howled with laughter, taunting, as they all continued their way up the path.

Meanwhile, the abandoned bento boxes floated downward, unseen and uncared for by the suburban punks, landing on top of what looked like a small bonsai tree.

The sounds from the disaffected youths faded into the distance, while a bird warbled distressfully, somewhere in the trees above.

Seeing that the rowdy young men had gone, a thin, cloaked woman stepped cautiously from the woods on one side of the path, then crossed to the area where the bento boxes had been tossed.

She appeared afraid of something, feeling the ground, sniffing the air, and checking behind and around her, until she finally made her way between two enormous pine trees. There, the trash had accumulated.

She gasped, "Ie!" and dropped to the ground. As if extracting pieces of wreckage from around a child in a wrecked car, she removed the trash from the ground and uncovered the tiny tree.

She watched it wilt in front of her eyes. Her breathing quickened and her hands trembled as she quickly lifted the tiny plant and stepped back.

Where the tree had been growing, a black shadow spilled out of the ground and spread outward in all directions.

Whimpering, the woman held the plant protectively under her cloak, turned, and ran!

* * *

Sirens from United Chemical's Gloucester, England factory continued to wail, as emergency vehicles crowded in the parking lot and along the road paralleling the stream that flowed nearby.

The two sides of the river could not have been more different. On one side, the trees of the Forest of Dean grew tall, covered with green and alive with the sounds of the forest. On the other was the enormous chemical plant, its numerous smoke stacks, refinery tanks, and barbed wire fences sitting on endless acres of asphalt.

Two men, in hazardous material clean up HAZMAT suits, stood on the roadside overlooking the stream and the thick forest beyond. Around them, dozens of HAZMAT clad clean up crewmen swept the area with detecting devices and dragged clean up equipment into the stream.

The first man, who filled his suit tightly, making him look like a space-traveling snow man, surveyed the area, darting his cuboid HAZMAT head sharply left and right.

"Damn business! Damn business this is!" the portly man complained, his voice muffled by the HAZMAT suit.

The tall, thin HAZMAT clad man next to him looked at a clip board then peered into the distance toward the crews entering the stream.

"Probably only three thousand gallons. Traces'll be detectable down stream, but nothin' there but trees and wild animals."

The fat man projected his belly forward and placed his fists on his hips.

"Environmental beetles will be all over it," he grumbled. Then his posture perked up.

"No. Wait. I can work the press angle like we did with the Overton spill."

The tall figure nodded. "That was a good one, boss. Spin it like they want to hear it."

"Yeah, we'll be heroes." The fat man held up a hand in front of his face and swept it as if he was creating a Broadway marquis. "United Chemical's products of modern medicine help nature and mankind. No expense is too good for the community and the environment."

A stifled laugh burst from the tall man next to him, his clipboard quickly rising in front of his HAZMAT plastic face shield.

The fat HAZMAT suit turned briefly in the tall man's direction, then focused on the clean up crew workers trudging through the stream. He watched as the glowing green liquid mixed with the water, which flowed all around the men, then swirled around a bend before disappearing into the forest.

"Yeah, that's the ticket," said the fat HAZMAT suit, pleased with himself. "When I'm done, we'll be the chemical Mother Theresa."

* * *

Kayla ran as fast as she could without tripping or letting her little sister, Siena fall. But they had both heard the Faeleriel crying and felt the Tree's pain.

Reaching outward they tried to hear the other Gardens and feel Taenoril sil, but no voices came and no energy filled the void. Their eyes briefly met, and both feared the worst.

Deep in the forest, the bright green chemically contaminated water swirled and flowed over the roots of countless old oaks, vines, and flowers.

One particularly large root extended up from the stream and connected to a much larger root system, belonging to an enormous old oak tree. Like large octopus tentacles, the roots at the base of the oak encircled a small enclave of very small plants, at the center of which was a tiny, leafless willow tree.

A pair of pale white hands surrounded the tiny tree and lifted it from the ground.

Siena's nine-year-old hands lifted the Tree toward her rosy cheeks, her red hair swirling into the tree's tiny barren branches. Tears rolled down over her pink cheeks as she looked over her shoulder at her red-haired, eleven year-old sister, whose flushed freckled face told her they were thinking the same thing.

"They are gone?"

Kayla forced a sad smile. "It'll be okay," she encouraged Siena.

"Will they come back? Are they gone forever?" cried the younger girl.

Before Kayla could answer, the forest became suddenly and ominously silent.

Both pairs of eyes shot toward the spot where the tree had been, each girl taking a step backward.

From the small hole, the black shadow spilled outward.

Siena gripped the tiny tree and whispered desperately over it, "Believe! Believe!"

Kayla clasped her shoulder, "It's too late!"

And together, the two girls turned and ran.

CHAPTER TWO

"I will go wherever the truth leads me...I am not afraid of truth."

-- Chaim Potok

Two days until ar' Ama Gedeon

"Stupid scholarship!" barked Sheffy Calbreath at the ceiling of the Fair Isle North Sea Remote Environmental Research Facility. His legs were extended, feet crossed and resting on the edge of the sonar control panel.

This was a violation of Cambridge University policy and Sheffy knew that if Professor Bibbits found him there, with his feet up on the instrument panel, he'd be calculating coordinate grids and wind speeds for a month.

But at that moment, Sheffy didn't care. For the hundredth time he cursed the "budget cuts" that had made his graduate school scholarship all but disappear, and forced him grudgingly to accept this thankless, menial research assistant position on an island that was miles from anywhere descent for humans to inhabit. Specifically, it was in the middle of the North Sea, halfway between Scotland and Norway.

'Fair Isle is hardly 'fair', he thought. But the North Sea Remote Research Facility certainly was 'remote'. Worse, Fair Isle was the definition of cold, dark and damp, he thought. "They don't even make beer!" he barked aloud. "Uncivilized."

Overcome momentarily with his desperation, he let his head fall backward and peered at the ceiling as if it would answer him. It didn't.

"I should be in Groundlings Pub with Charlotte right now!" he bellowed. But the ceiling did not respond to this either.

What did respond was a sensor light on the far end of the control panel. A yellow indicator light was flashing and a panel speaker beeped in time with it.

Sheffy came out of his stuporous mood and slid his chair down the control panel.

"What is this?"

His eyes rapidly took in data from one sensor, then another. "Water pressure rising, atmospheric pressure dropping."

He rolled to a screen along the panel with a radar display of the North Sea. It showed a uniformly pale blue. "Nothing on radar."

He slid to a curtain and peeked out, before rolling back to the panel.

Confused, he pulled out a hand held device, looked again at the control panel and studied a screen that scrolled a series of digits, then typed the numbers into the device. He spun his chair around, pulled a three ring binder from a bookshelf and flipped its laminated pages open to one baring a table filled with numbers.

His index finger ran down one column of numbers, then checked his hand-held device screen. He looked from the device back to the chart where his finger lay, then back at the device.

Uncertainty covered his face. His eyes returned again to the control panel screen and the series of numbers spread across it. Sweat began to trickle from his temples.

"This can't be right," he said as he wheeled his chair back to the curtain, where he peaked outside. After a moment, he slid once again to the far side of the panel. He flipped up an opaque plastic cylinder, under which was a blue toggle switch. "Recalibrate then."

He tripped the blue switch, and all screens momentarily went black. Seconds later, digital data began scrolling across the various screens, as each computer rebooted its system. One by one all the systems returned to their original configuration.

Sheffy pushed the black toggle switch that controlled the intercom and leaned into the microphone. "Professor Bibbits, can you come to...?"

A tall man with thinning blond hair and an anxious expression strode into the control room.

"What's going on in here!?" His voice crackled, his eyes instantly darting across the control screens. "Did you...?"

"I rebooted the system, professor," Sheffy confessed firmly.

"Why, may I ask?"

Sheffy rolled back to the screen where he had detected the anomaly. "Here, professor."

After examining the series of numbers Sheffy was pointing out, Professor Bibbits dropped his eyes to the binder and the table Sheffy had already retrieved. Professor Bibbits' own finger ran down the column of numbers until it reached the same value Sheffy had found.

"This can't be right," he stated then went to the control room's single window and threw open the curtains. The sky outside was clear but for a pair of wispy clouds.

"Yeah, doesn't make sense does it?" Sheffy agreed. "With these numbers, this should be the first step of a category one hurricane forming over us."

Professor Bibbits' left eyebrow twitched nervously. His eyes darted back and forth as if searching for a nonexistent explanation. "There have been instances," he mumbled to himself, "of barometric change without climatological effect."

The professor turned to Sheffy, "What we are witnessing is the interaction of a known variable that we simply can't measure."

Sheffy peered at Professor Bibbits like a second nose was growing from his face. 'What is he talking about?' Sheffy thought to himself. 'Something bad should be happening right now; I don't know what or why, but I get the feeling when it does happen, it is going to happen very quickly.'

"The data are still too isolated to be reliably accurate. We'll simply watch it for now and observe," Professor Bibbits decided. The professor nodded, slowly at first, then more rapidly as he appeared to convince himself this was the correct course of action. Then without explanation, Professor Bibbits gave Sheffy a tentative smile, turned and left the room.

Sheffy remained next to the control panel, the yellow warning light reflecting off his flushed cheek. 'Is Professor Bibbits going to do nothing?' he wondered.

To Sheffy, it appeared Professor Bibbits was going to rest everything on whether the numbers somehow showed up in some recognizable shift in weather patterns rather than make a decision based upon the unexplainable pattern of data in front of them.

Such unexplainable shifts in natural environmental patterns had been Sheffy's undergraduate thesis, however. In Sheffy's mind, most large scale shifts in weather were due to a cumulative effect of many small-scale almost nothings.

Sheffy knew Professor Bibbits had just received tenure, and he suspected the professor was still in the mode of keeping his nose clean on all fronts.

'I fear,' thought Sheffy as he stared at the empty radar screen, 'this could be the first of many small nothings.' Though he was sure these nothings would soon mount up to a very significant 'something' indeed.

CHAPTER THREE

"The marvelous richness of human experience would lose something of rewarding joy if there were no limitations to overcome. The hilltop hour would not be half so wonderful if there were no dark valleys to traverse."

-- Helen Keller

One day until ar' Ama Gedeon

Inside an Arizona Institute of Technology research laboratory a storm was raging.

"Enough, mother!" demanded Elizabeth Sinclair as she tried to focus her attention on her tablet computer controller. In front of her, a two foot long section of pipe mounted on her lab table was being bent in seven different directions at once by a series of opposing pistons.

On the controller tablet screen, a diagram showed the heptagonal cross-sectional shape of the pipe withstanding the force of the opposing pistons, the force for each represented by a number next to the corresponding piston. Elizabeth's fingers tapped on the screen next to each piston icon like an astronaut meticulously guiding her positional rockets to achieve the exact capsular alignment.

It had taken her nearly two years to theorize the shape and material of the piping, three months to devise her experiment, five weeks to get it on the schedule, and all morning to set up. Yet with one momentary loss of focus...

"You know how important this is," retorted Susan Sinclair from the other side of Elizabeth's engineering work bench. "And he's your father."

The comment caught Elizabeth off guard, and in a flash of incredulous surprise she looked up from her tablet computer controller. That moment was enough.

An ominous creaking sound arose from the metal tube. Elizabeth's eyes shot back down to her tablet screen. "No!"

Piston number two had lost momentary friction, turning potential energy into kinetic energy in the form of sheering forces. The sound was the agonizing battle between metallic gladiators, each out of sync with their proper stance, each lying exposed to their enemy, and each swinging hard to strike the deadly blow before they received one in kind.

Elizabeth frantically tapped the piston number two icon, which had now turned red. She hammered furiously on the electronic keyboard.

"Dammit, dammit!"

The moment Elizabeth typed in a computer command and struck the RETURN key was punctuated with a "crack!"

Both women looked at the experiment rig which had suddenly fallen silent. Elizabeth leaned over the device to inspect the damage. Number two piston's lever arm was bent forty-five degrees off its axis, and the pipe surface had a crude rent ground into it. The combination looked like a comet and tail.

Elizabeth stared stunned. It took her several seconds before she realized someone was talking to her.

"Is it broken?" asked Susan again.

Elizabeth felt the blood race to her face, as her chest heaved with emotion. "Yes, mother!" She slammed the controller onto the lab bench. "My thesis is broken!"

Without looking at her experiment, Elizabeth spun on her heels, covered her face with a hand, and strode toward her office. Susan skirted around the lab table in pursuit.

"It'll be okay, sweetie," Susan consoled, "You'll see."

Elizabeth stopped abruptly, spun around and leaned menacingly forward onto her toes, so that her five foot five inch frame was equal to Susan's five foot seven.

"Okay? You think this is going to be okay!" exclaimed Elizabeth. "You think you're talking to a five year old? Do you know how long I have been working on this!"

At that moment, the outer door from the hallway to the main lab opened, and a young man Elizabeth's age entered. His dark hair hung over his ears and had a natural curl that kept it above his blue eyes. He walked casually into the lab, then focusing immediately on Elizabeth's distress, sped quickly to her.

He tenderly placed a hand on Elizabeth's back and looked into her eyes. Without a word he glanced over to the experiment. His face told Elizabeth he understood.

"What happened?" he asked, returning his gaze to Elizabeth.

Elizabeth's eyes closed as she once again tried to control her breathing and her emotions.

"It was my fault," confessed Susan. "I distracted her, and the...". Susan paused, then looked back to the experiment, as if the device had its name written on it. Her face returned back toward the young man with a blank expression. "...thing...broke."

Elizabeth faced her mother, "That 'thing' was nearly two years of work, which broke, because you couldn't give me an hour of peace to finish my work."

"But this is important!" bellowed Susan.

"And my thesis isn't?"

Elizabeth was just beginning to turn again toward her office, the young man moving with her, when Susan gripped both their arms.

"Elizabeth. Aaron. I need you both to listen," Susan pleaded. Her own face, hardened with more than her fair share of lines from frequent scowling, relaxed.

"You know Martin and I were over years ago. Leonard and I have been together for most of the last three. This is our opportunity. Please for Leonard and I, do this."

Susan released both of them.

Puzzled, Aaron looked to Elizabeth. Slowly exhaling a breath, Elizabeth said, "Martin contacted Susan and told her that if we all came up to his cabin, he'd finally sign the divorce papers."

Aaron's grin took on a mischievous flair. "Hell freezes over at last, huh?"

"That's not the best of it," continued Elizabeth. Aaron raised a single eyebrow, reminiscent of Spock.

"Hell is freezing over at some remote cabin in the woods, in Montana!"

"Montana? Your dad disappeared and became a hermit in Montana?" Aaron mused, astonished. "Crazy."

"Oh, crazy hasn't even started," extorted Elizabeth. "He'll only accept the divorce and sign the papers if Susan, Leonard, you, and I all go. And we have to be there no later than tomorrow afternoon!"

"Tomorrow?" Aaron pondered. "But you're defending next week."

Elizabeth cranked her 'I told you so' puckered lips toward her mother, "Yeah, I know."

Susan shot a momentary icy glare at Aaron, who took a reflexive step backward, before settling her pleading expression on Elizabeth once again.

"I know it's an imposition, but I'm begging you. Do this and I guarantee we'll be back in two days, and you'll get the next two impossible demands you want."

Susan crossed her chest, then opened a tiny invisible box, tossed something imaginary into it, locked it with an equally imaginary key, and threw the key away.

Elizabeth looked at Susan like another head was growing from her shoulders. "I have no idea what the hell that was. But..." She looked at Aaron, who returned her anxious expression with eyes full of compassion.

"You know my vote. I'd never miss the opportunity to see my family." Aaron squeezed Elizabeth's hand, "And this may be a good thing...a way to view the events of your childhood through your adult perspective."

Susan gently laid three fingers over the back of Elizabeth's hand. "I know there's no love lost anywhere around, but we do this, and it's finally over."

"It's been over for a long time," retorted Elizabeth.

"Not for me," said Susan. "Please. Just come," Susan pleaded. "It'll only be a day or two, then we'll be back to our regular lives."

"How're we getting there?"

Susan's face brightened up. "He said there's a landing strip near him, so Leonard will fly us right there. We'll get everything signed and leave right afterward. Up and back...two days tops!"

Elizabeth scanned the lab, her analytical gaze coming to rest on the bent metal across the room. "Fine."

Susan's face relaxed.

Elizabeth exhaled, "But don't expect me to play nice."

* * *

In the historic architecturally styled neighborhood of Cambridge, Massachusetts, Doris Feinman swept the last of the dishes from the dinner table and followed her hostess, Louise Hart, into the kitchen. Despite the somber mood throughout most of the dinner, Doris managed a laugh.

"After thirty-five years of marriage," chuckled Louise, "I've learned this is Philip's way. If the sky can rain, it's falling. If it could ever happen, it's happening now." Louise turned to Doris. "Whatever is on their minds tonight will run its course, and still the sun will shine another day."

Doris placed a half full wine glass on the kitchen counter and nodded in agreement. "If I had not been around to temper Isaac's intensity over the years, he would have locked himself up in a bunker a decade ago over forecasts of doom."

The two women laughed lightly together, but their laughter was as somber as the dinner conversation had been. Both women hoped that whatever it was of such grave concern to their husbands would not be a problem for very long.

Louise removed coffee cups and saucers from her buffet and began pouring the dark liquid. "I have some very nice cheesecake," she said brightly. "We'll take this to the study and perhaps get the men to relax."

At that moment, both women were startled by the rattling of coffee cups on their saucers, and Doris subdued a scream as the wine glass toppled from the counter, shattered on the floor, and the remaining wine spread across the floor like blood.

Down the hall the grey haired professors sat in the study and gripped their arm chairs until the tremor finished.

From the kitchen, they both heard Louise say. "Don't worry. It was just a wine glass. We'll be there in a minute with coffee."

Ashen-faced, Professor Philip Hart appeared from the hallway and entered the kitchen, Professor Isaac Feinman close behind him.

Louise stopped pouring coffee, and Doris forgot about the broken glass and wine on the floor. "Philip, what is it?"

Philip gasped, "Innumerable insignificant factors, in time, create very significant effects."
The sudden ringing of the telephone stirred the tension in the room, causing everyone to jump once again.

Dr. Hart lifted the receiver and placed it to is ear. The voice on the other end began talking excitedly.

"Professor, this is Shalimar at the lab...very urgent, so I'm patching a call through to you. Don't hang up!" the voice demanded. Then the line crackled.

Louise and Doris looked at their husbands imploringly. Before either scientist could form an expression in response, another voice, sounding far away, came on the phone.

"Professor Hart?" asked the voice with a nervous British accent. "This is Michael Bibbits. Are you there?"

"Yes, this is Dr. Hart. Who is...?"

"You may recall I was one of your exchange post-doctoral fellows five years ago, from Cambridge."

"Yes...," replied Dr. Hart as he recalled Dr. Bibbits' face. "What can I...?"

"I apologize for the inconvenience, Dr. Hart, but I know your lab collects and coordinates seismic and infrared data from sensor stations throughout the globe. I'm conducting research at the Fair Isle Laboratory, and I've found a series of anomalies. Has anyone on your team been tracking the North Sea?"

"Yes, and other places," replied Professor Hart. "Though I admit, we have been having a difficult time understanding exactly what it is we are seeing."

"So have we," agreed Professor Bibbits. "However, a graduate student of mine and I have been making some calculations, and we think you can assist us in answering a crucial question."

CHAPTER FOUR

"The altar cloth of one aeon is the doormat of the next."

-- Mark Twain

"If you do not change direction, you may end up where you are heading."

-- Lao Tzu

Day of ar' Ama Gedeon

The century old grandfather clock struck 2 am, jogging the small group in the Massachusetts Institute of Technology graduate conference room out of their collective contemplation.

"The question is, 'What are we missing?'" explained Professor Hart as he finished writing the final variables of his integral equation onto the white board. He underlined four separate sections of the equation for emphasis.

"And each of these represent the anomalous data from the outlying sensors in Kenya, Southern Japan, the Central Amazon, and the British data measured at Fair Isle, but which appears to have come from the southwestern portion of England." He then turned and looked at the others in the room.

In chairs crowding the white board, were Professor Feinman and three graduate students, each bleary-eyed, terrified, and holding a tall cup of coffee. A television monitor mounted on the wall above their heads showed a twenty-four hour news program with the sound muted. Scenes of rough winds, high waves beating shorelines, mud slides, earthquake crumpled buildings, and riot after riot cycled across the screen. Professor Hart passed his scrutinizing gaze from one person to the other. Each in turn nodded silently but continued to stare at the equation.

The last was Professor Feinman. "There's no doubt. Everything has shifted, and it's only a matter of time."

He looked his friend Philip in the eye. "You should make the call."

* * *

William Beiner had been the Science Advisor to the President of the United States for over five years. Through the first campaign, the contentious election and its difficult environmental policy questions, the first term buffeting tactics they had suffered from the other political party, and the second election rife with ethical land mines. Through it all he was still the Science Advisor to the President of the United States.

"Good night, Mark," Beiner said with finality as he set the telephone receiver back in its cradle. He looked at his bedside clock, two-thirty in the morning, and rolled his eyes.

'Senior geologist,' Beiner scoffed to himself, 'from where? Iowa? 'Bench worker!'

Beiner shuffled his feet to a more comfortable position in bed and rolled away from his telephone. Presidential Science Advisor Beiner had taken personal pleasure in devising this particular epithet for scientists who knew only about their field of science and nothing about how to relate their findings to the *real* world.

These 'bench workers' never understood whether their work was significant or not in the real world. It was *his* job to determine what scientific data was important and ensure the President had access to it. Without him, entire fields of research would not be funded and their findings would not make their way into government policy and society.

The thought of the irritating bench worker he had just hung up on was still fresh in Science Advisor William Beiner's mind when his telephone rang again. Beiner groaned and cursed himself for not having turned on his answering service before retiring to bed. He vowed that after this call he would.

William Beiner rolled back over and lifted the receiver. "Dr. Beiner," He stated with a drowsy air of superiority.

"Bill, this is Philip Hart from MIT. Sorry if I woke you," came the voice on the other end.

"Philip...oh yes, Philip," he said, now fully recalling Dr. Philip Hart and the assistance he and MIT had provided the President in debunking several opposition claims during the previous year's election.

'I'll give him one minute,' Beiner generously thought as he stifled a yawn and returned,
"Not at all. What can I do for you at this late hour?"

"I need you to wake the President and set up a meeting immediately."

William Beiner did not mistake the urgency in Dr. Hart's voice, but he had not risen to such a high position without exercising some political wrangling. And at this late hour, with no good reason, Dr. Philip Hart was going to be wrangled.

"Philip, I can tell you have some important information. Let's meet on Tuesday morning. I have an open round table for specialists in..."

"Tuesday will be too late," interrupted Dr. Hart. "It may already be too late."

"Too late for what, Philip?" Science Advisor to the President of the United States, William Beiner knew this was going to be one of 'those' discussions.

The last call had been one of 'those' discussions. The professor of geology from University of something, somewhere in Iowa, or was it Indiana, had been convinced that a fault line had formed in the middle of the North American tectonic plate and could become unstable. He had demanded an audience with the President as well.

'They all want to talk to the President,' chafed Beiner, 'but they fail to appreciate that I am the only one who talks to the President.'

"Hasn't anyone else notified you?"

"It's late, Philip. What is on your mind?"

"We have collected data from laboratories, sensor systems, and outposts around the world, and discovered there are a series of destabilizing waves spreading ..."

"Philip," Beiner interrupted with his authoritative voice. His placatory tone was good for smoothing over misunderstandings and misdirecting overzealous energy, but fanaticism required direct authority. And MIT or not, Dr. Hart was in no position to make any demands with him.

"I'll have my secretary call you personally in the morning to set up a one on one with me." He began to release the pressure of the receiver against his ear in preparation for hanging up the phone. "We'll go over everything in de..."

"Damn, Bill, Listen! The mantle is destabilizing, and it's progressing exponentially. We don't have time!"

William Beiner took a relaxing breath to keep his voice calm. "I tell you what, I have a nine o'clock briefing with the Chief of Staff. You still have my email from last year. Send what you have over your secure network, and I'll address your concerns at the meeting."

"You don't get it! I've chartered a flight. We're boarding now, and we'll be in D.C. in a few hours."

"That's not necessary, Philip."

"Call the NGS. We've already uploaded our projections. And have them sync with the NOA database. From there, we'll be able to make assessments of the full damage."

"Philip," Beiner grumbled, about to hang up.

"Do it, now!" And the line went dead.

'He hung up on me!' Beiner realized with astonishment. "How dare...!" the Science Advisor to the President of the United States of America grunted.

Beiner flung the covers from his feet, which he slid into his slippers. Infuriated, he paced twice across his bedroom. Finally, and with the intent of debunking any and all conclusions he found, Dr. William Beiner made his way to his study, turned on his computer, accessed his secret level portal to the National Geographic Survey and National Oceanographic Administration data repositories, and began to download Dr. Philip Hart's assessments.

* * *

Twilight of dawn and lightning reflected off ominously grey cumulus clouds, as the FEDEX 747, its two pilots, three crew members, and one hundred fifty thousand pounds of overnight cargo descended into the clouds and the flight path for final approach into London's Heathrow International Airport.

The pilot toggled his transmitter. "Heathrow Tower at three thousand feet, three degrees declination and final approach."

The radio replied, "We have you FEDEX One Zero Seven. Stay on course, and be advised, the barometer is dropping. Ground conditions foggy. You'll ... instruments for landing."

Though the radio was beginning to emit frequent static, Captain Steve Leinert was not concerned.

"Roger that, Heathrow," replied Captain Leinert. He turned to his new copilot. "You gone into Heathrow on instruments before?"

First Officer Jefferson Arnold shook his head with a flick, "Nah. A dozen times in good weather. Been into Edinburgh a few times blind, but not Heathrow. I know the cross winds can be a ... challenge."

"Good word for it. Why don't you lead her in?"

First Officer Arnold nodded respectfully and began his landing cycle without hesitation.

"Minimum VRef speed set, altimeter check, brake setting set, flaps one, speed two ten, flaps two, speed one eighty," Arnold recited aloud as he went through the usual landing routine.

Tonight though, he allowed the thought to permeate his process, 'Blind, night landing, into a Class Bravo airport...that makes tonight a three-for-one. Play it right, and I could make Captain by this time next year.'

First Officer Arnold smirked and allowed his mind to wander just a bit as his hands used muscle memory and habit to click off system after system in preparation for landing.

He knew there was fog outside, but because of his distraction, he did not register the change in cloud color from white and grey to black.

First Officer Arnold was holding the yoke of the airplane with one hand when the nose of the aircraft suddenly dipped downward, like a canoe going over the falls.

Both Captain Leinert and First Officer Arnold felt the familiar lump in their throats, with the sudden loss of atmospheric pressure and resulting loss in altitude, that every pilot had experienced either during their training or the rare real world mechanical failure.

"FEDEX One Zero Seven to Heathrow Tower, loss of barometric pressure, dropping altitude at sixty meters per second," called Captain Leinert into his transmitter.

He received only static in reply.

First Officer Arnold scanned the electronic instrument panel, but it flickered and went black. He gasped, then reflexively turned his eyes to the physical compass above him. The needle did not point in the westerly two hundred seventy degree direction they had been traveling. The magnetic compass was spinning like a top.

Despite the useless instruments and compass, both pilots could feel they had leveled the plane, though they could no longer tell if they were over land or sea.

Outside the windshield, the black clouds pelted the airplane with their condensation. Wiper blades swished back and forth, enabling the pilots inside to attempt some form of visual identification of land points of reference.

Both pilots looked out the window now, but neither saw anything they recognized. What they did see were apparent black crystals forming on the windshield, traveling across and through the glass, and over the instrument panel.

Stunned by the bizarre crystalline formations, Captain Leinert did not notice the blackness form over his shirt sleeve until it was traveling up his arm. He slapped at the blackness as if it was fire. Then, perplexed he stopped slapping and watched the black crystals spread across his hand and disappear into his skin, turning it an ashen grey.

A gagging sound distracted Captain Leinert, causing him to look toward his copilot. It was First Officer

Arnold gagging, he discovered, for the black crystals had traveled up his neck, into the naturally dark skin of his face, turning it pale and his eyes grey.

"What is going on?" Captain Leinert grunted.

First Officer Arnold at first struggled to breath, then released what to Leinert sounded like the death gasp his mother had made when she had passed away. Leinert turned back to himself and saw he was completely covered in the black crystals. His breathing became more and more labored, like breathing through a straw, and his vision clouded with tears and a greyish film.

'I'm dying,' he thought. He reached for his seat harness buckle. 'I have to get out of here. I can't breath!' He panicked.

Then a growl distracted him. Just as he released the seat harness and began to stand up, his attention was drawn to his copilot's seat. There, Arnold sat facing him, his eyes grey as stone, his skin pale as death. Captain Leinert opened his mouth to plead for help from his First Officer, but nothing came out but a growl. Arnold growled in return, filling Leinert with an uncharacteristic hatred and loathing, not just for First Officer Arnold, but for every copilot who had ever sat in that seat.

'Hangers on!' he thought maliciously. "Worthless..." he grunted aloud.

At that moment, the grey eyes of First Officer Jefferson Arnold flared open. He bore his teeth in a snarl, and shrieked, "My plane!"

He lunged at Captain Leinert, catching the copilot yoke with his leg, causing the plane to turn sharply.

The Heathrow Tower was a concert of confusion. Controllers were hailing all their points of traffic, and airplanes were issuing inaudibly panicked calls in return.

The controller who had been tracking FEDEX 107, initiated his transmitter, "FEDEX One Zero Seven, this is Heathrow Tower, we show you altering course to one eight zero and dropping altitude. Climb and maintain to heading zero one zero and maintain altitude at five thousand feet."

The controller switched on his receiver, but heard at first only static.

He turned to the radar screen where he had been tracking FEDEX 107 as a white blip on a green back ground. The blip continued its course away from Heathrow, and out to sea.

"FEDEX One Zero Seven," the controller said again. "Do you copy? Acknowledge by voice or squelch. Do you copy One Zero Seven?"

As if in response, static was replaced by savage grunts and screams. The other controllers looked his way.

"One Zero Seven are you in distress? What is your condition?"

Then with one final primeval scream, the speaker gave nothing but static, and the radar beacon disappeared.

* * *

Mary Darisher had waited her entire life to make the journey to Paris. She had no idea she would spend the rest of it there.

Retired for the past four years and atop the Eiffel tower at last, she exited the elevator and serpentined her way among the many tourists exploring the top landing of the tower until she found what she was looking for.

She was now as high as she had ever been, higher than all the most ornate edifices of the world's most beautiful city. She was literally on the top of her world. And at this moment, she wanted to look down on everything else. She placed a coin into the coin-operated binoculars, leaned her eyes to the lenses, and adjusted the focus.

The Arc de Triumph came into view and was spectacular. Notre Dame cathedral was breath-taking, and further into the distance...Mary paused, having difficulty seeing clearly into the distance. Uncertain if the problem was the binocular lens or not, Mary moved her head and looked with her own eyes. Again her view of the horizon was blurry. She buried her face once again into the binoculars and found the horizon was not just blurry, it was moving!

Mary lifted her face to look at it again and both heard and saw other site-seers had discovered this strange phenomenon.

"Look!" called out one Asian man, pointing toward the horizon.

"What is it?" asked a woman with a British accent.

Mary again used the binoculars, hoping to identify the dark rim of horizon that was rapidly growing. This time, in the binoculars, Mary could clearly see what appeared to be a shadow spreading over all the buildings of Paris from West to East, for as far as the eye could see North to South. And the shadow was moving very fast.

Some who had noticed the shadow began making their way back to the elevators. Others filed down the long chain of stairs. Mary could tell from the speed of the oncoming shadow that whatever that shadow was going to do, it would do it with her on the top of the Eiffel Tower. She could not manage the stairs, and the crowd scrambling to get on the single elevator was too rough for her to endure.

The shadow was less than a mile away now. The elevator that had risen to drop off a load of tourists, had arrived full of people who had also begun to notice the shadow. Once the doors opened, none wanted to leave. However, many of the people outside the elevator pushed to get into it. A battle of pushing, shoving, and frustration quickly ensued until the elevator operator took charge and began closing the elevator door.

The undercurrent of fear instantly metamorphosed into outright panic, as those on the elevator pleaded for the doors to close, and those on the landing demanded to be let on board.

Then, a scream pierced the chaos, "Ach, mine Gott!"

All eyes turned and watched as the shadow swept through the Palais de Challot, across the Sans River, and began climbing the tower. Everyone could now see that this shadow was not a shadow at all, but a wispy, crystalline blackness burying itself into everything it touched.

Panic burst out anew as the blackness shot up the Tower. In two seconds, it had swept up and enveloped the metal structure. As it did, the crowd stopped pushing into the elevator, as every person on the landing and in the elevator cried out and uselessly scraped and swatted their arms, their legs, and even their faces to get the spidery blackness off of them.

Moments later, yelling and crying had become grunting and howling. Every face was pale and every eye had turned grey.

The battle for the elevator was transformed into a death match, one that did not end until the shrieking elevator operator released the brake mechanism, the door still open, causing the elevator to free fall back down along its track, and dozens of people who had been trying to push into the elevator to plummet into the elevator shaft behind it.

Mary wedged herself into the corner of the top landing between the binocular device and the tower railing.

Around her tourists were going mad, growling at one another, beating one another, and either fighting to get down the stairs or standing their ground where they stood.

Mary giggled menacingly. She felt good. She felt powerful. She, for once in her life was higher than anyone in her little northern town thought she could be, and she knew she was better than any of them ever would be.

* * *

Racing through the South Pacific, United States surface ship, the USS Serenity, and ballistic missile submarine, the SSBN Kamehameha, simultaneously increased speed by four nautical miles per hour. The Kam, as the Kamehameha was known to its sailors, set the hatches of its sail, sounded the dive alarm and quickly disappeared beneath the surface.

On the Kam's bridge, US Navy Commander Michael Dorsett called for his next speed setting.

"Ai Captain," replied Lieutenant Scott "Shorty" Pine.

At the maximum allowable six foot two, LT Pine had just qualified within the maximum physical requirements for submarine surface, thus earning him his nickname. With six years in the silent service of submarines, he had qualified in every one of the ship's systems, stood every watch, and mastered, he thought, every submarine maneuver.

Seconds later the ship's radioman called out, "USS Serenity confirms matching speed and vector."

The Captain nodded.

"Anomaly identified, Captain," announced the sonarman.

"Distance to target?" requested Captain Dorsett.

"Anticipate breeching perimeter in four minutes, forty-five seconds," LT Pine called out.

"On screen," Captain Dorsett ordered.

Next to the Captain's chair, a solid state plexiglass screen illuminated into a digital map, marking the Kamehameha with an orange, bullet-shaped oval and the USS Serenity with a yellow ellipse, both on a blue field, separated by latitude and longitude grid lines. From the Northwest, the field of blue was being overtaken by a blanket of grey.

"Set perimeter course with target speed minus one-quarter knot," called out Captain Dorsett.

LT Pine replied, "Setting course. Speed minus one-quarter knot, Captain."

On the digital screen, the submarine and surface ship split in opposite directions, paralleling the border of the grey anomaly, but allowing it to inch ever closer.

"Sensors?" inquired the Captain.

"No infrared, no sonar signature," replied the sonarman.

"No displacement," replied the controlman next to LT Pine.

LT Pine spoke his thoughts, "How can it be moving with no substance? What is this?"

"That's what we're here to find out, lieutenant," reminded the Captain.

"Ai, sir," said LT Pine, coming out of his distraction. "Distance to target?"

"Four hundred meters, sir," replied the controlman.

"Helmsman, match target speed," ordered the Captain.

"Ai, sir, matching speed," replied the helmsman.

"Launch sensor buoy, Captain?" asked LT Pine.

Commander Dorsett, Captain of the SSBN Kamehameha considered this. The sensor buoy was a device designed to detect differences in density, sound, and pressure. It was attached to the submarine and trailed behind it, allowing the Kam to make its measurements at a distance, then reel it back in.

Commander Dorsett nodded.

LT Pine turned to the controlman. "Launch buoy."

And with an hardly audible "Swish," the buoy was away, trailing farther and farther behind the Kam.

The radioman called out, "Captain, USS Serenity informs us barometer above the anomaly is dropping, and a storm is forming. Winds now spiraling at sixty miles per hour, and climbing.

"Lieutenant, take the ship to General Quarters," ordered the Captain.

"Ai, Captain," replied LT Pine. Then into the one MC, he announced, so all on the ship could hear, "All hands to stations. All hands to stations."

Commander Dorsett trusted his crew. They were well trained, and at this moment not a single person was idle, every duty stationed was manned, and every damage control watch was ready to respond.

On the digital map, a thin white line trailed behind the orange oval of the ship and arched toward the grey of the anomaly.

"Ten seconds until buoy breech, Captain. Nine...eight...seven..."

Commander Dorsett watched with all who could on the bridge, as the thin white line represented on the digital screen trailed behind them and slid closer and closer to the massive grey anomaly.

"...Two...one."

And then it was in! At first nothing happened.

Then, "Captain!" called out the sonarman. "Pressure on the sensor climbing rapidly. CD plus three, five, six, eight..."

Pressure underwater was measured in multiples of atmospheric pressure. A person standing at the waterline of a beach lived in an environment of one column of air, which extended upward to the top of the atmosphere, pressing down on him constantly. If that person walked down the slope of the beach into the water (assuming he was still able to breath), every thirty-three feet of sea water depth added another atmosphere of pressure on top of and around him, pressing against his body and his lungs.

For a hallow submarine, there came a point at which the atmospheres of the mass of water pressure over and around it could crush the ship. This was known as "crush depth" or "CD," and it was a number every submariner respected.

"Captain, USS Serenity informs, surface waves now reaching fifty feet. They are turning about," panted the radioman.

At that moment a "crack" was heard on the bridge. The sonarman yelped and threw his earphones from his head, held his ears and writhed in pain. LT Pine leapt to the radioman's station and read the sensor readings.

"We've lost the buoy, Captain. Last recorded pressure was CD plus twenty-three."

Without hesitation, Commander Dorsett ordered, "Reel the buoy line, and come about to three thirty degrees, full throttle."

Those in charge of each station immediately acknowledged and engaged the order, as one man replaced the sonarman at his station and two others stepped onto the bridge to lead the injured man to sickbay.

"Distance," demanded the Captain.

"Four hundred meters, and closing, sir!" replied LT Pine.

Commander Dorsett called to the helmsman, "Full speed?"

"Ai, sir. Throttle full! But there's resistance on our baffles. I can feel it!"

LT Pine turned to the Captain. "Disengage the buoy line, sir?"

"Do it," replied Commander Dorsett. LT Pine spun and punched a yellow button on the sonar console.

"Line away, Captain!" he replied.

"Three hundred meters and closing, sir..." began the controlman, but his announcement was interrupted by an agonizing creaking of the ship's hull.

"Ambient pressure?"

LT Pine called out, "CD minus five atmospheres, but climbing, Captain."

"The storm's overtaking us, sir," called out the controlman. "One hundred meters!"

"Pressure CD minus two atmospheres!" announced LT Pine.

Commander Dorsett, third in his Naval Academy class, first in his submarine warfare class, and youngest in three decades to take command of a United States nuclear vessel, broke out in the first cold sweat of his career. His breathing quickened, as if his chest too was being crushed.

Suddenly he snapped his head toward the helmsman. "Surface the ship, emergency blow!"

The helmsman responded immediately, but could only manage a grunted, "Ai!..." as he heaved with all his might on the yoke. LT Pine slid alongside him and slammed his palm onto a green control panel button.

The One MC blared the breeching alarm, green strobe lights spiraled, and the ship sung a whales' song of pressurized pain and agony.

Any eye that was not glued to a sensor or monitor reflexively scanned the hull for leaking water.

LT Pine reached over the helmsman and added his strength to the yoke.

Above the chaos, the young controlman's voice called out, "Depth, sixty feet. Distance from anomaly, twenty meters!" Then, in a voice that cracked like a broken heart, "But pressure is still climbing, CD minus one atmos...we're not gonna make it!"

LT Pine and the helmsman grunted as they maintained the yoke at full rise.

"Forty feet!" cried the controlman. "But pressure's at crush depth, Captain! What's...?"

LT Pine's muscles contracted to their maximum force, the submarine arched toward its angle of escape, and LT Pine's war cry joined the countless war cries of warriors of every age long dead, as the ship's groan became a shriek, and ten feet from the surface, the pressure surrounding the submarine exceeded crush depth pressure, and the hull of the SSBN Kamehameha gave way.

At the surface, not even a ripple was evident as a tidal wave well over one hundred feet swept over the spot where the Kam would have surfaced, swallowing it and the USS Serenity to the depths of the sea.

* * *

The telephone next to the President's bed rang with the tone that always set his heart racing. He reached for the phone, but instead of feeling the firm receiver in his fingers, he felt a soft, slobbery mass.

"Belle!" The President grumbled. "No. Sit!"

The President flicked his hand and flung his family Irish Bull Dog's slobber on the floor. He knew not to wipe it back onto the dog, because she would just bury her face into his as a gesture of affection and get him even more slimed.

The phone rang a third time, as he drew the phone receiver to his ear.

"Go ahead," he said, doing his best to sound alert and actually be alert.
On the other end of the line, his Chairman of the Joint Chiefs for each of the United States Armed Forces spoke in the voice that he had long ago learned meant a worse-case scenario would somehow be involved.

"The battle group element has made contact. We received initial sensor readings, but the transmission was cut short."

"Interference?" inquired the President.

"We believe lost at sea, Mr. President."

"Hmm," replied the President, his stomach beginning to twist. "Attack?"

"Possible, Mr. President, but unlikely. A full briefing is being developed. We'll be ready in sixty minutes."

The President looked down at his bedside clock for the first time. 0430 it read.

"Oval Office, then."

"Yes, Mr. President. Out," and the line went dead.

The President replaced his receiver on the bedside stand and drew in a breath. He hoped he was ready for whatever challenge faced him and his country this day.

The four hundred year old grandfather clock behind the Presidential Secretary's desk chimed 0530 as the President entered the Oval Office.

Already present and standing at attention were the President's National Security Council, comprised of the Chairman of the Joint Chiefs, the White House Chief of Staff, the Speaker of the House of Representatives, the Chairman of the Senate, the US Ambassador to the United Nations, several members of his cabinet, and the National Science Advisor.

"Please, take your seats," said the President, seating himself at the head of the Oval Office sitting area. "What do we know so far?"

The Chief of Staff spoke up first. "Mr. President, the volume of data is enormous, but no one has yet been able to develop a cohesive picture of what is causing it all."

The Chairman of the Joint Chiefs added, "Vessels from multiple sovereign nations have been reported lost. We have several making accusations of war against one another."

The President turned to the UN Ambassador. "Where do we stand?"

"The G Eight are all concerned but communicating. No adversarial posturing at this point. China currently has North Korea in hand, and neither they nor South Korea believe the North capable of such widespread disruption."

The President then turned to his Secretary of State. "What are the damage estimates?"

"Thus far, mostly rioting in certain regions: Northeast Asia, East Africa, Northwest Europe, South and Central America. We are not sure why, but it appears civil unrest is rising to a fever pitch worldwide."

"This may have something to do with the earthquakes and weather patterns in those regions," broke in the Speaker of the House, his thick southern accent emphasizing his vowels. "Though we have not seen weather changes, I am informed my own state of Iowa has developed a new fault line."

The President wordlessly turned his gaze to the person sitting at the far end of the couch, half hidden by the Secretary of Transportation.

Dr. William Beiner, Science Advisor to the President of the United States, suddenly had the driest mouth he could ever recall. Wrenching his mouth open, he managed to say, "I...I spoke this morning with colleagues at MIT, who are compiling data from sensors worldwide. They may have found a correlation between anomalies. I have asked them to brief you in person. They are in the air now."

The President nodded, pursed his lips, and then looked up at the wall opposite him, where his famous painting of Prometheus hung. In it, Prometheus was shackled to a boulder, sentenced by Zeus to eternal torment for creating and championing humanity, then willfully disobeying Zeus by enabling the progress of mankind.

For his transgression of helping all, Prometheus alone suffered. Prometheus was the President's personal muse. His presidency, he had decided, when he was young and when he had first set himself on the course of becoming President, represented the triumph of good over evil, the just over tyranny, the wise over the weak minded.

"Until we know more," said the President confidently, "activate our National Security Plan; all federal agencies on high alert, all disaster relief organizations mobilized. This body will meet," said the President, turning to the Chairman of the Joint Chiefs, "with all service Chiefs, in the Secure Control Facility, at fifteen hundred hours."

The President scanned the faces in the room and received nods of ascent in reply.

The President stood. "Thank you all."

And the President of the United States left the Oval Office for the last time.

CHAPTER FIVE

"Those without true sight believe that all in their field of vision encompasses everything in the world."

-- Topper, Keeper (Ancient) of the Caeltis Garden

The Storm

Dr. Leonard Newman sat in the pilot's seat of his twin engine Cessna 320F airplane, completed the preflight checks, spotted the airfield wind sock (now nearly horizontal with the wind from a building central Arizona windstorm), and looked over his shoulder to see how Susan and Elizabeth were getting along.

"Susan," Leonard hailed. "I'd rather not wait any longer this morning. The wind is picking up. We should be in the air soon."

Susan Sinclair turned to Elizabeth, "We can finish the conversation in the air," and swept her arm toward the plane steps like a game show model.

Elizabeth rolled her eyes, gripped Aaron's finger tips, and climbed the stairs. She slid into one of the two rear seats as Susan and Aaron followed her; Susan to the right cockpit seat and Aaron to the rearward seat next to her.

Leonard lifted himself from the pilot's seat and came back to secure the side door. Before returning to the front of the plane, he gave an inquisitive thumbs up to both rearward occupants.

Aaron thrust out an exuberant thumb, while Elizabeth's thumb acquiesced a positive response, clearly in protest.

Leonard nodded understandingly.

Within minutes, the propellers were humming and the wheels were lifting off the tarmac.
An hour later, the small airplane having been cruising at maximum altitude and air speed, Susan exited the tiny toilet room in the rear of the airplane for the second time. She squeezed her way back to the right forward seat. After buckling in, she turned to Elizabeth.

"Do you want to talk about it?"

"No mother. I'm here," Elizabeth began, then looked at Aaron. "We're here. So we'll make the most of it." She looked at her mother. "You'll get what you want, and then we'll leave."

Elizabeth's words stated the basic facts of the trip in content, but their intonation spoke an undercurrent of accusation.

Susan's face flushed. 'Is she blaming me for everything?' she thought. Susan looked toward

Leonard, who with his earphone headset on had not heard a word Elizabeth had said. Susan turned back to stare out her windshield.

'Is she saying I walked out on the marriage to get some selfish thing I wanted?'

Susan felt suddenly breathless. She wanted to retort, but she would have to yell to be heard appropriately over the sound of the airplane's engine. To do so now would only make it more difficult for Elizabeth to do as she wanted later.

She turned away toward her own side window. The desert below was giving way to forests and the Rockies. Then the forests blurred into a watery version of a forest, until nothing was visible. Susan let the tears roll out of her eyes and down her face, feeling them splash on her forearms. She closed her eyes, hoping to sleep but not to dream and experience that same horrible nightmare again.

She had been having the nightmare of the fire for months now, and in it she often either lost Elizabeth or Leonard. But either way, in each she lost her life.

Susan wondered if this dream was somehow related to Martin. 'Was this the result of repressed guilt or something?'

'How could it be?' she allowed herself to think. Martin had walked out on her, put them through so much. Had Leonard not been there to help her, to befriend her, and to ultimately love her, she could not have survived.

In the rear seats, Aaron supportively squeezed Elizabeth's hand. Elizabeth smiled a weak thank you, then closed her eyes and hoped she would sleep and not dream. Neither she nor Aaron knew that they shared the same dream, the same vision, and feared the same loss of the other in a horrible, fiery death.

* * *

"We'll be back t'marra!" barked Silas Grummel at Justine and Lil' as he led their two men, Carl and Matt, and his woman, Wanda, with their baby, out the front door of the bunker.

Silas stomped toward his truck. Wanda walked close enough behind that she knew he could hear her footsteps, but far enough away that if he turned hatefully, he could not immediately slap her.

She climbed into the passenger side of the truck and saw Carl and Matt arguing with Justine and Lil'.

Silas roared the truck engine to life and punched the gas. The pickup kicked up dirt and dust, speeding out of the nest of boulders in the Montana plains.

The dust cloud enveloped the four as Justine coughed and yelled, "That's just great! End's comin' an' you just decide to up and git!"

Carl held up one hand in defense and another as a peace offering. "It ain't like that, baby. Just need more protection. You know how this is gonna go down. We need these."

Matt nodded to Lil', "Anything happens, you know what I showed you. You can take care of yourself. Besides, we'll be down to Cheyenne for the gun show and back before ya know it."

"Ah hmm," humphed Justine, who spun on her heels and stomped back into the house.

Matt waved to Lil', and Carl followed Matt to their truck. As they drove away, Lil' waved a final time, watching the departing truck until neither it nor its dust trail could be seen.

Alone again, except for the perpetually angry Justine, Lil' turned toward the bunker.

Silas called it the "bunker", reflected Lil', but she knew it was just a cabin wedged between boulders and buried with earth on top and three sides. She knew the men had built it into the side of a small hill among a large grouping of enormous boulders, because 'the end was coming'. That's what Matt said anyway. And Matt said it, because Silas said it.

But she worried like Justine. Did they have enough food? Could they really last a year? What if the bad times lasted longer? Was hunting going to be enough?'

"That's why we need more guns," Lil' said aloud to herself. 'When the end comes, it's kill or be killed.' That's what Silas said anyway.

Lil' looked down the road where it disappeared behind the boulders. Silas was mean, but he was smart. Matt was smart too, Lil' knew, and she was thankful for that. He would look after her. She would need that if the end was truly coming.

* * *

Carl Howard, the 'Bad Baron of Wall Street,' as Business Week Magazine had dubbed him, stepped from his private office elevator onto the corporate trading floor where his ninety traders fought in the pits for every dollar, yen, and Euro that had made Phoenix Investment Group the largest "pig" in the pen.

Every time he thought about the company name, Carl Howard sneered triumphantly to himself. The day he traded for his first million in commissions at the age of twenty-three, the age-old company he worked for had been indicted for securities fraud, eventually suffering tens of millions in losses. A fellow trader, claiming to be disgusted with his tactics for success, had called him a "ruthless pig."

Laughing all the way to the bank, as they say, he had left that firm to form his own investment group. Having risen from the financial ashes of the ancient firm he had left, he dubbed his company "Phoenix," the 'phoenix pig.'

Two decades later, the Bad Baron of Wall Street peered over his trading floor, out the floor-to-ceiling windows overlooking lower Manhattan, at the thick grey clouds circling New York Harbor.

The weather was hazardous outside, but it was nothing compared to the trading floor within. Carl Howard could smell the panic. And to Carl Howard, panic meant money!

Like a conductor, he peered over his stressed but hungry stock traders hammering away on keyboards, convincing under-educated buyers and stockholders to stay calm in spite of current market conditions and either buy or sell as he wanted.

On the floor, one stock trader, however, felt his stomach turn for the tenth time in as many minutes. Mounted from the ceiling, televisions showed market news reports and tickers, all confirming market after world market plummeting into the deep red.

Unsuccessful with yet one more trade, he clicked his phone device off and mentally shifted his attention to the television monitor above him. On it, a handsome man in a well-cut suit calmly narrated the worst day in his life.

"Unprecedented political and geological unrest over the past six hours," the well-dressed anchorman said, "has caused catastrophic uncertainty in key financial markets. The New York Stock Exchange is down twenty-three percent, the NASDAQ forty-three, NIKKEI thirty-seven, and Shanghai thirty-one percent. With less than an hour left in the New York trading day, the Securities Commission is debating whether to suspend trading until global events and recent catastrophic weather patterns throughout the world calm down. For more on this, let me turn you over to our weather guru. Mark?"

The trader remained transfixed as the television screen cut to the weather man, his Doppler screen covered in weather icons.

"Never seen anything like this," exclaimed Mark, the weatherman, in front of a blue screen image of the Atlantic Coast of the United States. White spiraling and circular arrows danced around him.

"The Atlantic jet stream is reversing, causing turbulent air..." Weather icons appeared like cartoon characters around him. "Tornados," he continued in a somber voice, "hurricanes, earthquakes, tidal waves..."

The weatherman's studio shook from a tremor, and both the weatherman and the set around him jumped.

"Whoa!," He said, catching himself, then regaining his balance. His focus returned to the television screen. "We felt that one!"

The blue screen image changed to an aerial shot of lower Manhattan on a sunny day.

Another earthquake began, with significantly more force than the previous one, lasting a full ten seconds, jolting the camera to the side, and sending the weather blue screen crashing to the floor. With no studio set barriers left in front of it, the television image now displayed a view through the floor to ceiling window of the TV studio over Manhattan.

The Phoenix stock trader could tell from the image that the studio was a West Side building, looking across the Hudson River into New Jersey. The studio camera was televising multiple sites where the ground had split and fiery red lava was geysering into the air.

On screen, the weatherman had turned to the studio window, viewing the real damage himself, dumbfounded. "...volcanoes?"

Mark the weatherman leaned against the glass, in awe, taking in the full view of destruction across Lower Manhattan and New Jersey.

Mark was from Los Angeles, the land without weather. He had come to New York to become a television personality, having failed in L.A., and weatherman was one more step on that ladder. "This can't be happening, he said to himself," panic beginning to build in his stomach.

Mark the weatherman allowed his gaze to migrate Eastward, where a blanket of darkness moved over the city, matched by ominous clouds overhead.

The wave of blackness crossed the East River, spread through midtown, down Lower Manhattan, across New York Harbor, the Statue of Liberty, and into New Jersey. From under Liberty Island, the harbor water appeared to boil, steam rising, until lava burst into the air from underneath it.

As the shadowy blackness crawled and spread across the city, traffic lights went out, car engines turned off, cars rolled and careened into one another, cell phones stopped working, and plants withered and greyed.

At one street curb, not yet hit by the wispy black shadow, a taxi cab pulled over. Both a man and woman reach for the passenger door from different directions. With reluctant chivalry, the man stepped back and gestured for the woman to take the cab. Without a second glance, the woman opened the door to get in, just as the shadow swept across them.

The taxi engine died, and the cab driver cursed, "Damn!"

The man, who had given up his claim on the cab, suddenly staggered backward for a moment, closed his eyes, then recovered his balance, and opened his lids to see the world through grey eyes.

He snapped his head toward the woman, who was about to close the passenger door of the taxi.

The man growled, then leapt at the door, pulling it open. He reached inside the cab, grabbed the woman, and tossed her to the curb.

Scraped, but not broken, the woman slumped to the ground. She had never been so harshly treated. For a flash of a moment, she felt scared. Then her blood felt it was boiling with anger. It felt good, and she wanted revenge. Like an animal she was up, scanning the hazy grey street around her, and shrieking as she dove at her attacker.

The sounds of their fighting were drowned out by the high pitched whistling of a suddenly violent wind. On a nearby television, the weatherman continued to look out the studio window over Manhattan. And now he pointed at a tornado about to hit a building.

On the trading floor of Phoenix Investor's Group, the worn out stock trader's dazed expression at the television metamorphosed to puzzlement. Something on the television was also in his peripheral vision and tapping at his subconscious to be recognized. The young stock trader allowed his gaze to move instead from the floor to ceiling windows.

There he saw the company CEO, Carl Howard, glaring down at him from the walkway that surrounded the stock pit. Carl Howard had used it often to preach his mantra, "Profits are for PIGs!" and motivate his troops through the financial battles that had won him exorbitant amounts of money.

Though the stock trader recognized Carl Howard's scowling expression, that was not the familiar sight that was tapping at his subconscious. Behind Howard, however, on either side of him, the familiar silvery white sight from the television expanded like a pair of angel's wings.

Carl Howard saw what was happening. He knew tough times, and he knew even more that the weak could not handle them. Even in his own organization there were sure to be some who would break. This would be a very challenging day, without doubt, but he would use this challenge to weed the weak ones from his herd.

He focused on one now, the stupid dolt staring blankly passed him, too overwhelmed with his own ineptitude and too stupid to realize his career was done. Carl Howard watched the mayhem of his brokers with his back to the window, and suddenly, one by one, they all began to look like the stupid trader staring passed him. Some brokers dropped their phones and some took stuttering steps backward.

On the television, the tornado about to hit the building had given way to "Breaking News". The news anchorman was saying, "The brightest scientific minds from around the world are meeting today in Washington, D.C. to determine if recent events could mark the end of the world."

Carl Howard, billionaire CEO of Phoenix Investment Group, scoffed, then turned toward the window, to do as he often did, view the domain over which he commanded.

"Every market rebounds," he said. "It's never the end of the..."

The tornado filled the window at last. Though its roar had previously been drowned out by the sound proof glass, its vibration now reverberated to a deafening pitch. With the unbridled force of an unscrupulous Wall Street robber baron, the tornado struck the building, blasted its windows inward, and ground it to powder.

CHAPTER SIX

"Perpetual devotion to what a man calls his business, is only to be sustained by perpetual neglect of many other things."

-- Robert Louis Stevenson

The Energy

An enormous spiral of grey storm clouds loomed over the White House from the south.

Fredrick Miter, recent Princeton graduate and third intern to the White House Chief of Staff, ran through the second underground level of the White House on an important mission. All Hell was breaking loose around them, and he had been trusted to bring the President's own dog, Belle, down to the White House Command Bunker.

As he ran, Fredrick Miter heard Belle panting and wheezing in the normal way bull dogs did. At the end of the hall was the secure elevator reserved only for Command Bunker personnel. Standing rigidly in front of its doors were two Marine guards.

Fredrick slowed to a walk and held out the leash to one of the Guards.

"The President called for his dog," panted Miter, bending over to catch his breath, sounding very much like Belle next to him. One guard received the leash, though neither turned away from Miter. Miter understood why. He was not authorized access to the Bunker, and they would not relax their guard stance until he either left or they had been given orders to allow him in.

'That wasn't going to happen,' thought Miter. A third possibility occurred to him. He could try to force his way down to the Bunker. That, of course, would result in the Marines taking offensively defensive action against him. That did not appeal to Miter. So, without receiving a thank you, or a beating, he stood, turned, and walked away.

* * *

Sixty feet below, the President took a deep breath and thought of his wife and daughter to calm himself. He could hear the hum of the elevator through the open briefing room door, down the hallway, through the open blast doors, to the elevator itself. His nerves were frazzled, and the inconsistent conclusions from his own staff did nothing to calm them.

He was not sure why he had called for his family dog. Belle was his daughter's dog actually. But with his wife accompanying their daughter back for her second year of veterinary school in Northern

California, the dog was the closest family he had available.

The President allowed the information presented to him thus far to run back through his mind. Frustrated, he stood up and slammed a hand onto the table.

"Dammit!" he exclaimed. "You're the brightest minds in the world. One of you has to have an explanation!"

The table at which the President sat at the head was surrounded by the men and women of his National Security Council and Joint chiefs, some in uniform, some not, and two additional members today in tweed jackets, looking more like college professors than advisors to the President. He knew that today they were both.

Dr. Philip Hart said, pointing to an electronic map of the world on the wall, "It's unexplainable, Mr. President. Every tectonic plate has shifted..."

On the map, animated continents appeared to float into and away from each other.

"...as if every string on a baseball had suddenly vanished, leaving the surface to..."

"Not suddenly," interrupted Dr. Isaac Feinman, looking older and more haggard than he had at dinner the previous night.

The President turned to Dr. Feinman, and Dr. Feinman shared a look with Dr. Hart. "Not suddenly," he said again, looking at the President. "Disturbances were detected in multiple remote locations as early as three days ago."

"Three days!" exclaimed the President, who reflexively turned to his National Science Advisor. Dr. William Beiner, Science Advisor to the President of the United States, felt his spine contract, though he resisted his cowering reaction.

Hoping to avoid an unnecessary diversion of the conversation, Dr. Hart said, "Dr. Beiner received our call and arranged for us to meet with you as soon as we began to understand what was happening, Mr. President."

The President faced Dr. Hart again. "And what is happening, Dr. Hart?"

"Are you familiar with Pangaea, Mr. President?"

"The primordial continent?"

"In essence, yes."

"But it's more than that," added Dr. Feinman. "Collectively, the sciences believe our Earth developed from a molten ball of lava into a carbon, hydrogen, and oxygen based, life bearing planet, when these elements were brought from meteors traveling through our galaxy, and trapped by Earth's gravity."

Dr. Feinman swallowed, and Dr. Hart continued, "Oceans formed and Pangaea was the continent that rose above it. Over time, the forces in Earth's core split Earth's mantle into multiple tectonic plates.

Pangaea split, separate continents formed and shifted..."

"Finally forming the continents we know today," the President finished.

"Ultimately," corrected Dr. Feinman, "but not finally."

The President pondered this statement a moment.

"What Dr. Feinman means to say," said Dr. Beiner, interrupting the momentary silence, "is that the tectonic plates are never in final position."

The President set his jaw in a way that silenced Dr. Beiner, then turned inquisitively to Dr. Feinman. "Is that what you mean to say?"

"Perhaps a better way of stating it," explained Dr. Feinman, "is that nothing happens in a vacuum. Everything in our world is both an action and a reaction, caused by something and in turn causing something else, simultaneously, billions of times a second."

"Our world is like a bee hive," continued Dr. Hart, the two scientists explaining events like professional tennis players hitting the science lecture ball back and forth. "It appears chaotic and random."

"But even apparently cataclysmic events: earthquakes, hurricanes, tornados...are part of a rhythm, a pattern, an energy, that keeps the Earth together."

Dr. Hart locked eyes with the President. "What you see now are waves of that energy disappearing."

"Disappearing? What do you mean?" asked the President.

"You are familiar with the physical laws," stated Dr. Hart.

The President opened his mouth to respond, but the sound came from further down the table.

"Excuse me, Mr. President, this is all interesting, but how is this related to any political unrest or natural catastrophes?" asked General Tom "The Tower" Hauer, Chief of the Army, stirring uncomfortably in his seat.

The President considered reprimanding the interruption, but under the circumstances and the limited time that appeared available, he said, "Perhaps we could cut to the chase, doctor."

"To us," continued Dr. Hart, "the total amount of energy throughout the world is finite. It merely exists in different forms. To this point, we have believed all energy can be measured and controlled."

General Hauer began to stir again.

Dr. Feinman turned to one of the numerous technicians manning computer screens surrounding the dark perimeter of the bunker Command Center.

"Can you play the simulation?" he asked.

On the screen, four grey circles appeared on the map of the continents and began to spread outward.

"This time-lapse animation shows the wave of events over the past three days," explained Dr. Hart. "The waves you are seeing appeared to originate from and grow outward from Yakushima, Japan; Gloucestershire, England; Kakamega, Kenya; and an uninhabited region of the Amazon rainforest."

"These are not weapons sites," stated General Hauer.

"No," agreed Dr. Hart. "As far as we can tell, their only commonality is that they are all very old forests."

"At the time the anomalies started," continued Dr. Feinman, "they were not even noted, seemingly insignificant. But like a wave, they've spread outward."

"Is it a weapon?" asked the President.

General Hauer shook his head, "No weapon has the energy for this kind of destruction."

"It's not energy," retorted Dr. Feinman. "It's the lack of it."

Dr. Hart turned again to the President. "This is why we were explaining the physical laws. The waves of destruction we are witnessing are not due to chaotic energy being added to our world. It appears to be the withdrawal of a stabilizing energy *from* our world."

"In the regions of these waves, nothing of any stabilizing technology works, as if the stone age crawled out of a hole and is sweeping across the world. It may even be affecting people," said Dr. Feinman with finality.

The President shifted backward in his chair and drew in a deep breath. The table remained quiet.

Then the President asked Dr. Feinman, "What's your specialty?"

"Probability String Mathematics."

"A math teacher?" asked General Hauer incredulously.

The President did not acknowledge the implication. Instead, he asked. "Can we fix this?"

The two scientists looked at each other in a way that told the President that these two scientists had been asking themselves this very same question. They slowly shook their heads, then looked up at the map.

Dr. Hart spoke what they both feared. "Sir, we only know that it has reached us."

All eyes shot to the map, which showed the upper edge of the South American dark circle covering Washington, D.C.

"My God," said the President. "What next?"

As the words came from his mouth, emergency bunker lights blinked yellow and red. A computerized voice from bunker speakers and red banners on the monitor screen announced, "Missile warning. Missile warning."

The Generals and Admirals seated around the table leapt up and ran to peer over technicians' shoulders as the technicians typed furiously.

Several began to call out coordinates. "Sir, multiple bogeys marked from ground based platforms..."

"Missile warning. Missile warning," the computer voice continued to say.

From the dark circle over Russia, the world map bloomed with numerous spidering yellow lines.

A sweet, almost motherly computer voice added, "Missiles activated. Launch in *thirty* seconds."

The President jumped up, moving toward his Chairman of the Joint Chiefs. "What the hell is going on? I didn't give the order to launch!"

The Chairman turned, pale, "We've lost control of the system. Any active silo, ours or theirs, is going to launch independently."

"Against who?" demanded the President.

"Between our allies and theirs," the Chairman explained, "it looks like every modern capital in the world is targeted."

The President searched the room until he locked eyes with Dr. Hart.

Dr. Hart slowly shook his head, his voice hardly a whisper, "Stabilizing forces dissipating faster than chaotic forces. There will be no contro..."

The White House Chief of staff moved to the Control Room door. "Not to worry Mr. President. We are locking down the bunker now. We'll be able to maintain all command and control from here."

With equally auspicious timing, all electronically powered illumination in the room went dead, leaving the group in complete darkness.

Moments later, the White House Chief of Staff drew a handful of chemical light sticks from a wall-mounted emergency case and cracked them to life.

A thump of footsteps made their way quickly at him and unceremoniously pulled the chem lights away. Like some panicked and drunken fire fly, the green glow bobbled to the Control Room door.

The President managed to see Dr. William Beiner's face momentarily in the green light, before the glowing sticks tumbled out the hallway door and down the hall, where several US Marine guards struggled to close the thick blast door.

Noticing the open Control Room door, the senior of the US Marine guards grunted, "Sir, there's no power. The blast door won't close!"

The disappointments and burdens were finally too much. The President of the United States collapsed into the chair nearest him. Over the course of his career, only one constant had been with him to calm his mind through tough times. Exhaling, the President of the United States closed his eyes, and thought of his wife and daughter.

* * *

Elizabeth was thankful to look out the window and see the flight was almost over, especially since they had been trailed by a towering wall of dark, ominous storm clouds for the past several hours.

She felt somewhat sorry about what she had said to her mother earlier. 'Sorry', because she liked Leonard and knew they would be happy together. 'Somewhat', because her mother was such a pain in the ass!

She had flown in Leonard's plane many times over the years. Once she remembered as a kid, when her mother and father were still together, and several other times over the past few years when her mother had begun dating Leonard and she had been dating Aaron. As crazy as the situation was, at least this part of the trip felt like family.

The thin door behind Elizabeth opened again, and Susan, looking pale, exited the tiny bathroom in the rear of the plane. She scooted toward the front passenger seat. She passed Elizabeth and Aaron holding hands, who had to let go for Susan to pass. Once she had, Elizabeth reached over and they held hands once again.

Susan lowered herself tenderly into the front right seat of the plane, looking somewhat green. "When will we land Leonard?"

Leonard tilted his head slightly toward a secluded landing field, about one thousand feet below, in the woodlands of Montana. "Nearly there," he said.

"Good thing," replied Elizabeth, looking back toward the bathroom behind her. "After eight hours, we're reaching maximum capacity."

Aaron chuckled and Elizabeth smiled with him. But the humor quickly soured for Elizabeth. She turned toward her window and looked down at the approaching woodland area where her father apparently now lived. She was faced with the reality of the impending reunion, but she could think of nothing else but the last time she told him good-bye.

It was four years earlier, her senior year in high school, and it was supposed to have been the best spring break of her young life. Instead, Martin had managed to guilt her into accompanying him on what he had led her to believe was a father daughter bonding trip to Florida.

At the worst, Elizabeth had harbored the possibility that if her dad became weird again, she could duck out from time to time to a nearby club or beach. The only problem was that they did not go to Daytona or Panama City Beach for her spring break. Martin had taken her to the swamps of Ponce De Leon, two hours from the nearest sand, and nothing but fresh water streams and reptiles for miles around.

She was in the woods, trees as far as the eye could see, and not a road for miles. Elizabeth remembered this trip, this day, the last day she saw her father.

Elizabeth recalled her seventeen year-old self stomping angrily away from Martin. She could still feel the roots of that anger even today.

"You dragged me out here to some Florida swamp, during my senior year spring break," she shouted, "to see some old tree!"

Martin stood in a small clearing, undaunted, a compassionate smile on his face. Next to Martin grew a three foot tall, knotted and twisted, nearly barren, willow tree.

"It is significant," he assured her, "and I want you to see..."

Elizabeth spun on him. "What! Why is this so important? What new revelation has come to you to embarrass me?"

He remained calm and consoling.

"It will make sense soon," Martin insisted. "Just be patient."

Elizabeth huffed defiantly and turned again to leave.

"It is important," explained Martin, "because everything begins and ends here."

"Yeah," replied Elizabeth condescendingly, "it does end here, Martin! Mom gave up on you years ago, but I held out, hoping you would either come out of it or at least get treatment. But no, you'd rather drag everyone down with you. I'm outta here. Enjoy your tree."

Now as she sat in the plane, coming closer and closer to a door she had long ago shut and locked away deep inside her, she knew she was supporting her mother, but she wondered if any good could come of this.

Aaron watched Elizabeth knowing this was going to be uncomfortable for her, but he knew equally well that she was working through it in her own way.

Still holding her hand, he looked out his own window behind them and had his attention caught by two images other than the approaching landing strip.

The first was a trail of dust and dirt being kicked up by what looked like two pickup trucks as they sped over the Montana plains just ahead of the storm's shadow. The second was ahead of their plane, not far from the landing strip. It was a recently harvested field.

"Good thing they got their crops in," Aaron remarked, "or that storm would've wiped them out."

Leonard regarded the ominous storm clouds behind them nervously and piloted the plane downward.

"Keep up, Carl!" shouted Silas into the CB radio, not for the first time.

He had seen the storm coming and turned the group from the gun show back toward their bunker. It burned him to admit it, but if they were going to hunker down, they had to do it now with the weapons they already had.

Hardened and weathered, Silas' face looked a decade more than his forty-three years. He drove the lead of the two pickup trucks with no intention of letting anyone keep him from surviving, not Carl, Matt, Wanda, the baby, or anything else.

Dirt shot out from under both sets of truck tires. Carl was sure Silas knew what he was doing. How Silas knew about the coming storm and the end of the world, Carl didn't understand, but Silas hadn't been wrong yet. And despite Silas' temper and apparent reckless ways, both he and Matt knew their best chance of survival was sticking close to Silas.

Silas let his anger push him on. Anger had always been his greatest strength. It had been his will and his means for success. When he was angry, he got what he wanted. It had been the same for his dad, and for his grandaddy before him. And now, when it counted most, Silas made sure his anger was at its peak.

Alongside Silas, Wanda held the baby to her breast hoping this time the milk would come and that the baby wouldn't cry. Last time it cried, Silas had hit her, hit her hard.

'I'm sure I deserved it,' she thought. 'It's my job to feed the baby and keep it quiet. The baby's crying made it hard for Silas to think of what we needed to do when we ran right up to the storm. Silas knew it was no use, and we had to turn back.'

Wanda lifted the bundling blanket to see if the baby was getting any milk. It was suckling, but with the truck jumping so much, she couldn't tell if the baby had milk or not. 'I sure hope it don't cry.'

Carl's panicked voice suddenly came over the CB radio. "The bunker's too far, Silas. We're not gonna make it!"

Silas pulled the rifle from his lap and thrust it toward Wanda, who had to shift her weight to hold it and the baby. He grabbed the CB hand set. "You don't make it, that's your problem. Ain't nothin' stoppin' me!"

Silas suddenly heard a humming sound and looked out his window as a small airplane flew overhead for a landing. He squinted his eyes. 'Others nearby,' he thought. 'Trouble happens, we'll be ready for 'em.'

Silas punched his foot down on the accelerator pedal and sped forward.

Carl saw the gap between their trucks increase and reflexively glanced in his rearview mirror. The storm was nearly over them. He gripped the steering wheel harder and slammed his own foot on the gas pedal, praying that luck was on their side.

* * *

The two most dangerous times in an airplane, Leonard knew, were the take off and the landing. This landing was going to be his most challenging to date.

The tail wind from the storm was turbulent and alternately pushed and pulled the small plane's tail, causing it to corkscrew as the plane descended closer and closer to the ground. On top of this pressure, Leonard had the sinking feeling in his stomach about what would happen when they had landed and he greeted Martin for the first time in three years, with Susan beside him.

Susan picked up on Leonard's apprehension. "You okay?"

Leonard said nothing. But when Susan placed a hand on his forearm, he said, "This is weird for me. We used to be colleagues, friends."

"This is weird for all of us," said Susan. "Let's just get this over with. We'll leave once he signs the paperwork and be home by tomorrow."

Susan pushed back into her seat, clearly tense, then closed her eyes. "I refuse to be sucked down the rabbit hole of his delusions."

Leonard couldn't think about tomorrow. Right now landing was everything. He looked momentarily and uncertainly at the storm approaching closely behind. 'Just land the plane,' he thought.

Leonard tried not to hold his breath. He needed to relax. To calm his nerves, he focused on the landing strip markers, keeping all his points of focus in his peripheral vision.

At two hundred feet of altitude, Leonard struggled to keep the plane level and in the landing strip. As he always did to get out of his own head, he internally sang his favorite rock anthems. Each had a driving, head banging beat that, between the music and his actual head drumming motion, kept him alert and focused.

Susan noticed the slight rhythmic nod of Leonard's head and smiled reassuringly to herself, knowing that he had gone to his 'happy place.'

Leonard let his mind go and allowed his muscle memory to take over.

Before he knew it, the plane's wheels had all engaged the ground, he adjusted the wing flaps to keep them there, and taxied toward the cabin at the end of the landing strip, where he now saw Martin exiting the front door and waving.

Martin was walking to Leonard's left and pointing toward the nearby woods. As the plane approached the end of the runway and began making the left turn, Leonard saw, on the edge of the woods, a hangar for the plane.

* * *

Minutes later, the plane was in the hangar, the propeller had just come to a stop, and Martin opened Leonard's door.

Leonard turned to see Martin, anticipating the worst. Instead he saw his old friend, very tanned, and grinning from ear to ear.

"I'm so glad you're here," Martin said, gripping Leonard's hand in both of his and shaking it energetically. "Thank you for taking such good care of them."

Leonard slid from the cockpit, and the others quickly followed. Leonard faced Martin nervously, but before Leonard could reply, Martin had turned to shake Aaron's hand.

"And Aaron, at long last," extolled Martin. "Such a pleasure."

Aaron, surprised by the praise, and having no idea how Martin could really know anything about him, opened his mouth to speak. But again Martin moved on.

Martin's face flushed, his eyes crinkled, and he appeared about to burst with either laughter or tears, when he faced Elizabeth. Elizabeth held her breath hoping for neither. Instead, Martin wrapped Elizabeth in a huge hug.

Stunned, Elizabeth stood frozen at first, like a 'doe in the headlights', then uncomfortably hugged him back. When he at last pulled away from her, his eyes were watery, and Elizabeth felt the twinges of tears forming in her own eyes. Then, as quickly as he had hugged her, he moved on and finally faced Susan.

Susan was the reason they were all there, but she was the most uncomfortable with the situation. As Martin opened his arms to give her a hug, she began to back away.

But the space too cramped and her reaction too late, his arms flew around her in a bear of a hug before she could resist.

Elizabeth could not help but smile. Watching her mother and knowing how uncomfortable she was at this moment, having dragged her all the way to Montana just before she defended her undergraduate thesis, this was some kind of karma justice.

Susan stood stiffly, her hands at her side. "Yes, we're all here, Martin." He released her and stood back to get a good look at her face. "But to be honest..." she continued.

"You must be starving," Martin interrupted, as he suddenly came to life and shuffled through the small group. Before anyone else had moved, Martin was already at the hangar door. "Please, come into the house. We have so much to catch up on!"

Martin scurried away, waving for the family to follow him out of the hangar and toward the cabin.

Susan stepped out after him, "About that..."

Martin paid no attention, however, and did not stop until they were all on the cabin porch.

Standing at the porch railing, Martin had turned toward the landing strip and the broad expanse of wilderness beyond, when all four of the others stepped up to meet him. No one spoke, as apparently Martin was lost in thought. The others looked outward also, wondering what had captured his attention.

Leonard broke the silence, "Hey, what is he doing?"

All eyes followed Leonard's gaze toward the hangar, where a Native American man pulled their small suitcases from the back of the plane and loaded them into a wheel barrow.

Susan turned to Martin more defiantly. "Martin, we're all here, like you asked. But, really, can't we just get this over with and sign the papers? We'll get back home, and you can..." She looked around disapprovingly. "We'll all have a new start."

Martin had not acknowledged their questions or reactions. He continued to stare mysteriously at the horizon and the approaching storm.

'A new beginning,' Martin thought, his heart beating faster and his breath becoming shorter and more rapid. 'I must be strong. If they do not believe...'

He stopped the thought there and focused on the horizon. To him the distant storm looked like a giant Saharan dust storm ripping up the ground from below, joined to the ominous clouds above in a wall of destruction. And it was coming closer.

He inhaled a deep breath and released it slowly, before turning back toward the cabin.

"Yes," said Martin, entering the cabin, "a new start."

The others looked at each other, then at Susan, but she remained on the porch. She had picked up on Martin's apprehension and wanted to ensure nothing was out of sorts. Scanning the horizon, she saw only the dark clouds above, blanketing the land in shadow.

She sighed and looked for cues from Leonard, who shrugged and encouraged her to enter as well.

Elizabeth bit her tongue and turned to Aaron. "Sorry about dragging you into all the weirdness."

He wrapped an arm around her and kissed her. Taking in the scenery he said, "This is cool." Aaron squeezed her hand and the two entered the cabin.

As the last of Martin's family disappeared, Askuwheteauachachak Kitchi, last of the Hashakochi Iti tribe, turned the wheel barrow away from the cabin and toward the woods.

* * *

The two pickup trucks raced across an open pasture toward a stretch of trees.

In the lead truck, Silas gritted his teeth. 'Damn them!' he thought, seeing the clouds bearing down on them. 'Damn them for slowing me down!'

Wanda scanned out the window frightfully, but saw only the shadow from the overhead storm bearing down on them.

Wanda swallowed hard. "Somethin' don't feel right, Si."

She opened her window and searched the approaching shadow, not more than a hundred yards away. In it, she saw darkness saturated the air, trees covered by it instantly withered, and in places the ground rent open.

'It's going to cut us off!' realized Silas, punching the accelerator one last time in the hope of outrunning the darkness. But it was on them.

"Aaahh!" Silas screamed.

From the CB, Carl's voice cried, "Not gonna make it!"

The rim of the storm above and the wave of darkness below overtook Carl's truck.

Carl and Matt watched the wispy black lines swim into the metal and plastic of the car. Carl screamed, "Noo!" turning the steering wheel side to side, and causing the car to lurch left and right, as the blackness traveled from the steering wheel to his hands, and from his hands up his arms.

Matt, next to him, jumped around in the seat, trying not to let the blackness touch him. When it finally did, he too could do nothing but see his skin turn pale and the world around him become a washed out grey.

Then with a "blam blam", the truck's tires exploded, careening the truck into a skid and a tree with a "crack"!

Silas heard the crash and knew the darkness was on them. He saw the wispy black lines crawl inside the truck and through the dashboard. A second later, the electronics of the truck went dead. Then, *his* tires exploded. Next to him, Wanda screamed, the baby cried, Silas spun the steering wheel, and the truck slid into an embankment, launching Silas out the driver side window!

Wanda hung nearly upside down, still clinging to the baby. She could hardly breath, and something was wrong with her eyesight. With one hand, she grabbed for the door and her seat belt. Free from both, she crawled from the truck, gasping, and clinging to the crying baby.

Safely away from the truck, she looked back toward the bushes where Silas had flown. "Si!" she pleaded. She could barely see. She was terrified she was left to survive alone. "Siii!"

As if in answer to her call, the bushes thrashed, and Silas stumbled out toward her and onto the top of the truck. He was hurt and gasping.

Wanda stepped fearfully forward, then was relieved when Silas did not fall. Instead, he looked up at the storm and yelled with about as mean a voice as she had ever heard, "I hear you!"

Silas lowered his face toward Wanda, and she saw he wasn't hurt. He looked powerful, hungry, and the whites of his eyes were now grey.

Silas drew in deeper and deeper breaths, feeling the anger flaring, and the power building inside him. It built inside him until he could almost hear it talking to him, until it felt the power in him would explode. Arching his back, he lifted his face to the sky, before releasing a blood curdling scream. "Aaaarrggh!"

* * *

Martin smiled like any dinner host, and handed five tumblers of cocktails to his guests: a double malt scotch to Leonard, a Mohito to Susan, a Coke and Malibu to Elizabeth, and Coke and Captain Morgan to Aaron.

In the fifth glass, he poured a little water from the sink, then raised it in a toast, "To family."

Susan, more than a little disturbed by this, set the glass to her lips and greedily drank its contents. Leonard nodded nervously to Martin and did likewise. Aaron tapped Elizabeth's glass and chugged his, while Elizabeth took a mere sip.

Martin raised his glass one more time to the open door, "To possibilities."

Martin could now see the wave of destruction just a few miles away. Animals were running in advance of it. And it was closing in quickly.

* * *

Justine and Lil' watched the storm clouds spread over the boulders surrounding the bunker, and with the clouds, their shadows. Lil' whimpered and ran inside.

"Yeah, go an' hide," Justine grumbled. "That'll do good."

Justine could feel something coming, but she knew it was not a storm of the usual kind. No wind blew, and the air did not have the static electricity in it before a tornado.

'This is something else,' she thought, and she resolved to stay outside and witness it. She did not have to wait long.

She saw the shadow did not cover the bunker so much as 'crawl over' it, and, she discovered, her. She held out her hand as the wispy black lines swam through her hand, up her arm, and throughout her body. She breathed deeply as the anger and rage unleashed inside her, heard Lil's whimpering from inside the bunker, and saw the entire world around her turn grey.

Lil' whimpered again, 'but this time it was different,' she thought. 'Was that a growl?' Justine wondered. Had Lil' challenged her?

Justine walked toward the bunker door prepared to answer that challenge. In fact, Justine was prepared to answer Lil' for a whole lot she had done over the years.

As Justine swung the bunker front door open, she was definitely hit with a fierce growl. She was also hit in her stomach by a hammer. Justine shrieked with anger, stepped through the door, and leapt forward.

The high-pitched, raging sounds of battle were soon lost in the piercing whine and blackness of the storm overhead.

* * *

"Can we get on with this?" Susan asked, placing her empty glass on the counter, glancing out the door passed Martin, and seeing only the storm clouds. "A storm is coming."

Elizabeth peered out the front window, seeing the clouds and shadow, but to her the land and trees below were hazy. She squinted, unsure of what she was seeing.

Aaron collected her glass and walked toward Martin, as Susan shot a knowing look at Leonard.

Leonard stepped beside Susan. "Uh, Martin, it really is good to see you again, but we should be getting on, you know."

"Yes," Martin agreed with a sad smile. "Things have changed, and the storm is coming."

Martin collected the glasses from each person and placed them and the alcohol bottles into what appeared to be a small cabinet. He closed the cabinet door, flipped up a panel, and pushed a button. The sound of a motor hummed quietly, then faded into the distance, then silence.

"And with any luck," continued Leonard, "we can make it to Denver before it hits."

Martin did not respond, walking instead to the back door of the one room cabin. He held the door knob and turned to the group.

"Follow me and we'll get this all settled."

Leonard and Susan began to follow, but Elizabeth remained at the front door studying the horizon. Aaron stood supportively next to her.

"Something doesn't feel right," said Elizabeth. Martin was distracted by Elizabeth and loosened his grip on the back door.

Exasperated, Susan at last pulled a manila legal envelope from her purse and threw it onto a table. "Martin, just sign the papers!"

"There is something you must see first," Martin explained.

Elizabeth looked worried and moved closer to the front door, feeling the air in front of her.

Susan bargained, "If we see this...whatever...will you sign and let us leave?"

Martin replied, "Once you see, I will do whatever, and you can do whatever, you want."

Susan bit her lip to keep from saying what she truly felt, and instead picked up the envelope and nodded.

Martin looked to Leonard who nodded as well. Then at Aaron, who, surprised to be included in the visual contract, chuckled.

"Sure," he said. "I'll stay as long as the party lasts."

Martin smiled and turned finally to Elizabeth. His smile faded as he saw the wave of destruction breaching the nearest hill on the far side of the runway.

Elizabeth looked terrified as she searched the clouds and underlying shadow for some physical confirmation of the terrible feeling she had. She could find nothing, but worse, she could no longer ignore the overwhelming sense of impending doom.

She turned, nodded to Martin, grabbed Aaron's hand, and pulled him quickly toward the others.

"Done," confirmed Martin.

Martin opened the back door, but not onto a back porch. The other side was a finely polished steel room, the size of a freight elevator.

Martin entered and gestured for the others to follow. Leonard did, and Elizabeth marched directly into the room, guiding Aaron in quickly.

When Elizabeth turned, Susan remained stubbornly in the cabin, her back toward the destruction, which was now only a hundred yards from the air field.

"Get in, mother," demanded Elizabeth.

"I'm not going any further," retorted Susan adamantly.

Panicked animals ran from the forest across the open space. And even Aaron and Leonard began to sense the feeling of impending doom.

"Honey," offered Leonard. "I think you should."

Martin now saw the destruction at the very edge of the field.

"I will not!" said Susan vehemently.

Aaron nodded to Leonard. "I think you should..."

Having had enough, Elizabeth gritted her teeth. "Get in! Now!" And grabbing her mother by the collar, she yanked Susan into the small room.

Martin immediately hit a button on an electronic panel, and whispered, "ar' Ama Gedeon."

Martin watched the outside destruction slam into an invisible wall at the edge of the landing strip, just as two metal doors closed the small room. The lights in

the room faded to a pale green, everyone gasped,
and the room...dropped.

CHAPTER SEVEN

"Rise above the storm and you will find the sunshine."

-- Mario Fernandez

The New World

Susan screamed.

She could feel her stomach churn, hear metallic clanging noises outside the small room, and felt the rapid descent.

On the other side of the metal walls, the room fell down a deep elevator shaft, just as two thick, metal blast-doors slid together, locked, and pressurized with a SSHHHT...BOOM!

"Martin!" Susan demanded. "What's going on?"

Martin said nothing, but pushed a glass panel that opened to reveal a series of buttons. A digital screen counted: 8, 9, 10...

Elizabeth nodded her chin toward the cabin. "What was that?"

Martin smiled reassuringly to Elizabeth.

Susan placed one hand on the metal room wall. "My god!" she exclaimed, "Martin! Are we in an elevator? Are we under ground?"

The numbers next to Martin on the display screen slowed down: 17, 18...19...and then stopped on 20.

"We are here," Martin announced.

The doors opened once again.

* * *

The next space the family saw was nothing like the one above they had just left. Martin held his hand across the elevator threshold, inviting the family into the new space.

Beyond the threshold was a very large circular great room. Though one room, it was tiled and decorated into five distinct spaces.

Stepping from the elevator, Elizabeth's eyes were drawn naturally to her left, where the space held earth tones and living room furniture. On the opposite right were the lighter tones of a kitchen. Beyond the living space was a cozy area with floor to ceiling books, and beyond the kitchen a dining room.

Bringing the far spaces together were a baby grand piano accompanied by violin, guitars, and assorted rare musical instruments.

Peering out from the elevator, Susan stammered, "What is...?"

Elizabeth and Aaron stepped tentatively toward the middle of the great room, still holding hands, followed by a dazed Leonard.

"What was...?" started Elizabeth, her mind stuck between questions of what had just happened and what was happening now.

"Your mother was right," answered Martin. "A storm is coming."

Aaron spotted the musical instruments and feeling grounded by their presence, wandered absently towards them, letting go of Elizabeth's hand.

Susan, with one foot in and one out of the elevator, was the only person who had still not entered the room. Martin looked at Leonard and invited, "Shall I show you around?"

Leonard turned back to Susan and offered his hand, who, tentative as a deer, stepped from the elevator. As soon as her second foot crossed the elevator threshold, however, its doors closed behind her with a "Shht," and disappeared.

Susan spun around and ran her hands along the wall to find the opening, demanding, "Where's the door? Martin!"

Martin said nothing but moved into the living room, gesturing toward a couch. "Please, sit down."

Elizabeth and Leonard followed Martin and sat, taking in the room. But Susan, unable to find the opening, stubbornly kept her back to the wall and scanned the open room from her vantage point near the elevator.

"Here is where I have been, mostly," began Martin. "Here, we can be safe from the storm."

"Is it just a storm?" asked Leonard. "It felt odd up there."

Martin opened his mouth to answer, but paused, noticing Elizabeth's expression had changed to an intense stare.

Susan, still at the wall, said, "It feels odd in here. I want to leave."

Martin spoke calmly to Elizabeth, "I'll explain, but your trust would be helpful." Then to the others, "It's no accident you are here."

Susan stomped from the wall toward Martin. "We know, Martin! You forced us to come. It's been seven years since we separated and three since you dropped off the face of the earth. I for one have had enough... a lifetime of enough."

Her final epithet was interrupted by a rumbling that shook the room. But Martin paid no attention either to it or Susan. He instead moved toward the library area beyond the living space, and waved casually for the others to join him.

Susan bellowed, "I want the divorce final, Martin! Now give us what you forced us to come all this way to get, so we can..."

But the rumble that interrupted her this time reverberated through the structure, causing her to lose her balance slightly and the lights to flicker.

She regained her footing, held her breath and her harsh words, and decided to follow the others.

"Earthquakes?" she asked. "In Montana?"

"Please come," Martin invited somberly. "There is much to do...to show you, and then you'll understand."

Aaron saw the others gathering by the books and moved from the instruments toward Elizabeth. She held out her hand.

Just beyond the bookshelves was another, though very much smaller, elevator. Martin entered it, and Elizabeth, Aaron, and Leonard followed. Susan remained back, her temper flaring.

"Leonard!"

"I want to know what's going on," he replied.

Elizabeth was not so accommodating. "Get in the elevator, mother." And, biting her tongue, Susan did.

"I think you'll find this interesting," said Martin.

The door closed.

* * *

The elevator door opened again, as Susan was lecturing Martin. "...and what can you possibly show us of any significance that will...?"

But her words faded to silence and her face filled with wonder as she stepped from the elevator. The rest of the family followed behind Susan, jaws dropping in awe. They were now in a forty foot tall compartment of wooded forest.

Susan laid her hand on the side of the tallest of many trees growing from sapling to forty feet in an orchard at four foot intervals. Every bit of space was occupied. Between the trees grew stalks of wheat and corn, while moss-covered panels lined the walls.

"What do you think?" asked Martin.

"Holy sh..." began Elizabeth's reply.

But Susan cut her off. "This bunker we are in...I assume this is the bottom floor." Susan's anger morphed into professorial condescension.

Martin raised an eyebrow. Elizabeth nodded, understanding what her mother was referring to. "Carbon dioxide is heavier than air," she explained, "and naturally vents downward from upper floors."

Susan continued, "Plants convert carbon dioxide and water vapor to oxygen and organic biomass."

Elizabeth, seeing Aaron's confusion, moved her finger from her mouth toward the trees, then from the trees toward her mouth. "Out with the bad air. In with the good."

"This bunker is sealed then?" asked Leonard. "Self-contained?"

Martin nodded.

"Clearly you plan on hanging around here for a while," remarked Susan to Martin. To the others she explained, "A single mature tree can absorb carbon dioxide and release enough oxygen to support two human beings for as long as the tree survives."

Elizabeth pointed to a light at the corner of the wall and ceiling. "A reflected light source, I assume."

Martin nodded again, the trace of a smile at the corner of his lips. "Each floor," he replied, "has six photovoltaic systems that collect the light from above and direct it through the shielding where needed."

Aaron shifted his feet on the soil, feeling it compress, touched the roughness of the bark, and smelled the chaff of the grains. "Fantastic!"

"Foolish," admonished Susan. "Now at least I see what you've been wasting your...?"

"Are there others?" asked Elizabeth, nodding toward the trees.

"This floor supports ninety trees," explained Martin. "Similar floors throughout the complex support an additional one hundred twenty."

"Complex?" asked Aaron.

Martin continued. "Yes, this is not the only silo. When done, the complex will function without mechanical assistance and provide as much oxygen as needed."

"When done?" added Leonard.

"Like I said...a lot to do." Martin plucked a spikelet of wheat from a stalk and ate it. "Everything is used. Plants of all kinds for wood, medical applications, oxygen formation, crops..."

"Where?" asked Susan enthusiastically.

"Other levels. Like this, everything supports everything else."

Leonard allowed a chuckle. "Your farm just needs a few cows."

Martin nodded his head toward the elevator, "Our next stop."

Minutes later the group leaned over a metal railing staring at four dairy cows, a dozen goats, as many sheep, six pigs, and pens of chickens, turkeys, pheasants, and quail.

Elizabeth and Aaron pet a goat as it munched on alfalfa.

Leonard fed a hand full of alfalfa to a dairy cow. "Noah had nothing on you."

Martin smiled, "There are a few other things Noah didn't have."

The group exited again from the small elevator into a new but now familiar circular space. This floor was far brighter than the others and lined in row upon row of concentric circular racks of plants from floor to ceiling.

Susan stepped further than the others into the room, then turned back. "Hydroponics greenhouse," she said astonished, and wandered among the rows, examining the greenhouse's life support systems.

Elizabeth followed Aaron into the vast room, and slipped her arms around his waist from behind. She placed her head apologetically against his back. "I told you this was going to be nuts."

He turned so they were hugging face to face. "You should see my family at Yom Kippur." He kissed her then chuckled, "So your dad's a prepper. Incredible!"

Susan emerged from a row opposite the one she had entered. "You gotta see this. It's amazing! Thousands of shelved and hanging plants, receiving redirected carbon sources, water condensation, and reflected light!"

She pointed to the more numerous reflective panels along the ceiling, walls, and rows, which cast light in every direction.

Leonard stepped up to her and whispered, "Look, the storm has clearly hit. We'll just wait it out here and leave when it's over."

Susan at first caught her breath to protest, then regarded the hydroponics. "Fine," she allowed, studying the plant arrangements.

Susan fixed on Martin. "You've arranged your bunker in a Bujuan Tower configuration," she announced.

Everyone else looked puzzled.

"A what?" asked Aaron.

"In areas with limited resources," Susan explained, "optimizing spacial arrangement enables the waste or by products of one organism to be the food of another."

Aaron's nose wrinkled unpleasantly.

Picking up on Aaron's distaste, Susan continued. "It's not used much in modern agriculture, but these hydroponics can feed ..."

Elizabeth stirred impatiently. "Why all this, Martin? This is more than some mid-life crisis get-away."

At that moment, a wall panel near them slid open, and the Native American man who had moved their bags entered.

Martin held a hand to him in greeting and introduction. "Everyone, please let me introduce to you my friend, Ask. Ask, this is my family."

Ask, tanned with black hair, appearing in his mid-forties, nodded respectfully.

Aaron inquired, "Ask? Is that short for something?"

He replied, "Askuwheteauachachak Kitchi."

"Ask," said Susan. "Got it."

Aaron laughed, "Awesome."

Ask whispered to Martin, "Elu, it has begun." Without another word, Ask exited back through the door in which he had come, and Martin took a measured breath.

Susan felt her temper rising again. "What is going on? The truth!"

Martin followed Ask, and without looking back said, "The truth...come with me."

Aaron began to follow, but stopped when he saw none of the others were following.

Susan stamped her foot. "I want answers, Martin!"

Martin stopped at the door and turned.

Susan continued in a slightly less angry voice, "Not more mysteries, and spirits, and hallucinations! I'm done with all that. The judge certified you insane..."

Aaron looked at Martin concerned. Martin casually told Aaron, "Only temporary. Diagnosis was changed to 'brief psychotic episode.'"

Susan shook her head and appeared about to burst. "I won't be dragged back into your crazy world. Sign the papers. I'm leaving!"

The floor rumbled again, and the reflected light throughout the room dimmed. Everyone gasped, and Aaron wrapped an arm protectively around Elizabeth.

With wide, pleading eyes, Elizabeth asked, "Martin?"

"Come, sweetpea," he said, "and I'll show you everything."

* * *

Aaron and Elizabeth followed Martin together through the door Ask had used, and Susan reluctantly joined Leonard. The group found themselves on a metal grate landing which separated the one foot thick metal room they were just in from a concrete cylinder which incased it.

All eyes were naturally drawn up and down. Through the grating it was easy to see they were near the middle of, and had been inside, a cylindrical building over three hundred feet tall, or rather, deep.

A metal grate walkway also spiraled circumferentially around the silo, rising four meters every complete circle. From where they stood, they could switch back up or down the stairway or walk the spiral walkway.

Leonard was considering both when Martin began descending the stairs. "Martin," he asked, "is this a missile silo?"

Martin glanced backward, "*Was* a missile silo." Leonard and Susan followed, while Elizabeth considered the structure more closely.

Aaron asked, "Not a bunker?"

Without looking back, Martin said, "This complex is much more capable than any bunker," then promptly disappeared though a door at the seventeenth floor.

Susan and Leonard followed behind Martin, peering inside. Then, Susan gasped, "Oh my...", stepping backward.

Leonard braced Susan up, mesmerized, before both entered the room beyond.

Elizabeth looked to Aaron, distressed, and when Susan screamed, "Oh my God!" they both ran.

CHAPTER EIGHT

"The most devastating attack is that which comes from within, unseen and unexpected."

-- Pipperion, Protector of the Caeltis Garden

The Destruction

Elizabeth and Aaron ran through the door and had to stop quickly. They were now in a room built more for electronic gadgetry than people. Elizabeth saw a dozen television monitors lined atop a wall over a seventies-era control panel with hundreds of buttons, switches, lights, and levers. She assessed to herself, 'If we are in a missile silo, this must be the missile control room.'

Ask sat at a computer terminal on the far side of the panel, typing on a keyboard.

The monitors above displayed scenes of tornados tearing up cities, volcanoes erupting in the middle of freeways, and earthquakes knocking down buildings.

Aaron could not understand what he was seeing. "What the...?!"

He was now realizing, in the nine hours since they had left Arizona, events of enormous proportion had been going on all over the world.

"Did that cloud have anything to do with...?" He began to ask, but stopped short.

Susan cowered into Leonard's chest, and Aaron noticed that no one was looking at the monitors. All gaped at the center of the control panel. There a modern large flat screen table top displayed a digital map of the world.

Most land masses were dark green and oceans dark blue. Extreme north and south had remained lighter shades of these colors, and several cities across the map (among them Washington D. C.) were covered by red circles.

Hundreds of yellow lines spread over the oceans from one continent to the other. Arching toward the yellow lines were as many white lines. Many began from the Midwest United States, while others originated from Russia, China, Pakistan, India, and Europe.

Elizabeth analyzed the screen, then studied Ask's keystrokes.

The pattern of lines on the screen was a web crossing every land mass and every body of water over the entire planet.

Elizabeth's attention was drawn back to the screen. Along its near edge were a series of coupled numbers scrolling rapidly.

"Martin?" Elizabeth asked. "Are you going to explain?"

Elizabeth's attention was drawn back to the arching lines as finally many of the yellow lines were intersected by the white, causing both to disappear.

Martin moved closer to Elizabeth.

One of the wall monitors overhead showed a view from the cabin above. In the distance, several rockets launched into the air.

The walls rumbled.

"Not every silo was converted," Martin explained.

On the computer screen, a new white line joined several others that had originated from Montana. Over the Pacific, another white line missed a yellow line, which then struck the West Coast of California and turned red over San Francisco.

All eyes searched the monitors above.

A monitor, showing the Golden Gate Bridge from the Sausalito shore, suddenly flashed with a piercing white light.

Susan covered her mouth and snapped backward reflexively.

As the light faded, a mushroom cloud rose over San Francisco. The wave of destruction instantly spread through the city, then struck the Golden Gate Bridge, bursting its cable connections and shattering its supports apart. Seconds later the blast wave hit the near shore and reduced the picture to static.

The family gasped.

Martin explained, "These are all nuclear strikes."

"What?!" exclaimed Aaron, who rushed to the table top and scanned the locations. He placed a finger over Trenton, New Jersey.

Nearby, two white lines intersected several yellow lines approaching Manhattan and disappeared. However, one white line over Philadelphia missed the yellow, and a red circle covered the city.

Trenton lay at its outer rim.

Aaron scanned the monitors in tears. "Is this happening now?"

"Yes, Aaron," Martin consoled.

Aaron turned desperately toward Martin."We've gotta do something. My family lives in Trenton!"

Aaron searched the monitors frantically again, then fixed on the static screen, as Ask adjusted a knob, and caused the static filled monitor to show a new feed.

On the monitor, appeared a parking lot outside a convenience store along interstate 95. A sign stating "Trenton Next Exit" and "Philadelphia 31 Miles" was clearly visible.

The crowd in the parking lot covered their eyes from the intensity of a distant point of bright light. As the light faded, the grey storm clouds above were lit up by the mushroom cloud that rose to meet them.

The crowd ran to nearby cars and buildings. But in seconds, the light and shock wave swept over the countryside, until this picture too was lost in static.

"No!" Aaron screamed. He turned frantically to Martin and Ask. "Turn it back on! That didn't just happen!"

"I'm sorry, Aaron," said Martin. "Many places are gone. Many more will be gone in a few minutes."

Elizabeth placed a soothing hand on Aaron's back, and all watched, horrified, as yellow and white lines collided, while many yellow still got through to bloom as red circles across the globe.

"This is partly why I brought you here," explained Martin.

Susan trembled. "The dreams...the voices?"

Martin looked at her but said nothing.

Aaron spun on Martin, "You knew this was going to happen? And you did nothing!"

Elizabeth stepped up and laid a hand gently on Aaron's forearm. "Wait Aaron." Then to Martin asked, "Is this what you saw?"

"I only knew an end was coming."

Leonard waved a hand, indicating the silo. "But all this?"

Martin shrugged, "I thought it best to be prepared."

Aaron buried his head in his hands, pulling at his hair. Elizabeth wrapped her arms around him.

Leonard studied the map of the world as few lines now remained. Hundreds of red circles had blossomed and covered the globe. The nearest to them were Seattle and Denver.

Leonard looked up and met eyes with Martin.

Leonard's heart raced. If Martin had done what they had asked of him, the family would have been flying within eyesight of Denver when it was wiped off the face of the Earth in nuclear holocaust.

If eyes could ever say 'thank you,' Leonard's did. "What now?" he asked.

"Now," said Martin, "you must learn."

* * *

Not long after, as the man made machinery of human destruction exhausted its fury, the family was left bewildered and exhausted. Aaron slumped over the table screen, where only glowing red dots remained.

Aaron listed city after extinct city, "St. Petersburg, London, Moscow, Mexico City, Beijing, Tokyo, Taipei, Sydney, Rio, New Delhi, Istanbul, Cairo, Riyadh, Berlin, Rome, Washington, D.C., Philadelphia..." he paused, held his breath, and finished, "Trenton...all gone."

Martin stood next to him. "I'm sorry Aaron." Then to the group Martin instructed, "But, we don't have much time."

"Time for what?" asked Susan.

"I must show you the complex," he explained. "We will all have jobs to do if we are to survive. If you have any questions, please ask me or Ask."

Susan raised an eyebrow. "Ask Ask?"

Ask smiled understandingly. Martin knelt next to Aaron, who's forehead rested on the table screen. Aaron looked up, saw everyone looking at him, then stood up.

"May I?" asked Martin sensitively.

Aaron stepped back, and Elizabeth once again wrapped her arms around him.

Martin tapped the screen in a corner and the map of the world was replaced by a schematic drawing with five circles, like the dots on a dice.

Martin began, "These are the five underground silo towers."

Leonard asked, surprised, "Five?"

Martin pointed to the middle circle. "We are in the center silo, which is 360 feet deep. The other four silos were not meant for such a large rocket and are about half the size."

"That's a lot of square footage," pointed out Leonard.

Elizabeth shrugged. "Not as much as you might think."

Then, receiving puzzled looks from Leonard and Aaron, and a reassuring smile from Martin, she continued, "Look at it like an engineer. A self-sustaining design must have all that we have seen and more: Power plant, air and water purification, hydroponics, you name it. All require vertical space. Not every floor is twelve feet high.

Susan added, "Truly impressive Martin. But how long, really, can we survive here?"

Martin and Ask shared a contemplative look, then Martin answered, "That depends on what you believe."

"Positive thinking?" clarified Leonard.

Martin forced a smile. "Night is falling, so we will begin again in the morning. For now, dinner, then rest."

Aaron took a breath, "Then what?"

Martin said simply, "Survive."

Martin moved back toward the stairs, then said, "We'll avoid the elevator for the time being, to conserve energy."

He opened the stairwell door again and was gone.

Ask followed and before he left, said, "Your rooms are not far, but I will take you to eat first. Do you have any questions right now?"

"Only about a million," said Susan.

Elizabeth put her engineer game face on. "Energy is always a premium. What is the energy source here?"

Ask smiled wanly to Elizabeth, as if he wanted to answer but did not, and disappeared, without another word, up the spiral walkway.

CHAPTER NINE

"You have chosen unwisely, Faeleriel Queen! Your Thaen will mock you, distrust you, then set your house on fire. They will build cities on your bones and forget that you ever existed."

-- Gulandian, at the Battle of Thaen's Fall

The Faeleriel

The engineer in Elizabeth was burning now more than ever. She had been less than two months from her degree, but now there would be no defense of her thesis, no graduation. There would be no theoretical problems for which she had to propose theoretical answers. Now she would only face real problems that if solved incorrectly would cause real disasters and harm those she cared about.

They were locked into a tin can, buried in the ground, with a campfire burning over it. The pressing thought burning in Elizabeth's mind now was life support, and life support was not possible without sustainable energy. Ask had eluded her questioning on the issue, and now Elizabeth, Aaron, Susan and Leonard sat at the dining table eating, while Ask worked in the kitchen.

Elizabeth talked through her concerns with the others, as Susan sliced cheese and offered it around the table.

"I'm just saying," said Elizabeth in hushed tones. "Martin showed us production sites, but no maintenance, most important, power."

"Are you concerned?" asked Leonard.

"This is Martin we are talking about," pointed out Susan.

Ignoring Susan, Elizabeth answered Leonard, "If the power source here is not sustainable..." Her expression was dire, and they all understood the result would be devastating.

Aaron felt a sinking in his stomach discussing the topic, and wanted to talk about something else. He quietly stood and moved over to the kitchen sink's counter top.

He regarded Ask. "How do you and Martin get along?"

Ask, who was now finishing in the kitchen, replied tentatively, "Elu and I have a...relationship."

Everyone turned toward the kitchen a bit shocked.

Elizabeth waved it off, "That's none of our busi..."

Aaron continued, "Elu?"

"Eluwillusit," said Ask. "His name in my language. It means, 'Holy Man'."

Elizabeth attempted to return the conversation, "We were talking about..."

But Susan interrupted, "Holy man?"

Leonard continued his thought, "Your relationship?"

Ask replied, "Elu maintains me."

"Completes you?" Aaron tried to clarify.

Ask shook his head. "No, you have the wrong...Martin is the Keeper of the Faeleriel. The Gardener. As I once was. His efforts make it possible for me to help maintain the systems here."

Susan stiffened noticeably with these words, appeared uncomfortable and flushed. She began to shift in her chair until Leonard placed a hand on hers to calm her down.

Aaron asked, "Fernal Keeper? Is that the hydroponics garden?"

But before Ask could answer, Susan slid her chair away from the table with a screech, stood up and strode across the great room toward Ask.

"Where are we sleeping?" she asked curtly.

"Your rooms are the next floor up," Ask replied.

Without a further word, Susan spun around and strode out the stairway door.

Aaron watched her exit, shocked. Hoping for an explanation, he turned to Elizabeth, who was clearly uncomfortable as well.

Leonard stood, "I know today has been a bit much. Perhaps she'll feel better after a shower." And he followed after Susan.

"I don't think she wants to hear about Martin's gardens," explained Elizabeth to Aaron.

When Aaron gave an 'Are-you-going-to-explain' look, Elizabeth returned with an 'I-don't-want-to-talk-about-it' shake of the head.

Elizabeth stood and inquired of Ask, "I imagine we should limit our use of water until we know more about our resources."

"Wise," replied Ask, "but you all deserve refreshment and relaxation after ...your day. There is water enough for showers. And tomorrow is a new day."

* * *

Leonard entered the room that was to be their living space for the time being. He was surprised that it was more like an apartment than a room.

But he paid no attention to anything except the sound of water running. He followed the sound as it drew him through a bedroom and to an adjoining door. He entered cautiously.

Inside, Leonard noted the amount of steam and knew Susan was literally letting out steam of her own. He listened and could hear quiet sobs above the background of water. He stepped closer to the shower and asked quietly, "May I come in?"

No reply came. Leonard held his breath and straightened to back out, when the shower door parted slightly. Susan's hand appeared in the gap.

Leonard wrapped her hand in his, and she leaned her face toward his. Her nose dripping water onto his, he said, "I can see he frustrates you."

Susan shook her head slightly and whispered, "I don't want to talk about him." She squeezed Leonard's hand. "Join me," she said.

* * *

Elizabeth and Aaron opened the door to their apartment, entering a small living room. Both explored the spaces with their eyes, but neither was engaged with their brain.

They explored the small kitchen, hallway, several small bedrooms, and their bedroom, their small suitcases sitting next to the bed.

Elizabeth was frustrated and well on her way to getting pissed off. 'Ask said Faeleriel!' she thought angrily to herself. The memory of the last time she had seen Martin raced back to her. 'Seventeen and my last time with friends, and he demanded I join him during my spring break...for what?...chasing Faeleriel!'

'Is that what this is about?' she asked herself. 'Ask appears to know about Faeleriel too. Did Martin convince him somehow? What's he hiding?'

Elizabeth stopped where she was, closed her eyes, and breathed in slowly to relax her nerves.

Aaron had been equally distracted, his thoughts taking him back just three days earlier and his last telephone conversation home. His sister, about to graduate high school had confessed that she had boxed up his old bedroom, was using it as her walk in closet, and was that ok? His mother was excited to see Elizabeth again, and wondered if she could bake her a cake for her college graduation. And his dad had asked if she was 'the one'. He had responded with the same answer in each case.

'Now they're gone,' Aaron told himself.

He wanted to think of something else, anything else. Aaron mindlessly walked into the bathroom and stood in front of the sink. Elizabeth stood next to him, her eyes closed.

Aaron had to get out of his own head, so he asked, "What did Ask mean by Keeper of the Fernal Garden?"

When Elizabeth opened her eyes, she saw that she was in a bathroom, a toothbrush laden with three times as much tooth paste as she needed in her hand.

"Faeleriel," she corrected, and scraped some of the toothpaste into the sink.

"What is it?" Aaron asked.

Elizabeth shrugged. "Voices," she stated matter-of-factly.

"Voices? From where?" Aaron asked, trying to get interested. "The 'Garden'?"

Elizabeth leaned over the counter shaking her head, "I'd rather not talk about it." Then after a pause, she offered, "The trees, I suppose. If you want to get biblical, it's the 'Garden'...of Eden!'

Elizabeth, unsatisfied with her explanation, jammed the laden brush into her mouth, and vigorously scrubbed.

With a pause, she added in a frothy gurgle, "Or the Ark or whatever..."

She glanced at Aaron, who stared into space. She noticed his distraught demeanor.

"Are you alright?" she asked.

Aaron dropped his toothbrush onto the counter and went back into the bedroom.

Elizabeth toweled off her mouth and followed. She found Aaron sitting on the end of the bed, bracing himself.

"They're all gone," he said. "Everything and everyone."

Elizabeth sat next to him and wrapped her arms around him.

"I'm sorry," she consoled. "I'm here. You're here. And we'll get through this. As long as the sun rises each morning, we'll take it one day at a time and get through this."

* * *

Six floors above, on the tenth floor, Ask laid on a carpet of green moss, eyes closed, surrounded by Queen's Anne, each of the tiny flower buds closed.

Nearby, Martin laid on the ground with his head at the base of a very tiny, barren willow-like tree that stood less than two feet tall and rose just above his head. The tree's roots had grown along the surface of the ground, over Martin's shoulders, and down around his body.

Where the roots contacted Martin, he emanated a soft pale green glow.

Together, wordlessly, Martin and Ask sought to contact the other Gardens, reciting for the countless time the story of the Gardens. And so, the energy of Taenoril sil flowed for one more day.

* * *

Dreamlike, Martin visualized beyond the walls of the silo's tenth floor and the walls of the silo complex. He saw the surface, the airfield and forest, which had remained as they were the moment the elevator and its occupants had descended into the silo complex, as if protected by a bubble of energy.

Background to this imagery was Elizabeth's voice saying, "As long as the sun rises each morning, we'll take it one day at a time and get through this."

Her words gave flight to the imagery, which flew higher into the air and found, on the other side of the bubble, the countryside was a scorched wasteland.

Martin continued to visualize, and the imagery flew over the continent, where volcanoes burst lava into the air and rolled it out in streams like neon nets, across the dark, night-time landscape of the western hemisphere.

The lava crawled into lakes, streams, and the ocean, causing the water to rise in steam. The lava burned forests, cities and fields, and the smoke rose into the air to join the steam.

Across the continent, the morning sun dawned along a patch of Eastern coastline, revealing the remains of a once great city, now burned and blown off the map.

In its harbor, a granite island held two remnants of the legs to the Statue of Liberty. Protected by one statue leg, a sooty, battered flower opened hopefully at morning's first light, with its face toward the sun.

But the smoke and steam rose from the destruction to meet the rays of the sun, blocking out its light, in a blanket of perpetual night. The battered flower was covered in darkness again and closed.

The imagery flew once again toward a far distant volcano as it erupted. Closer and closer the volcano came, until at last Martin imagined he flew down into the magma, along its internal streams of lava, to enter a single vein. The vein narrowed into a finger of lava, encased in hard earth's crust. The very tip of the lava stream inched through the blackened, hard rock until something unseen stopped it flat.

The rock on the other side of the invisible barrier was not blackened and dead, but vibrant. Suddenly, the invisible barrier shifted a few inches. The few inches of rock that was previously vibrant turned grey. And as the lava ate its way forward, and the grey rock turned dead black.

The imagery moved once again, this time up the invisible barrier, to the earth's surface, back in Montana, to the silo complex.

Far to the East, the glow of morning light rose, but the curtain of smoke, ash and steam did also, shading the sun's light to a lifeless, dark red.

CHAPTER TEN

"Solving a problem requires a higher level of thinking than that which created it."

-- Kenbo Ichi, Keeper of the Japanese Garden; similar quotation also attributed to Albert Einstein

The Puzzle

Elizabeth turned in bed impatiently. Aaron was still very much asleep. She wanted to remain next to him, but Elizabeth could do nothing but stare at the ceiling, frustrated.
'It's no use,' she thought, looking at Aaron.

Her words from the discussion the previous night came back to her. 'I'm just saying,' she had said. 'Martin showed us production sites, but no maintenance. Key among these, power.'

She got up and dressed. Her thoughts continued, 'If the power source here is not sustainable,...'

Unable to finish the thought, she looked at Aaron. Her face held the same dire expression it had the previous night. And with a desperate hope, she left.

* * *

Minutes later, Elizabeth found herself in the control room, sitting where Ask had been. She toggled switches and pushed buttons on the control board as she had watched Ask do.

She initially focused her attention on the overhead monitors and discovered that Martin and Ask had been able to tap into a network of public and private cameras across the country. She used these now to view the destruction.

Screens showed ruined cities, broken and deserted freeways, and where cities had been blown away, camera static. She found nothing alive.

Trying to remain hopeful, she said aloud, "Let's see what's left above us then."

She pushed a button and the last monitor screen overhead revealed the cabin above. It, and the woods outside it, appeared untouched.

'How?' she wondered.

Her hands and fingers moved over the control board, toggled a camera near the airfield, and illuminated a monitor screen with the runway and the forest beyond.

"How is the air so clean up there?" she asked herself. "What is protecting...?"

Without finishing her thought, she slid her chair across the floor to the flat screen monitor.

'Okay, begin at the beginning,' she couched herself. 'Analyze.'

She tapped the screen in the center, and it came to life showing the map of the world. No missile tracking lines remained, and nearly every major city worldwide glowed red. She tapped the corner of the screen as Martin had done the day before, and the screen revealed the schematic of the five silos in the complex. Using finger pinching and spreading movements, she created a sidelong view of the silos.

Encouraged with her progress, Elizabeth searched the screen and found several icons on its perimeter.

'Come on Beth...systems algorithm,' she chided herself. She tapped an icon that looked like cogs. Six more icons appeared underneath.

'Environmental control and life support systems,' she deduced.

She tapped an icon with arrows pointing in opposite directions. 'Influents and effluents...no air comes from the surface. It's all recycled,' she discovered.

She pushed the icon of a fan. Azure blue lines appeared, traversing up and down all silo floors. She traced these with her finger. 'Ducts, leading to...'

Her finger hovered over a blue square comprising most of the second floor. '...ventilation.'

She studied the system intently. "Air is scrubbed and recirculated," she said aloud. "That has to take enormous amounts of power."

She found an icon looking like a lighting bolt and tapped it.

Green lines coursed outward from the tenth floor to every other floor but the tenth floor itself remained a black void.

'Hmmm...a power source of some kind,' she thought.

She tapped the different icons again, this time focusing on the tenth floor.
'Nothing goes into the tenth floor except ventilation. Power is coming from the tenth floor, but no resources are going in or waste products coming out.'

She leaned back. 'How is that possible? What can possibly be making energy, and why can't I see it?'

With a flash of inspiration, she leaned forward.

"Wait a minute!"

She tapped the fan icon and studied the ventilation system again, focusing on the second floor. Excitedly she pointed to a box on the schematic.

"Got it! A power relay!"

And with new hope, she headed up the stairs.

* * *

At the tenth floor landing, Elizabeth stopped for a breath. She gathered her energy, but intense curiosity was growing inside her. This was the floor that appeared to power the silo, and did so by some means she had never seen before.

Cautiously, she examined the door, then tried the knob. It did not turn.

She turned from the door, certain that the ventilation system power relay would help her solve this puzzle. But after climbing only a few steps, she paused to look back. The locked door challenged her, and what was inside she knew was the difference between life and death in the silo.

With the determination to return and not just solve, but conquer this puzzle, she continued up the stairs.

But no sooner had she gone, a soft glow emanated from the cracks around the door.

* * *

In their bed far below, Aaron awakened to find Elizabeth gone.

Moments later, Elizabeth opened the door from the stairwell and entered the second floor of the silo. She knew the type of structure in this space well.

The second floor actually comprised elements of the first and third floors, themselves a network of shock absorbing beams that deadened the vibrations generated by the two metal cylinders on the second floor.

Each cylinder was twelve feet in diameter and eight feet tall.

"Ventilation fans," Elizabeth confirmed.

She placed her hand on one of the fan casings and looked at the three stories of beams and vibration dampening arrays for the two spinning ventilation systems.

Elizabeth scanned the room and discovered a small control panel, the size of a podium, on one wall. She moved to it and inspected the controls. There were buttons and control switches, but no computer screen. She opened the cabinet doors underneath the panel and discovered its controlling wires.

She scanned the room again and spotted a tool box fixed to the floor next to the second fan. She crossed to and opened it. Excitedly she pulled a hand held meter and several other tools from the box, then crossed back to the panel and climbed under it.

She attached the meter's alligator clips to several wires under the panel, making the needle bob.

"So what can possibly be making energy, and why can't I see it?" she asked herself. To her surprise, she received an answer.

"Both excellent questions."

Elizabeth nervously craned her head outside the panel and saw Martin smiling at her.

Elizabeth flushed, feeling sheepish.

"No. It's okay," Martin encouraged. "You need to understand."

* * *

Far below, Aaron entered the great room to find Susan and Leonard just sitting down at the table.

Ask nodded a greeting as he made coffee in the kitchen. "Please sit down," he invited. And in minutes coffee and plates of fruit and cheese had been set out.

Aaron blinked his eyes and looked around, feeling something had changed. Peering up, he realized the reflected light had dimmed.

"I know it's early," he said, "but shouldn't the lights be a bit brighter?"

Susan looked up at the reflectors and asked, "Have the solar cells been damaged?"

"No, explained Ask. "The sun has been obscured." He raised a hand toward the solar light panel. "This is what remains."

Leonard was puzzled. "Obscured?"

Ask explained further, pouring more coffee. "Smoke, steam and clouds have covered the sky and hidden the light."

The group was silent.

Susan nervously thought about the implications of massive destruction obscuring the most important energy source for life on the planet. No light meant no photosynthesis. No photosynthesis meant no oxygen. How long would the skies be obscured, and how long would their reserves last.

Ask spoke as if in answer to Susan's concerns. "Conservation of energy is more important now than ever. Lights and electronics only when and where we need them, and only at the intensity we need them."

Aaron nodded, "Anyone seen Beth?"

Ask lifted his eyes toward the ceiling and his expression turned blank. When he returned his gaze toward the table, he said, "She is in the ventilation control center, learning the engineering of the complex."

Ask dried his hands with a towel, and spoke to the group, "It's a good time then to begin our own adventure."

* * *

Elizabeth stepped from the small ventilation control stand and gestured toward the fans. "Ok, but something must be producing power on the tenth floor.

Martin replied, "Not some...*thing.*"

Elizabeth turned back toward Martin, puzzled.

* * *

Below the solid, vibrant rock that supported the silo, a finger of magma and its surrounding demarcation line of black, brittle rock advanced a fraction upward, with a mild tremor.

* * *

Susan, Leonard, and Ask entered the hydroponics greenhouse from the stairwell. As Aaron stepped onto the landing, he stumbled from the unexpected jolt of a tremor.

Leonard looked back. "You ok?"

Aaron caught himself, then looked up the stairs. Waving he said to the others, "You go ahead. I'm going to see what they are up to on the second floor."

Leonard and Ask both nodded as Aaron continued up the stairs.

* * *

At the ventilation control panel once again, Elizabeth listened to Martin's explanation.

"Each floor can receive power in isolation," he said.

"You need someone in the main control room, then, coordinating," she contended.

Martin shook his head. "Look at everything as if you alone will need to operate it."

"Alone?" Elizabeth puzzled.

Before Martin could respond, Aaron entered from the stairway. Elizabeth's face brightened as he entered, distracting her from following up her question, and he smiled at her, relieved.

Aaron wanted to join Elizabeth, but he saw the look on her face. She was in her 'discovery mode'. Aaron knew Elizabeth could be very intense about solving a problem. He was the one who had dubbed it her 'discovery mode.' More accurately, though, she was like a predator on the prowl. He did not intend to get between her and her kill, so he chose not to disturb them. He turned his attention instead to the rest of the room.

Elizabeth dove right back into her discussion with Martin, while Aaron walked around the second fan, noticing the various beams arrayed like some kind of spider web.

Aaron thought aloud, "Wow, all this for two...fans?"

Elizabeth responded without drawing her attention from the control panel. "These are the same types of ventilation systems found on sky scrapers," she said matter-of-factly. "Their vibrations can rip a building apart."

Aaron turned back toward the beams, suddenly aware of every weld and rivet. He drifted around the fan absently, nearly tripping over the tool box fixed to the floor.

"...which is why 'all this' is here," Elizabeth continued.

She glanced toward Aaron, and her attention was drawn briefly to the base of the fan.

Martin added, "If the control room is the brains of the complex, these are the lungs."

Elizabeth looked at Martin and nodded toward the foundation under the fan. "A gimbal plate? Expecting earthquakes?"

Martin shrugged. "Just covering the bases."

Elizabeth returned her attention back to the ventilation control panel. "I assume this combines scrubbing and ventilation."

Martin nodded.

Alone again, Aaron looked from the tool box to the top of the fan.

Elizabeth continued her explanations of the ventilation system to Aaron, as she studied the control panel. "Without these fans, contaminants would build in our air, and the pressures going downward within the silo would unevenly distribute what little breathable air remained. Within days, we couldn't survive."

Then, to Martin, she asked, "Still thinking like an anesthesiologist?"

Martin retorted, "Not just an anesthesiologist."

A gasp from atop the second fan system pulled both their attentions immediately.

Aaron had used the tool box to crawl atop the fan casing to get a look inside. He had been surprised to find the top of the fan was not a solid covering, but a sheet of metal grating, which served as an air intake. Aaron was pinned onto this top vent by the powerful suction forces.

His attempt to protect himself and break his fall had resulted in his arm extending through the open metal grate, and the suction kept him there, drawing his hand and body closer to the fan blades.

Elizabeth rushed to him and grabbed his belt, halting his further slide, but she could not bring Aaron down without getting sucked in herself. Martin held onto Elizabeth, then placed his hand on the fan casing. He calmed his thoughts, closed his eyes, and focused his energy.

CHAPTER ELEVEN

"Energy is the essence of life. Belief is the conduit for energy. And in the nonbeliever, belief begins with the words."

-- Lunataella, Queen of the Caeltis Garden

The Words

"We met in Florida," Ask explained, "but after discovering that we see the world in the same way, we decided it was time to come here."

"You hallucinate too?" asked Susan.

Leonard gasped, "Susan!"

Ask waved it off laughing, "We both..." Then his smile disappeared and his pupils dilated.

Leonard's medical reflexes engaged, wondering if Ask was experiencing a seizure. "Ask, are you okay?"

In a moment, Ask blinked and returned from his trance.

"Quickly!" he commanded. "We must hurry!"

Ask ran to the stairs, Susan and Leonard following close behind.

* * *

Ask, Leonard and Susan entered the ventilation room, gasping.

"The emergency stop!" yelled Elizabeth's voice.

Ask sprinted to a far wall and hit a black button, while Leonard ran to Elizabeth, stepped on the tool box, and grabbed Aaron.

Aaron struggled as his hand, with Leonard's initial added weight, was drawn even closer to the fan blades.

Ask ran to the fan and held onto Leonard. "It will take too long."

Leonard climbed the casing to get a better grip on Aaron, but he too was drawn toward the fan intake.

Susan pleaded to Martin, "Do something!"

Martin's energy was extended fully into the machinery as he maintained his grip on the fan casing, and his concentration intensified to control its momentum.

Leonard focused his struggle on keeping Aaron's arm from being sucked into the blades. He set his body weight against the fan and pulled on Aaron's arm firmly and steadily.

Martin felt the kinetic energy and internal torque of the electrical motor, and gasped from the effort of trying to reverse it.

In protest, the fan released a loud, wrenching whine. The gimbal plate on which the fan rested tilted back and forth, as the internal forces were being unevenly hindered. The jolting nearly tossed Leonard.

The casing shuddered violently as internal portions of the fan slammed into the outer casing. Each time Leonard bucked and slipped a little further off of the fan.

Martin could feel his firm grip on the energy of the machinery, but he could not control the gyroscopic after forces from the slowing process. He had to give Aaron a chance. Now dripping in sweat, his face pale, he extended his energy fully against the momentum of the blades. The forces thrust back at him like a blow to the ribs. He gripped the fan casing as the jolting portions of internal fan collisions narrowed closer and closer to his position.

Leonard knew the moment was near when he would not be able to hold Aaron any longer. Then suddenly the forces changed, and he felt the opportunity for one last effort. He gripped Aaron as hard as he could and heaved backward. Miraculously, the forces from the fan continued to slow. And as if a rope had snapped, Aaron's arm shot from the vent, Aaron pealed off the fan, and both men, along with Ask and Elizabeth, fell to the floor of the ventilation room.

Martin's hand remained on the casing as it shuddered violently again. Martin now felt the internal forces in complete disarray. If he did not control them, the fan blades would dislodge and shoot like a grenade from within at all angles, potentially killing everyone in the room.

'...must concentrate...forces,' Martin thought as a single blade slammed into the metal opposite Martin's hand and blasted through, throwing Martin across the room.

Elizabeth fell to the floor again. Susan helped Leonard up and both saw the gaping hole in the fan casing, then looked from it to Martin.

Ask started to move toward Martin, gasping, "Elu!" He struggled to stand and breathe.
Amid the chaos, the fan screeched to a halt.

Elizabeth screamed, "Martin!" and ran to him.

Elizabeth shook him desperately, but Martin did not open his eyes. "No! Not again!" she cried.

Leonard scooted Elizabeth aside and opened Martin's shirt to examine him. He palpated along Martin's side and pulled back a bloody hand.

"He's bleeding!" Elizabeth exclaimed.

Leonard rolled Martin over enough to exam his flank and found his side was massively bruised, with blood streaming from a wound. He placed a hand over it and applied pressure.

Ask closed his eyes and chanted in whisper. Martin exhaled a long slow breath, then moved his lips soundlessly the same words Ask was chanting.

Lifting his hand, Leonard observed the bleeding stop, the bruising disappear along Martin's side, and the wound seal.

Leonard gasped, "Martin!"

Martin breathed deeply again, but did not open his eyes. Ask breathed identically, opening his eyes, and managed to stand.

Susan cried, "What's going on?"

Leonard panted to Ask, "Where is your infirmary?

Ask replied, "This...way."

* * *

Leonard and Aaron carried Martin from the elevator into the infirmary and lifted him onto a gurney. He did not appear conscious.

Martin had withdrawn inward, utilizing only those body functions he required to survive and to maintain connection with Taenoril sil. And he was struggling to do so. Thus far, his connection with Taenoril sil had enabled him to redirect a significant portion of his life energy, begin to reorganize his damaged tissue, and stem any further loss of blood.

Elizabeth passed gauze to Leonard, who took her hand and pressed it over the wound. Leonard then rushed to a glass medicine cabinet, searched, found a vial of medicine, and rummaged through a nearby shelf for a syringe.

Martin extended his energy outward enough to feel Leonard's. Martin knew that for Leonard to run through his trauma algorithms properly, the patient would need to be sedated. But as the Keeper, his loss of conscious connection to the Garden through Taenoril sil meant he could not sustain himself, protect the silo, the entire group, and the Garden.

Martin fought against Elizabeth to sit up as Leonard approached.

Leonard soothed, "Relax Martin. You're in shock," and drew the liquid from the vial into the syringe. Into an intravenous bag of saline next to him Leonard injected the syringe contents, then he held the bag out to Susan.

"Hang this IV bag," Leonard instructed.

"What's in it?" asked Susan.

"Sedative," replied Leonard. "I need to check for internal injuries."

Martin gasped, "Need..."

Leonard held Martin down at the shoulder. "Your body needs to relax for me to help you." He wrapped a tourniquet around Martin's arm to insert the IV catheter.

Martin struggled weakly, "Awake!"

As the needle approached Martin's arm vein, Martin closed his eyes, the lights in the room flickered, and he slumped. He moved inward, preparing to counter, as best he could, any sedative that made it into his system.

A hand reached in, however, and grabbed Leonard's, stopping the needle.

Leonard turned to see who had grabbed him. The hand was Ask's. In Ask's other hand was what looked like a small laptop computer, which he offered to Leonard.

"Why not use this ultrasound machine to see what damage may exist?" invited Ask.

Leonard was at first unsure, but Martin's breathing had relaxed. Leonard observed Martin a moment, and since he appeared more stable, Leonard took the device.

Ask released his own grip, then stumbled backward slightly.

Leonard opened the device, removed a pen sized probe, and ran it along Martin's side. The device screen immediately lit up with an ultrasound image of Martin's organs.

Ask struggled to stay on his feet, but managed to lean against another nearby gurney.

Leonard studied the device screen with equal amounts anxiety and confusion.

"What's wrong?" asked Susan. Leonard explained, "His spleen is fractured. He should be bleeding to death internally..."

"But...?"

Ask shakily laid down on the second gurney and closed his eyes. Elizabeth moved to him, "Ask? Are you alright?" But Ask did not respond. Elizabeth observed Ask's breathing slow and placed two fingers over his pulse. "Ask's heart rate is dropping!" she exclaimed.

Leonard nodded toward the medicine cabinet he had already used. "Go to the cabinet and get a vial called Atropine. Draw a syringe full to three milliliters."

Elizabeth did as Leonard had said. She was familiar with medicines and IVs, having lived her early life with Martin while he was still a practicing anesthesiologist. She found the vial and began her task.

The silo lights flickered again.

Aaron gripped a counter, white-knuckled, knowing that this was his fault. He didn't know what to do, or how he could help. And not for the first or the last time, he asked himself, 'Why am I here?' Though the only word to escape his mouth was, "Sorry."

The walls creaked, and Susan clung to the rail of Martin's gurney. "Leonard!" she said, in a tone that demanded to know what was going on.

Leonard shoved the ultrasound device and probe into Susan's hands. "Take this," he said, "and keep it right there so I can see the screen." Susan froze in the position he had set, with the additional result of the task freezing her speech.

Leonard took a stethoscope hanging on the wall and listened to Martin's abdomen. He then examined with his hands, especially Martin's left side and flank.

Martin continued to lie with his eyes closed. 'Aelialtha to Aeleriel, Aeleriel to Faeleriel, Faeleriel to Thaen, for the Garden to remain,' Martin recited his thoughts, ensuring his heart rate was controlled and his body could repair with minimal use of his life energy. 'Taenoril sil, da Luna Fael, Aelialtha mur, tul malia Hael.'

Leonard studied the ultrasound screen again. "No. This is not possible," he told himself. But he watched as the tissues in Martin's body did the impossible.

Susan whimpered, "Is he dying?"

Leonard looked up, desperate and perplexed. "No."

He scanned the room and all the puzzled faces. "His original injuries, in the ventilation room, were spleen and kidney lacerations. He should have been dead in minutes. Here," Leonard pointed to a portion of the ultrasound screen, "I saw his organs..." Leonard removed his hands and lowered Martin's shirt, "...healing themselves."

'...Faeleriel to Thaen, for the Garden to remain.' Martin finished the mantra on an exhale, then drew in a long breath and opened his eyes. Mirroring Martin, Ask took a similarly controlled, deep breath and opened his.

The lights brightened and steadied once more. Martin slowly sat up.

Elizabeth rushed to him. "Da...," she almost exclaimed, then caught herself.

Susan trembled, dropping the ultrasound device to the gurney, and extending her arms with clenched fists.

"Martin. What. Is. Going. On!"

Leonard placed a hand on Susan's elbow, hoping to calm her, but she shirked him off and flushed with anger. "This is all too much. Natural disasters, nuclear holocaust, secret bunker, coming back from the dead. Explain. For God's sake, no more lies!"

Martin took another deep breath and closed his eyes.

'Are you well enough, Elu?' Ask communicated to Martin.

He replied, 'Well enough, yes. My body is stable, but I will require sustenance for energy and further repair.'

'I will see to it,' began Ask.

'But,' interrupted Martin, 'I will not now be able to sufficiently lead the others on their path. The situation has changed. They must learn sooner than anticipated, and for that there will be risk.'

'You maintain the Garden, Elu, and I will lead them to it.' Ask sat up suddenly.

Everyone startled. But before anyone could vent their surprise verbally, Martin opened his eyes again. "We will tell you everything," he said. "But right now, I think we could use something to eat."

Susan, still infuriated, was not buying it. "No one's hungry Martin. You're stalling."

Martin gripped Susan's hand. "I need energy...need something to eat."

Then he and Ask both stood up mechanically, and walked toward the door to the short hallway that connected the stairwell and the elevator on this floor.

Aaron stepped in front of them. "What about the ventilation system? Elizabeth said..."

Martin smiled calmly, "Only one fan need work at a time. Do not be alarmed." Martin paused and turned toward Elizabeth. "I must rest, but you might find it instructive to remember the lessons I taught you." And without further explanation of his injury, his recovery, or what the others were to do now, Martin and Ask left the floor.

Aaron turned to Elizabeth and silently lipped, "What the...?"

Elizabeth turned imploringly to Leonard.

Leonard shrugged, "I can't explain what I saw. I could feel his wound healing underneath my fingers and see the tissues mending on the ultrasound. This is like nothing I've ever seen."

"Is he going to be okay?" Elizabeth asked.

Leonard shrugged again. "So it appears, but I'm a surgeon, not a mystic. I think the bigger question is how..."

Susan shook her head. "I just can't... I can't stay here!"

Elizabeth turned to her coldly. "Yeah mother, leaving, ...excellent decision. Good luck with that." Then turning to Aaron and taking his hand, she said, "C'mon."

Aaron looked at her hand holding his, then up at her meaningfully. She squeezed his hand tenderly, then determinedly, she led him out of the infirmary.

CHAPTER TWELVE

"The search for truth is the courageous journey one takes to find himself."

-- Eluwillusit Kowianu

The Search

Elizabeth and Aaron peered into the hall and saw Martin and Ask standing in front of the stairwell door.

The two looked at each other, nodding alternatively, as if communicating silently in some way. Finally Ask turned, then both disappeared through the stairway door.

Elizabeth walked down the hall, still holding Aaron's hand.

Aaron asked, "What did Martin mean by 'remember the lessons I taught you?'"

Elizabeth quietly opened the stairwell door, and both lean out onto the landing.

"He could have meant the power grid for the ventilation system," she said.

"Why do I get the idea there is more to this story than anyone is telling?" Aaron replied.

Both peered through the stairwell grating and saw Martin enter the great room below, while Ask entered the door on the tenth floor landing above.

Elizabeth whispered to herself, "What's on the tenth floor that's more important than the ventilation system?"

* * *

Elizabeth released Aaron's hand and began climbing stairs. 'Discovery mode,' Aaron thought, and followed.

After a flight of stairs, watching Elizabeth's face become more and more intense, he said, "You're thinking."

Elizabeth blinked and emerged from her own thoughts. "I want to check out the damage to the ventilation system."

"So do I," Aaron replied, 'but I know you... always two steps ahead."

They arrived at the tenth floor landing. Rather than continuing immediately up the stairs, Elizabeth stood in front of the door to the tenth floor space. Aaron nodded toward it. "After you."

To his surprise, Elizabeth continued up the stairs instead. Aaron raised an eyebrow and followed.

"The ventilation system has your interest," he said nodding toward the tenth floor door, "but my real money was on number ten."

"We'll get there," answered Elizabeth, adding energy to her steps, "but first I need the answer I was looking for."

* * *

Aaron watched Elizabeth as she inspected the gaping hole in the second fan casing of the ventilation system.

Inside the casing, Elizabeth noted that all the fan blades seemed intact but one. She recalled the gyroscopic motion that had occurred and completed some calculations in her head. Intuitively she knew, but her rough calculations confirmed to her, that it was impossible for all the forces working on the fan to have caused damage to only one blade.

Both visually followed its path to where it still lay, broken and bent, against the far wall of the ventilation space.

Elizabeth shifted her focus to the control board, then stood and crossed to it, leaving Aaron kneeling next to the casing.

Aaron could not tear his attention from the fan blade, lying bent and bloody outside the casing hole. He felt guilty and ashamed thinking of the injury he had caused Martin and the danger he had placed the group in.

"I'm sorry," he whispered again.

Elizabeth's legs protruded from under the small control board. Intent on her inspection of the control board's electrical system, she responded to the sound Aaron had made, "What?" though she had not registered what he had actually said.

She finished attaching alligator clips to the wiring system and read the hand-held meter.

Aaron stood, picked up the fan blade and placed it near the casing. He turned from the fan and took a deep breath. 'Wallowing in my own pity won't do anyone any good,' he reasoned, and decided he might as well see how he could help Elizabeth.

"Found what you're looking for?" he asked.

"Yes."

"What is it?"

"I don't know," Elizabeth replied excitedly.

Aaron wasn't sure how to respond. Confused, he replied, "You said you found what you were looking for."

"I was looking for something that I don't know, something unexpected," she said as she crawled out, "and I found it."

"Who's on second," Aaron replied deadpan.

Elizabeth gave him a blank stare. Aaron raised a single, questioning eyebrow, like Spock.

Elizabeth explained, "I'm measuring the amount of power this ventilation system is drawing as part of a larger estimate of all the energy requirements in this complex."

"And what will that show you?"

"Whether this silo can sustain itself," she said. "In this place, energy is life. Without power, we're all in one giant coffin."

"Happy thought," he returned. But he could tell from Elizabeth's expression there was more to her theory. "And?"

Elizabeth continued, nodding toward the ventilation fans, "And, the silo complex requires more power than it is receiving. I need to know if whatever generator is on the tenth floor is sustainable."

She began walking back to the stairs. "And now that I know what to look for, we'll find that answer back in the main control room."

She opened the stairwell door and paused. "By the way," she said. "Who's on first."

Then she exited. Aaron smiled and followed.

* * *

Leonard led Susan into the great room and toward the living room space. There, they found Martin sitting at the dining table with a small plate of fruit and cheese in front of him.

Susan tried her best not to look at Martin. She had worried about and for him again, and that angered her. He had left her emotions hanging out there so many times over their marriage, exposed, like raw skin, only to be injured over and over again.

'This obsession of his...this hallucination, I want no more of it.'

She felt her heart begin to race again and knew she had to think of something else. 'But what else is there to think of? The end of the world?'

She felt Leonard's hand squeeze and saw he was inviting her to lie down on a couch. She gratefully did so, intending to expend no more energy than she needed to. Moments later, Leonard had placed a cool wash cloth over her forehead and lifted her head onto his lap.

Her breathing relaxed. With deliberate effort she sought something she could think of that would not ignite panic or anger in her again. A vision of the green house came to her.

'Wonderful!' she recalled. 'Simply wonderful.' At first glance it was an excellent example of high efficiency energy transfer. She knew that in closed ecospheres efficiency of energy transfer was paramount. Both the forest floor and the Bujuan tower in the green house were masterful, and as soon as Martin recovered, she wanted to know more.

* * *

In the main control room, Elizabeth leaned over the touch screen computer, and with the finger movements she had used before, recalled the schematic of the silos from the side.

She tapped the cog icon. "This displays the control systems for the silo."

She tapped the lightning bolt icon. "Here is the power grid."

Aaron nodded.

"I discovered," she continued, her fingers tracing the green power lines as she looked at Aaron, "the system is using more power than is being generated."

She tapped the tenth floor. "And the difference is coming from here, but it remains a black void."

Aaron offered, "Perhaps something is keeping us from seeing what is making this energy."

Elizabeth's face brightened, "Exactly!"

Aaron, uncertain how his suggestion really worked, was confused again. He realized, however, that he had tripped a switch in Elizabeth's brain, as her gaze began to drift away.

Elizabeth recalled that she had said, 'Something must be producing power on the tenth floor,' and Martin had answered, 'Not something.'

Aaron tried to break into her thought process. "What did Martin tell you?"

But he saw she was no longer there. As much as one part of her tried to make sense of the present world through the logic of engineering, another part seemed to repeatedly search back in time for the fragments of a lost childhood. Aaron knew she was in that never land now.

She was lost in a memory from ten years earlier. Elizabeth was one of two people sitting on whicker chairs in a beautiful backyard garden. A younger Martin held a rose bud in front of his face and pointed to the top of the petals.

"So where will the next petal emerge?" Martin asked. He waited for a response but heard none.

Elizabeth remembered why.

"I don't want to do math," twelve year-old Elizabeth pouted from the chair next to Martin, her arms crossed and legs pulled in tightly toward her.

Martin pointed to an equation in an open math book on the table in front of her. "It's not just math. It's a key to an entire world of adventure, unlocking..."

Preteen Elizabeth deadpanned, "...the mysteries of the unseen universe," her expression bitter. "You can't tell me what to do. You're not even my real dad!"

Martin lowered the flower. "We adopted you as a baby, yes. We've talked about this before. Do you want to talk about it again?"

She wrapped up into her arms even further.

"You know how much your mother and I love you," said Martin.

Elizabeth's eyes began to well with tears.

"I understand why you are upset," he consoled. "Dancing is wonderful, Lizzy. But understanding how the world works will save lives."

Young Elizabeth took several defiant breaths, then relaxed, and glanced toward the text book.

Back in the control room, twenty-two year-old Elizabeth continued to stare into space through watery eyes.

"Martin has told me a lot of things," she told Aaron. Then to herself, "How the world works."

"Sorry?"

She shook her head and focused back on the computer screen.

"It has to be in the math. Martin suggested the energy differential was not caused by something."

"Someone? You mean a person is creating energy to keep this place running? Do you think this 'Faeleriel' is a living being?"

Elizabeth considered Aaron's words, then sprang to life over the screen, tapping icons and moving from screen to screen.

Aaron watched, as always amazed by her ability to place all the puzzle pieces together once she understood the picture.

As she manipulated the silo diagrams and analyzed the data, she coached herself, "Where is all the energy going?"

She froze. "Yes! *All* the energy." And she tapped the screen excitedly. "Not just electricity. Not just the silo. All energy...everywhere. Here!"

An image of the silo complex with multiple colors appeared, and Elizabeth studied the image closely.

"Much of the silo energy comes from geothermal and biothermal sources," she explained.

Aaron looked puzzled.

"Hot rocks and gassy plants," she clarified.

Elizabeth leaned back from the screen, taking in the entire schematic. Multiple shades of yellows and oranges filled the inside of the silo complex, while a circular purple rim surrounded the complex.

She typed into the keyboard, and numbers appeared along the bottom of the screen.

01 days; 00 hours: 02 minutes: 53 seconds

The numbers scrolled downward by milliseconds, seconds, and minutes, to the hour.

Elizabeth pulled her hands back as if from a hot stove.

"What?" asked Aaron.

Elizabeth caught her breath.

"This graphic shows the total amount of energy being used throughout the entire silo complex," she said.

"What's wrong?"

Elizabeth traced a circle with her finger around the purple edge of the five silos on the computer screen.

"It can't do that," she explained.

"What do you mean?" asked Aaron.

Elizabeth stabbed into the air with a finger. "The First Law of Thermodynamics is being violated."

Aaron replied facetiously, "Sorry, I meant to say, 'So what?'"

"Look," said Elizabeth. "Energy can neither be created nor destroyed. But within a system, all energy forms must balance out."

Aaron replied with a blank stare.

"It means we shouldn't be here."

Aaron, still confused, asked, "You think we should leave?"

"No," said Elizabeth. "The system is using more energy than it is taking in."

Aaron sighed, "You've said that already."

"But it's worse than I thought," confessed Elizabeth. "Energy is being created, not just for life support systems, but to create some kind of protection field."

Aaron's face screwed up like he had been eating lemons, struggling to understand.

Elizabeth pointed to the purple circle outside the silo complex on the digital schematic.

"This is the force pushing in from outside the silos." She focused on Aaron. "Whatever is adding energy and counter-balancing those outside forces shouldn't exist. We should all be dead."

Elizabeth cast her glance to the row of monitors that had shown the outside devastation.

Aaron's expression showed a hint of understanding. "You think Martin's got some generator hidden somewhere that we don't know about?"

Elizabeth raised an eyebrow. "I can see the energy coming from every piece of machinery, except the tenth floor. The math doesn't add up." She took a breath. "It doesn't make sense. It could be his fairy dust for all I know."

"You think it's Martin... himself, some kind of power... he has?"

When she gave him a smirk, he amended, "...Or controls?"

Elizabeth shrugged, "What I know is...if whatever this is stops adding energy, the silo systems will fail, and the forces outside the silo will overcome those within."

"Meaning?"

Elizabeth's face drooped. "It will get very bad for us very quickly."

Aaron's voice dropped to a whisper. "Like, 'no air' bad?"

Elizabeth shook her head slowly. "Like a submarine sinking below crush depth bad." And she slapped her hands together.

Aaron's face turned ashen.

"The Earth around this silo is incredibly unstable," she explained. "My calculations show that this field is failing..."

She pointed to the countdown on the computer screen, which turned over at that moment to 23 hours; 59 minutes: 59 seconds.

"...and that's how much time we have left."

CHAPTER THIRTEEN

"Perception is the foundation of Thaen memory. No Thaen views with infinite perception, thus, no Thaen truly remembers."

-- Rhana, Faeleriel

The Memory

Martin finished chewing and swallowing a grape and could feel its energy adding to his metabolism. He would have liked to have focused on healing his internal organs completely, but did not have that luxury under the current circumstances.

It was more important that he sustain the Tree and the Garden, even as they hibernated, so long as he had the energy to do so and remained alive.

During Omladine, an Age of Belief, he knew energy flow of Taenoril sil was so efficient, the symbiosis between he and the Garden would heal his wounds in minutes and enable him to rejuvenate countless Faeleriel. For now, he was resigned to eating as his only form of energy replenishment, unable to do more than prevent the loss of the silo and its inhabitants.

Elizabeth entered from the stairwell, scanned the great room, and marched toward Martin, Aaron not far behind. Leonard looked up, while Susan laid on the couch with the wash cloth on her forehead.

Martin sat motionless with eyes closed at the dining table, the small tray of fruit and cheese in front of him. Elizabeth stomped angrily toward him.

"How are you adding energy to the system?" she demanded.

Martin opened his eyes but did not come out of his trance. She slammed her hand onto the table next to him.

"We should be dead right now!" she exclaimed.

Susan sat bolt upright at this. "What?"

Martin startled back to full consciousness, as the lights momentarily flickered. Elizabeth and Aaron shared a look.

Leonard was perturbed, "What's going on?"

Susan turned to Martin, "Martin?"

Aaron scanned the room, however, and noticed that Ask was not present.

"No, wait," Aaron pointed out to Elizabeth. "It's Ask." Then, to Martin, Aaron inquired, "Isn't it?"

Susan was becoming more frustrated by the moment. "What about him? What is Ask doing?"

Aaron spoke accusatorially to Martin, "He's adding power to the system."

Elizabeth continued, "And without him, the walls cave in."

"Cave in?" whimpered Susan. "Will someone please explain what you are talking about?"

Elizabeth picked up the television remote and scrolled through the screen commands until she found "Monitor." She selected it, and the television projected the computer monitor image showing '23 hours; 51 minutes: 06 seconds.'

Elizabeth turned to the group, "It appears something..."

"or someone," interrupted Aaron.

"...is creating enough energy surrounding this complex to keep the walls from imploding," finished Elizabeth.

Susan demanded of Martin, "Is this true?"

Martin spoke matter-of-factly, "That depends on what you believe."

"Please, Martin!" Susan pleaded, "Enough of the mystic cra..."

Elizabeth shot Susan a glare.

"I mean, can't you, for once, just speak in normal sentences?"

Aaron pointedly asked, "Do you and Ask maintain some kind of energy field?"

"And what is on the tenth floor?" added Elizabeth. And Leonard finished, "And how did you heal...?"

Martin's interest was peaked by Elizabeth's question. 'She knows about the tenth floor,' he marveled. 'Can she feel it? Does she believe?'

From the back of the great room, Ask's voice broke in, "All will be explained..."

Everyone turned, surprised, as Ask entered.

Ask saw the count down on the television screen, then closed his eyes. 'Eluwillusit, what do you see?' He asked through their mental connection.

'The melting is upon us. I can maintain until then, but may not be able to protect once it hits,' Martin replied mentally.

'But if they see and do not believe...,' Ask warned.

Yes, the risk is great. They can each be a savior or a harbinger of evil and death,' thought Martin. 'Their ability to understand will decide. But there is no choice now.'

Ask continued aloud, "but Elu...Martin, must rest. I will show you so you can begin."

"Begin what?" asked Susan.

"Learning the duties that will..." Ask looked at Elizabeth, "...keep the silo from imploding."

Martin casually ate a grape with a "pop".

* * *

Ask climbed the stairs and began explaining the necessary tasks at hand. "To best understand the systems..."

But Elizabeth was well into her 'discovery mode'. "I want to go to the tenth floor," she said firmly.

Ask opened his mouth to resist.

"Nothing you or Martin say will mean anything until we have explored the tenth floor. Now take us there."

Ask cocked his head, wondering if Eluwillusit was right. He regarded Elizabeth and her exuberance, then nodded in assent.

* * *

The entire group, except Martin, had accompanied Ask. "Everything begins here," Ask announced as they approached the tenth floor landing.

Elizabeth strode ahead of him, not listening, and immediately tried to open the door. The door knob did not budge.

Elizabeth grudgingly moved aside, as Ask casually walked up, gripped the door knob, and twisted it, opening the door easily.

Ask held the portal open for Elizabeth to enter first, and with a sigh she stepped through.

* * *

Elizabeth took four steps into the room and slowed to a halt. Old, shriveled, grey vines completely draped the circular wall of the large open space, many hanging like beaded curtains from the ceiling.

The floor was not flat. It rose and fell in mounds, like a north coast beach. Brown, brittle moss clung to various defoliated plant stalks and small, barren tree trunks.

"Ugh! My God!" exclaimed Susan. She had stopped on her second step into the room, disgusted, because the room before her eyes was not just brown and shriveled, but rotted and decayed. "This is the largest compost pile I have ever seen."

She turned to Elizabeth, "There's the mystery... energy from decay and rot." Susan started to turn and leave. "The methane alone could kill us."

But before Susan had reached the door, Ask had closed it. He walked past her nonchalantly.

Susan gripped the door knob, but it didn't move.

Everyone turned and watched Ask as he stepped comfortably to the center of the room. He sat down in a small clearing, perhaps twelve feet in diameter, and gestured for the others to follow.

Elizabeth and Aaron entered the clearing and sat uncomfortably. Susan and Leonard remained standing at the edge of the clearing, which looked to Susan like a carpet of dark sludge.

Elizabeth noticed that all of the shriveling plants in the large open space appeared to emanate from or focus on a small lump of wood sitting next to Ask.

Susan spoke to Elizabeth, "Why is this so important?"

Elizabeth looked around her, disappointed and confused.

Aaron whispered to Elizabeth, "Are you okay?"

"I've seen this," she told him. "I mean something feels familiar." She scanned the room, searching for a grounding image for her memory.

"It will all make sense soon," Ask assured. "Just be patient. Everything begins and ends here."

Elizabeth snapped her head toward Ask. Something in this room *was* familiar. She had heard before the words Ask had just spoken.

'Everything begins and ends here.'

'Where? And what?' Elizabeth wondered.

She expanded her perspective to consider not just Ask but the area and room around him. Her eyes naturally moved to the lump of wood near him.

And in that lump of wood was a vision of her past.

Her thoughts drifted instantly and transported her mind to the last time she saw Martin before these past few days, and as she now realized, the last time she saw this tree.

She was in the Florida forest again, her seventeen year-old self stomping away from Martin.

"You dragged me out here to some Florida swamp, during my senior year spring break to see some old tree?!" The words were as hot in her mind and heart now as ever.

And Martin stood in the small clearing as annoyingly imperturbable as ever...his compassionate smile infuriating.

Now however, Elizabeth focused not on Martin or her feelings, but on the three foot tall, knotted and twisted, nearly barren, willow tree.

"It is significant," he assured her, "and I want you to see..."

But young Elizabeth spun on him again as she remembered the day. "What! Why is this so important? What new revelation has come to you to embarrass me?"

"It will make sense soon," Martin insisted. "Just be patient."

Elizabeth huffed defiantly and turned again to leave.

"It is important," explained Martin, "because everything begins and ends here."

"Yeah," replied Elizabeth condescendingly, "it does end here, Martin! Mom gave up on you years ago, but I held out, hoping you would either come out of it or at least get treatment. But no, you'd rather drag everyone down with you. I'm outta here. Enjoy your tree."

Now, in the tenth floor of the silo, Elizabeth looked down at the tiny tree, clearly not the same one. Yet something about it reminded her that that day had been the last time she had seen Martin until yesterday. They had spoken on the telephone several times, and she remembered having been very unkind to Martin. But that was the last time they were in the same place.

She spoke the words to herself, "Begins and ends here?"

Elizabeth studied the twisted, knotty piece of wood next to Ask. It was about a foot and a half tall, one foot wide block of knotted wood, with a slightly narrower mid portion, and protrusions from bottom and top that could equally be either roots or branches.

Ask raised a questioning eyebrow to Elizabeth.

"This reminds me of something I once saw in Florida," she explained.

Ask nodded his head. "It reminds you, because you are looking at it."

Elizabeth shook her head disbelievingly. "This can't be. It's so small!"

Ask shrugged. "Perhaps our perceptions change over time."

"This looks like a dried out bonsai tree. The one I saw wasn't big, but it was certainly bigger than this," her words fading as she drifted into thought.

"If this once lived," Susan added compassionately, "I don't think there is much of a chance of recovery. I hope you have others?"

Elizabeth mumbled as she tried to figure out how else she could know this plant in front of her.

"Begins and ends here," she mumbled.

"Yes," said Ask, as if he was responding to a query from Elizabeth. "Life energy is circular. It may seem linear - a beginning and an end, but all life is infinite. You will see. Like ar' Ama Gedeon, itself the end of one and the beginning of another, a Thaen life cycle gives up its failing body to travel through the Tree and join with Aelialtha before returning again to another form."

Elizabeth looked at Ask, puzzled. She had clearly heard some of this when she was younger from Martin. But none of it meant anything to her now.

Irritated with Ask's apparent diversion into Martin's fantasy world, Susan interrupted, "Perhaps she is thinking of an entirely different tree."

Ask said, "It is the only one of its kind we have here." He then took a long breath, briefly studying each of the others in the room.

Elizabeth knew about Martin's belief, or at least that he believed in 'something'. But Elizabeth was bitter about her childhood experiences. Susan was far worse, and to bring them up only invited her anger. Leonard seemed capable of dealing with a discussion of Martin's philosophy, but would likely follow however Susan reacted. Aaron was the most creative of the group and had a great capacity to accept differing, even fanciful, ideas. But Ask knew Aaron did not believe nor see now.

'None of them see,' realized Ask, weighing his options, 'There is so little time. I can explain where they are and what it means, but if they reject it and hold to their disbelief, there will be less time still.'

Then, an idea occurred to him.

Ask changed his demeanor to show fatigue and resignation. He stood.

Ask stated, "As you know, this complex was redesigned to sustain life. We hope to soon show you all the life forms we maintain, but for now let me show those in artificial hibernation."

Susan suddenly came to life herself. "You have an embryo lab?"

"With thousands of species," Ask replied.

"Where?" Susan inquired.

Ask walked through the debris of the tenth floor to the far side of the room. "In another silo."

Susan immediately followed. "Are they in cryo or anhydrobiotic form?"

Leonard followed silently behind Susan.

Elizabeth, who had been lost in thought about the tree to this point, came out of her trance and followed the group.

Elizabeth recited, "Anhydrobiosis has too high a regeneration failure rate in eukaryotes. It has to be cryo."

Ask moved a curtain of vines to one side at the far wall of the room and opened a door to a long hallway. He gestured them through the door. "This will take us to silo number two."

Then without a pause, and still engaged in a discussion of the possibilities surrounding reanimation of cryogenic tissue, they walked through the door, closing it behind them.

Aaron watched them leave without a glance backward, leaving him alone in the dead and withering space.

He saw the room as Elizabeth had, infested with overgrown plants now devoid of life. The silence was as dead as the plants.

The feeling of death suddenly overwhelmed Aaron. The silence was dead. The plants were dead. His family was dead. And in less than a day they and the planet would likely be...

Frustrated and feeling ill, Aaron left through the stairwell door from which he had entered.

CHAPTER FOURTEEN

"We shall not cease from exploration
And the end of all our exploring
Will be to arrive where we started
And know the place for the first time."

-- T. S. Eliot

The Reason

Minutes later, Aaron reentered the common living area.

He spotted Martin, who appeared a little sweaty and pale to Aaron. Martin had apparently not moved from the dining table. His eyes were still closed, though he was apparently not asleep, but rather in deep concentration.

Aaron peered at the television in the living space, which showed the countdown: 0 days, 21 hours, 26 minutes, 37 seconds and counting.

Aaron despondently picked up the television remote and switched the screen graphic to the silo schematic showing the balance of outside versus inside forces.

The outside purple color had intensified further.

Aaron looked again at Martin, who appeared not to notice or care about the impending destruction.

Feeling ill himself after looking at the monitor, Aaron scanned the room for some other distraction and found the instruments once again. He was drawn to them in the natural way a bee is drawn to flowers.

Sitting at the piano was comforting, like donning a well-worn pair of shoes, and placing his fingers over the keys was refreshing, like a cool breeze on a hot and humid day. Feeling as close to home as he had felt in the previous twenty-four hours, Aaron relaxed, released his breath and played.

At first, he played short, popular tunes he would play for Elizabeth and their friends for fun. But his mood was not there. He journeyed on through his feelings into a complicated and crescendoing melody, his emotion spilling out in a tapestry of sound.

The sentiment evolved from melancholy to anger, with Aaron hammering his fingers on the keys as he played, then desperation, until finally the melody mellowed into the musical equivalence of acceptance.

Martin meanwhile was in a three-way stalemate, balancing the energies in and around him. He had stabilized his injuries, but made no advance with his healing. He had secured the protective shell to the silo complex, but the outside forces were bearing down on them. And he was maintaining the life support systems within the silo to keep everyone alive. He was maintaining the status quo, but no more.

Then a stream of light had approached him in the darkness. It offered him a taste of its energy. It was enlivening.

As the calming refrain of music filled the room, Martin's tenseness relaxed and his breathing eased. The light in the room brightened slightly.

Then, as it had begun, Aaron's melody resolved into a dissonance, stopping as Aaron's fingers sunk into the keys.

Aaron sucked in a deep breath, got up, and paced the room, frustration coming back to his demeanor, along with the realization that he did not belong here.

'I'm not like them,' he complained to himself. 'What can I do here?' He lamented, thinking of the family he had lost, but guilty that he did not necessarily want to join them by dying himself.

He suddenly felt he was not alone. Looking toward the dining table, he discovered Martin's eyes were now open and studying him.

Aaron faced Martin, his internal struggle bubbling outward. "Didn't Beth say something about the air going bad and us not being able to breathe in a few days?"

Martin nodded calmly, "We have another ventilation system."

"But it's been a day."

"Only one is required to maintain the complex," said Martin.

Aaron's frustration would not be appeased, however. "Ok, so Noah has an ark," he said waving an arm around the room animatedly, "with life support systems, hydroponics, computer and mechanical gadgetry, all run by my engineer girlfriend, her biologist mother, two doctors, and an all knowing...whatever Ask is!"

Aaron paused as if that was question enough.

Martin looked at him expectantly, but gave no reply.

Aaron at last finished his question, "So,...why the musician?"

"What do you mean?" Martin replied innocently.

"I get the feeling there was more to this than just prepper refurbishing of a missile silo," Aaron expounded. "I know it was you who pushed Beth into engineering instead of dance. And you who introduced Leonard to Susan before you disappeared?"

Aaron circled in toward the table where Martin was sitting. "And now we all arrive, as you insisted, conveniently just before Armageddon."

Martin appeared more concerned. "A father wants his child to be happy, to grow up..."

Aaron crossed his arms defiantly, while Martin continued, "...to preserve the next generation."

Aaron wasn't buying it, and was about to turn away. But Martin stood and placed a hand on his elbow.

"I knew," he said warily, "when Elizabeth was young, that there *wouldn't be* a next generation. That is, unless *she* was the next generation."

Martin turned toward the door, then looking back over his shoulder at Aaron, "Let me show you something," and led Aaron to the stairwell.

* * *

Aaron was not sure what Martin had planned to show him, but Aaron had certainly not expected this. Two levels above the common living level, Martin and Aaron entered from the stairs onto a circular floor divided into four distinct spaces.

The first, which they had entered, was an open gym and dance studio. It was essentially half of the circular silo floor, about twenty feet high, surfaced in beech wood, with a basketball hoop and markings at the far end and gym equipment at the near. Dominating the middle of the room were ten foot tall mirrors along both the divider and curvilinear walls, giving the room a feeling of infinite spaciousness. A dance bar railing protruded out from both walls.

The center wall was not an uninterrupted divider. At the floor's exact center was a fifteen foot diameter glass room. Martin led Aaron there, and opened the glass door to allow Aaron inside.

From inside, Aaron could see that the other half of the circular silo space was divided equally into a movie theater and a multimedia recording studio. The center glass room that they were now in was a mixing control room and held an unobstructed view of all three other spaces.

Martin stepped up to the mixing board and pushed a button.

On the movie theater screen in the next room a movie began to play, and in it, a high school teacher was reciting poetry to his students and imparting more than just its literary meaning. He was giving them an important life lesson as well.

Aaron watched the scene engrossed in it, having seen the film while he too was in high school. Unseen by Aaron, Martin winced in slight pain.

The professor told his class that poetry was not a meaningless endeavor. Creative passion, in whatever form is why we exist. That passion, that beauty fills us, drives us, and gives our lives meaning.

The young professor quoted Walt Whitman, but Aaron did not need to watch the movie.

"O me! O life!" said Aaron, "... of the questions of these recurring; Of the endless trains of the faithless — of cities fill'd with the foolish; Of myself forever reproaching myself, (for who more foolish than I, and who more faithless?); Of eyes that vainly crave the light — of the objects mean — of the struggle ever renew'd; Of the poor results of all — of the plodding and sordid crowds I see around me; Of the empty and useless years of the rest — with the rest me intertwined; The question, O me! so sad, recurring — What good amid these, O me, O life?

"Answer.

"That you are here — that life exists, and identity; That the powerful play goes on, and you will contribute a verse."

Martin pushed another button, and the image disappeared. "Survival," he said, "is just survival. You can help us maintain music, art, religion, laughter...life."

Aaron stared at the empty screen.

Martin pressed on. "Aaron, what do you believe?"

"Huh?" puzzled Aaron.

"I am not talking about religion. When you create, what brings you inspiration?"

Aaron pondered the question. "I write about...the world, the human condition, what binds us...or separates us."

Martin's voice picked up, "When you play then, what is your hope?"

"That we can," began Aaron, then he corrected himself, "*will*...all live together peacefully."

Martin pushed further. "That we all believe...," his expression coaxed.

Aaron finished, "...in each other."

Martin smiled.

Aaron pondered his own answer, then looked at Martin understandingly.

Martin nodded, pleased, and led Aaron back toward the door.

* * *

Elizabeth marveled. Susan and Leonard were beside themselves.

Elizabeth stood next to Ask as Susan and Leonard wandered down rows upon rows of microtube incubation canisters reading the labels on each.

"Panthera leo, hyaenidae, Giraffa camelopardalis. That's a giraffe!" exclaimed Susan, like she was six years old explaining the toys in her room.

Elizabeth whispered to Ask, "Looks like she'll be happy for a while."

Ask merely smiled.

Elizabeth scanned the laboratory again and considered all the work it had taken to build and stock it. "I wasn't far off when I called this silo Noah's Ark," she said colloquially.

Ask nodded, "Over three thousand species in deep freeze."

Elizabeth looked at him astounded, "Three thousand!" Elizabeth knew that the math by itself was not truly impressive. Earth had certainly lost most of the nearly nine million species over the past day or so, but she knew the work involved to accumulate so many DNA and embryonic forms was staggering.

'Not to mention,' she thought, 'having to decide which three thousand species were the most representative to save, to one day initiate the process of world repopulation.'

That question in itself was daunting, considering the importance of symbiosis between species and the role each played in world evolution.

It suddenly occurred to Elizabeth that Ask was not unlike these specimens. He was the last of his tribe. She had not bothered to consider before what or who he had lost.

"Did you have family?" she asked carefully.

Ask looked at her. "Yes, though my parents moved on when I was very young. I was raised by my grandfather."

Elizabeth heard the pride in Ask's voice as he said this. She was sure he must miss his grandfather dearly. She could not think of anything appropriate to say now.

Ask filled the silence. "It was my grandfather who taught me to prepare for this time, this moment, this beginning that comes from the end."

"Beginning?" puzzled Elizabeth.

Ask nodded toward the lab. "This is but a fraction of the life that exists."

"You have other labs?"

Ask stifled a chuckle. "Life energy is very powerful in its natural form. It can..." he searched for the right word, "...hibernate as long as needed, if preserved appropriately."

Elizabeth felt Ask was now speaking in perhaps his tribe's spiritual terms. She did not make an issue of it or debate the forms of energy that existed in the physical world.

Unlike the real world, the heart did not need proof or fact to have its own truth. 'And if his family energy is in hibernation to him and not dead, who am I to say otherwise.'

"The Hashakochi iti, my tribe, were very good at preservation. My grandfather passed the way to me, and I passed this to your father."

Elizabeth snapped toward Ask, surprised. "Passed this to...Martin?"

Ask nodded. "Yes. The knowledge of the life energy cycle is very important. As the last of my tribe, it was, and is, important that this knowledge carry on."

"But you're young."

Ask chuckled again. "Ah, not so young. In fact, I am much older than I look, and I have lived as the last of my people for many years."

This saddened Elizabeth. She imagined that since Ask only looked in his early forties, he must have lost his family at a young age and forced upon him a lonely life.

Hoping to offer him something, she said, "We can learn too, so your tribe knowledge won't be forgotten."

Ask turned toward her, smiling broadly. "Thank you, Elizabeth. My tribe would consider your assistance a great honor."

* * *

Martin stood on the tenth floor stairwell landing with his back to the door.

"Are they still gone?" asked Aaron.

Martin briefly closed his eyes, expanded his senses throughout the silo complex until he could feel the energy from the others, then replied, "In the embryo labs. Yes."

Martin then paused and looked inquisitively at Aaron.

Aaron returned his expression, as if to say, 'I have no idea what you're thinking.'

Martin glanced over his shoulder toward the tenth floor door.

'He means the dead plants,' realized Aaron, catching on. "But I just left here. There's nothing to see."

"See again," offered Martin, "this time through the eyes of your...inspiration."

Martin fixed Aaron with his stare.

Aaron was at first puzzled, then allowing himself to consider thinking creatively, he closed his eyes.

Martin continued, "Consider what you *believe*," explained Martin. "Center your energy on what you believe is *possible*. Focus your belief on those you most believe *in*. Think of the world as music of your own composition. Imagine in that song, your feelings for Lizzy."

And Martin opened the door.

* * *

Aaron entered blindly, guided by Martin, into the space he knew was laden with dead, matted grasses, decomposing palms, and shriveled vines. He could feel the softness of the dirt beneath his feet. Still he focused on his feelings for Beth and tried to ignore everything else.

Aaron had walked about fifteen paces into the room when Martin stopped.

Martin began to chant softly, "Taenoril sil, da Luna Fael, Aelialtha mur, tul malia Hael. Taenoril sil, da Luna Fael, Aelialtha mur, tul malia Hael..." repeating the nonsensical phrase over and over.

Aaron thought something sounded familiar about these words, though he was not sure why. They reminded him of Beth in some way, and for that, the words were beautiful. He imagined Beth as he always did, with the look on her face as they leaned together to kiss.

She almost always kissed with her eyes open as they leaned in toward each other, then just before their mouths touched, she'd glance at his lips, and close her eyes slowly and seductively. The vision never ceased to get his heart pumping or tune everything else out of his brain. Now, however, as Martin had instructed, Aaron imagined Beth as a song, painted like a portrait, but by notes instead of pigments, and that somehow the room he was in served as the canvas to hold that music together.

Aaron knew that whatever he saw when he opened his eyes, he would not be disappointed, because rotten plants or not, he was going to see through his belief in Beth.

Without making the conscious decision to do so, Aaron began singing in his head a song he had written for Beth and him to play as a duet.

Martin finished the mantra and exhaled. Drawing in a casual following breath, he said, "Now open your eyes."

Aaron did so and noticed nothing at first except a steady glow of emerald light. It emanated from the center of the tenth floor space, silhouetting most of the plants in the central clearing. As Aaron moved to the light's source, he continued to sing his song for Beth in his thoughts, noticing less and less of the silhouetted plants and more of the light which cast its glow.

Stepping into the clearing, he felt more than saw that he was walking on a soft carpet of moss which shown a deep forest green, not because of the clearing's green glow, but because, "It's alive!" The words escaped from Aaron's mouth without his realizing it.

Aaron's eyes followed the moss to its edges and examined the plants growing all around him. They too were alive, lush, and glowing with iridescent color. From his vantage point at the center of the clearing, Aaron could see the entire tenth floor of the silo was covered with living foliage. Though there were no flowers, every inch of floor, wall, and ceiling was covered with some shade of green, yellow, orange or brown plants.

Aaron was astounded. "How?"

"How do you think?" replied Martin.

Aaron considered this for a moment. "Has this been here all along?" he asked.

Martin smiled but did not answer. He drew his attention instead back to the center of the clearing. Aaron followed his gaze to the small, withered tree or bush Ask had sat next to earlier. Aaron remembered how dead and rotted it had looked before, but now, thinking of Beth as he sang his song for her in his head, he saw a small, barren but brilliantly gleaming mahogany-colored willow tree.

Aaron observed that not only was this tiny leafless tree at the approximate center of the room, just about all the plants in the room were oriented in relation to it. Roots, branches and leaves throughout the floor all seemed to use it as some form of compass, growing as if they wanted to be connected with it in some way.

Most astounding to Aaron, as he focused on the tree, he saw that the glow throughout the room was emanating from around the tree itself. Dumbly, Aaron's mouth fell open as he tried to focus harder and harder on the tree to define its traits and glean from where the glow was coming. Try as he did, however, the tree itself remained simple, even if Aaron's feelings did not.

Martin nodded upward and replied, "You asked before, what happened to cause such destruction?"

Aaron thought of Martin's instructions when they entered the Garden and the strength of what bonded him to Elizabeth. From the very first moment, it had been one thing.

"Belief?" Aaron asked.

Martin nodded encouragingly.

"In each other?" Aaron continued.

Another nod.

"You mean all that," said Aaron, pointing toward the surface, "happened because people stopped believing in each other?"

It seemed to Aaron that in that moment Martin's expression changed only slightly in form, but somehow gained the appearance of immense wisdom.

"Energy," he explained, "is the foundation of all universes and the purest essence of life itself. Our civilization has only been consciously thinking about how our world works for a tiny fraction of its existence. Though our science has spawned from our observations and developed from experimentation, it is important to understand," he said soundly, "that not all forms of energy can be measured with a device or proven with a theorem."

"Belief connects us to this energy?" Aaron asked.

"Taenoril sil, it is called," Martin said.

"When we entered, that was one of the words you chanted."

"The chanting helps me focus the living energy that flows between all who believe. Taenoril sil is the flow of that energy."

Martin walked along the periphery of the clearing and held a hand over the tall grasses growing there. As his hand passed over them, the plants leaned toward it. He turned and look at Aaron.

Aaron gaped, astounded by what he had just seen.

Aaron was excited, but he concentrated, not only on what he was learning from Martin, but maintaining his thoughts of Beth and the song he was singing in the back of his mind. Controlling his breathing, he ran his own hands over the same plants. They did not lean. Aaron was not surprised, but felt a little disappointed.

Suddenly a thought occurred to Aaron, and he turned to Martin.

"If a form of energy exists that we cannot yet measure," Aaron pointed out, "few will believe it exists."

Martin nodded.

Aaron continued, "And one who insists it does exist may be found to have..."

Martin tilted his head.

"...a 'brief psychotic episode,'" explained Aaron.

Martin smiled and nodded slightly again. "Yes," he said, "that could very well happen."

"We have to bring everyone back here. They have to see this!" Aaron said enthusiastically.

Martin said nothing, but his face became somber. He moved again toward the small Tree and sat beside it. Uncertain what he had said to disquiet Martin, Aaron dutifully followed.

Aaron watched as Martin laid a hand gently on the mossy floor, beside the base of the Tree, and closed his eyes.

Within moments, and to Aaron's surprise, a thin gleaming root slid from the side of several thick roots at the Tree's base, toward Martin's hand. Like an octopus tentacle, it reached for, touched and slid over his hand, illuminating a pale green light between it and Martin's skin. Another slightly larger root followed.

Aaron could not believe it! As that thought came to him, he admonished himself, 'What a terrible saying that is.' And he focused on Beth and her song as he controlled once again his thoughts and his breathing.

"So," he stammered, "the old legends and fairy tales...are true."

Martin looked at Aaron, "I suppose that depends on what you call truth."

Aaron was puzzled.

"What we call 'Truth'," explained Martin, "is little more than a collective point of view. If the world appears flat, and that is the common wisdom, then such is the truth."

Aaron replied, "But it still doesn't make the world flat."

"No," agreed Martin, "but it does affect how we live our lives together on the face of that round world...and it affects what we believe."

Martin looked down at his hand placed next to the Tree, and Aaron felt a deep desire to do likewise.

"During times of Duadine, the common wisdom is that of disbelief, and disbelief is the truth," said Martin.

"Earth has an enormous amount of energy within it and lies in a position to our sun that is ideal for life. The Faeleriel discovered this long ago and through Taenoril sil were able to direct Earth's energy away from volatility and toward tranquility."

"Who are the Faeleriel?" Aaron asked.

"The beings who inhabit this Garden and assist the flow of Taenoril sil," Martin answered.

Aaron looked around the Garden again. He saw the brightly colored plants but no flowers or other beings. "What happened to them?"

"They await the fall of Duadine and the return of Omladine; the fade of disbelief and the rise of belief. It is the cycle of life on our world, the world of Thaen," explained Martin.

"And this is the end of the cycle?" asked Aaron.

"Yes," replied Martin, "ar' Ama Gedeon: The New Beginning."

"New beginning?" puzzled Aaron. "How many times has this happened before?"

"Many," replied Martin. "But the time between each cycle depends on whether belief and the flow of Taenoril sil survives from the previous one."

"So if we and this Garden survive this, what comes next?" Aaron asked, a lump firmly placed in his throat.

Martin said nothing.

Cautiously, Aaron placed his hand at the base of the small Tree.

"Taenoril sil, da Luna Fael, Aelialtha mur, tul malia Hael," Martin chanted. He nodded to Aaron for him to recite with him.

"Taenoril sil, da Luna Fael, Aelialtha mur, tul malia Hael," Aaron recited with him.

"Consider what you *believe*," explained Martin. "Center your energy on what you believe is *possible*. Focus your belief on those you most believe *in*."

Aaron closed his eyes, as a tiny tendril slid from the base of the Tree, across the narrow space, and over his hand.

Just as the first wisp of tendril contacted his skin, Aaron gasped from the sensation. In that instant, Aaron felt his body had been charged with electricity.

'No,' he thought. 'Not electricity, not a shock...energy. It's like I can feel the energy from everything else in the room.'

Gathering all the varying and individual sensations of energy around him, the darkness from his lack of vision was replaced by an image built from the iridescent energy he was sensing. Keeping his eyes closed and his mind open, Aaron expanded his focus until the image included not just the plants in the room but he and Martin as well.

'There is something odd,' thought Aaron however.

He scanned the image in his mind trying to find what did not make sense. Then, he noticed, he was seeing the entire tenth floor, not from his vantage point in the center of the room, but from all angles, simultaneously!

And...he and Martin were both glowing.

Aaron's heart pounded. He realized at that moment that he was no longer singing the song in his head, nor focused primarily on Beth. Still, with his eyes closed, he sensed, felt, and saw everything around him. Aaron felt revitalized, energized, more than he could recall since the day he had met Beth. He focused deeper into the sensation, and the image in his mind of the tenth floor and the glow within it expanded, extending outside the room, to incorporate the entire silo complex, radiating outward in all directions, like a sphere, until its faded edges met a harsh, black, cold wall of nothing.

Aaron shuddered. The blackness on the other side of the energy Aaron inhabited did not feel evil or violent. It was worse than that. It was a pure, unfeeling absence of energy, with no desire or purpose but to devour whatever energy it encountered.

Aaron felt exposed and alone at the edge of the glow and pulled his focus back toward the silo and the tenth floor.

'That,' came Martin's voice into Aaron's thoughts, 'is the world with no belief in it.'

'And it destroyed our world?' replied Aaron, returning his consciousness back to the Garden.

"No," said Martin aloud. "It is a scavenger. It can devour what is passive and weak, but not the united and strong."

Aaron blinked uncertainly, trying to comprehend.

"Aaron," said Martin emphatically, "this Garden you are in once covered the entire surface of the Earth."

Martin paused as Aaron looked around the room, taking in the scope of what Martin had just said, trying to imagine a world with such vibrant colors and living energy.

"Duadine?" asked Aaron.

"The dark energy comes in many forms," explained Martin, nodding. "That which hovers outside us, is its most obvious. But it influences energy in many subtle ways. 'Doubt' is its keenest tool. And it uses doubt along with greed like the two opposing pincers of a pair of pliers, to wrench away the faith we have in each other and leave only disbelief. It sews greed and doubt into sentient beings, creating strife and division. The being, if it allows the dark energy to grow, soon more than disbelieves, it fears and distrusts its neighbor, isolates itself and builds its defenses with violent intent."

"Then just tell them," retorted Aaron. "Just explain what they're doing and what's happening to them."

"A person believes what they sense from their own point of view. It is our nature. We discount what others sense and believe, when it is not obvious to us. That is the nature of Duadine."

Aaron began to make another argument, but Martin continued.

"One cannot force another to see nor to believe. The effect in fact is opposite to the desired belief. If one is not ready or willing to accept what exists, they will not see. They will not believe. And they will instead become an empty vessel for dark energy to inhabit and control."

Aaron's gaze drifted away from Martin, as he considered his next encounter with Beth.

"The darkness within will then feed on the energy around it," said Martin, "until all energy is fragmented into the entropy you have seen above us."

Aaron focused on Elizabeth, closing his eyes. He extended his consciousness and his heart out to her.

"The darkness above is the entropy where eventually nothing survives, until..."
Suddenly, Aaron did not just think of Elizabeth, he felt her. "Beth!" he gasped.

Martin studied Aaron. "What do you feel?"

"She has moved. They are all in the control room now."

Aaron's eyes flashed open. "Something's wrong!"

* * *

Aaron had tried to focus on Elizabeth's energy during his run down the stairs to the seventeenth landing, but his worry and effort would not let him. He and Martin arrived and immediately entered the control room.

Elizabeth's expression was one of shock as she turned from a monitor and saw Aaron enter. Around her were Susan, Leonard and Ask. Elizabeth crossed to him, but not with dread. Her face lit up with excitement.

"Something amazing just happened!" she exclaimed, placing both hands on Aaron's chest.

Aaron exhaled with relief and wrapped his arms around Elizabeth firmly.

Elizabeth was surprised at first to receive his show of affection, then seeing Martin over Aaron's shoulder and the remnant concern on his face, she realized what Aaron might have been thinking. She hugged him back.

"We're ok," she said.

Aaron leaned back and looked at Elizabeth, and then at everyone and everything in the room. His overt concern on entering had not allowed him to notice, but there was no mistaking now, that everyone in the room had some kind of aura.

Elizabeth's was a very faint glow, like the fading light of sunset. But in her case, more lavender than yellow. Both Susan and Leonard glowed with a rim of faint violet, Leonard's a slightly lighter shade than Susan's. Not surprisingly, Martin and Ask both shined with bright auras. Martin's was the yellow of sunrise, while Ask's was the same green as in the Garden.

"It was shrinking," came Susan's quavering, emotional voice from the other side of the control room, distracting Aaron from his thoughts. "And the countdown was progressing quickly, until just a few minutes ago, when..."

Susan peered over Ask's shoulder at the computer screen, her eyes watering.

Elizabeth finished, "The countdown slowed!"

Exhausted, Susan pointed to a video monitor overhead, "And look."

The monitor displayed a topside demarcation line between healthy and burned out surface foliage.

'The glow,' thought Aaron. 'Everything beyond it is destroyed or being destroyed.'

Everyone saw the sun was beginning to set outside.

Susan continued, "A few minutes ago, that line was moving... inward...fast enough for the human eye to see, like a bubble contracting around us." She looked over at the flat top monitor and the countdown. "They were both moving."

Aaron slowly shook his head. "I can't see it moving at all."

"Exactly!" replied Susan, relieved.

Aaron was confused, but Elizabeth added, "It still is moving, just slower than we can easily see."

Elizabeth pointed to the countdown clock on the screen, scrolling slowly.

02 Days: 23 Hours: 16 Minutes: 42 Seconds

Aaron asked, "What do you think it means?"

Susan replied eagerly, "It's a protection field, but like nothing I've ever seen."

Leonard looked at Martin, "What is it?"

Aaron also focused on Martin, for they had both seen this field and knew from whence it came. He could explain it in a few words in fact. At that moment, he wanted nothing more than to explain everything that had happened to him in the last hour.

But Martin cranked his head very slightly, "No."

Elizabeth caught a glimpse of the communication between Aaron and Martin, then studied them both suspiciously.

Aaron picked up on her suspicion and asked Elizabeth, "What do you think?"

"I think," said Elizabeth with a hint of accusation, "'whatever' happened to the protection field gave us time."

'Whatever happened,' thought Aaron. 'What did happen?' He asked himself. Then, without realizing it, he answered himself with a whispered, "Belief, in each other."

Martin placed a hand on Aaron's shoulder encouragingly. But Aaron felt Martin was also bringing his focus back to the room in front of him. Had he said his thought out loud? He pursed his lips, wishing he could tell Elizabeth everything, but not knowing how he could tell her that would enable her to believe it.

Elizabeth raised her eyebrows, "If someone understood this, it would be nice..."

Then he knew how! Aaron turned to Elizabeth, wrapped her in a hug and kissed her passionately.

The room was suddenly and shockingly quiet. Leonard, Ask and Martin stared at the two in embrace, while Susan remained focused on one of the monitors.

As Aaron and Elizabeth slowly separated, Aaron smiled. Elizabeth was confused.

"Okay," she said slowly.

Then, looking into his smiling face, she saw the eyes and smile she had seen several times before over the past few years together. 'This was his distraction kiss,' Elizabeth realized.

Elizabeth's mind was transported at that moment to a college engineering lab two years earlier. The windows into the lab revealed the darkness that marked the late hour.

Inside the lab, Elizabeth paced in front of a chalk board littered with equations, while Aaron dutifully slumped in a chair nearby.

'The end of my sophomore year,' she recalled of her memory.

The Aaron of the memory fingered the desk top in front of him like he was composing on a pretend piano.

"What am I missing?" complained the student Elizabeth.

Aaron looked up from the lab desk.

Elizabeth appeared about to pull her hair out. Frustrated, she strode back to the board, ticking off the elements of her equation one by one.

"I have accounted for all the forces, aligned all angles, ensured compliance with all physical laws...why doesn't this make sense?"

Her voice had tightened up and risen to a higher pitch as she spoke, until exasperated, she spun and bumped face to face with Aaron, who had stood up beside her.

She would have been startled, had Aaron not wrapped her in a passionate hug and kissed her.

The anxiety and frustration melted from her into the warmth of his lips and passion of his kiss. She relaxed and kissed him back.

When finally he leaned his head away from hers, he whispered and caressed her hair.

"It's all in there. Just let the pieces fall where they may, until a picture presents itself."

Elizabeth studied Aaron's eyes, mesmerized and in love. She passionately kissed him this time, releasing herself and her worries. One by one, the frustrations broke off and flew away from her consciousness, until...

Suddenly, she leaned back.

"Yes!" she exclaimed.

Elizabeth turned back to the board and an empty, or nearly empty, portion of it and began writing furiously...giggling the whole time.

"Obviously!" she laughed. "How could I have missed it?"

Aaron casually returned to his chair, humming his concerto and playing his invisible piano.

Elizabeth looked into Aaron's eyes now, remembering this and other times when he had used his kiss distraction to get her out of her own head, enabling her to think clearly.

"The protection field," Elizabeth thought out loud, "has to do with belief?"

Aaron smiled.

"Belief in what?" she shrugged.

But before she could received his response, Susan interrupted.

"What was that?"

Everyone turned to the screen Susan was pointing toward.

Through the dimming surface light on the monitor, just as the final rays of sun light were fading away, the group saw, stepping into the protected area above them, a man.

CHAPTER FIFTEEN

"When people fall into danger, they are then able to strive for victory."

-- Sun Tzu

The Others

Carl's chest heaved, and he felt like crying, or screaming, or 'ripping the damn thing apart!' He was hungry and angry. He had been, since the storm had overtaken them on the way back to the bunker.

'The bunker,' he thought for a moment. Something about going back to the bunker had made him angry, he remembered, but he was not sure what or why. They had all walked from the crashed trucks back to the bunker and found the bodies. 'That was it,' he recalled. The two women had clawed each other and bled to death. 'Yes,' he recalled again, 'she was dead!'

The anger flashed back to him, because he had lost someone he had wanted. Then the memory of his feelings was gone, and only the anger remained. Now he remembered his hunger. The food they had stored in the bunker couldn't quench it. They needed something else, so each of them had set out to hunt.

Disheveled, with mucus running from his nose, spit from his mouth, and his body covered in dirt, he struggled to catch his breath. He had been chasing the rabbit for nearly two miles, and that had started near the end of the trail he had already been on for most of the day. All told he figured he must be seven, eight miles from the bunker on foot.

"And nothin' ta show for it!" he yelled aloud.

His scream, however, had startled something, pulling Carl's attention back to the shriveled and burned bushes and trees around him.

He was a thin, muscular man, with thinning black hair and several days of spotty growth on his chin.

He swiped his forearm across his face, smearing the mucus and saliva over his cheek, out of his airway. His breathing eased a bit as he scanned around him. Pacing slowly through the burned out trees and underbrush, looking for a camouflaged brown coat among the grey and ashen surroundings, he suddenly saw the impossible...color.

As if he was looking from an ancient black and white movie into a modern one, he saw in front of him a border between dead and living forest.

Cautiously, he stepped to the edge of the scorched land like a shadow wary of crawling from the protection of a dark alley into the exposed light.

Letting his anger drive him forward, he slid a foot across the divide.

To his shock, his dirty boot appeared more alive. He felt mesmerized at first, by the light and the color. Then he felt anger. Why had this been kept from him, from them?

'Silas will want to see this,' he thought. Carl did not know what caused the light, but he knew Silas would want it.

But Carl knew better than to go back to Silas unable to answer his questions. And about this, there would be questions. He needed to learn more.

Carl shifted his weight and stepped all the way into the light and color. He inspected himself to make sure he was okay, that the light had not done anything to him. He felt the same. He looked the same.

More confident now, he sniffed the air. 'The air is clean,' he thought. 'It doesn't choke.' Then, with eyes closed, he inhaled a succulent lung full.

Suddenly, his eyes snapped open, and he dropped to the ground in a defensive posture.

He had gained power since the storm and the truck crash. Silas, Matt and he all had. He thought even the woman had, but he didn't care. What he knew was that he felt stronger and he could sense things better now. He had been a hunter since he could first lift and aim a gun. But he could track an animal now just by smelling its blood. He sniffed the air again.

'And this blood is human,' he smiled.

Stealthily, he made his way to the edge of the clean green trees, where they abruptly ended and an edge of grass grew. Beyond that appeared the end of a street, or so it looked.

Carl recognized the dashed white line along the road's center, then followed it with his searching eyes. He recognized then, that he was looking at the end of a private airplane runway. And at its far end, stood a very intact cabin.

'Cabins have people,' he thought hungrily, 'and cabins have food.'

He grinned and sneered, then pulling his shotgun from behind, he stepped quickly back into the grey world from which he had come, disappearing back into the sooty darkness.

* * *

Susan paced the open floor of the great room nervously.

Aaron watched her aura turn darker the more she brooded. He played the piano nearby, as the rest of the family ate a simple meal at the dining table.

"...But there are clearly survivors!" Susan argued. "Don't you think we should bring him down here? That's what the other silos are for, right?"

"Bring a crazy man down here?" retorted Elizabeth. "With a *gun!*"

Susan walked toward Elizabeth, her palms out and forward in a pleading gesture. "He could just be defending himself, or his family."

Elizabeth stood her ground. "Or bringing more crazy people down here, and out number us."

Frustrated, Susan halted in front of the table and just as curtly stopped her breath in a 'humph!'

Martin spoke calmly from the dining table, "He left, but now that he has seen the cabin, he is likely to come back."

Elizabeth turned back to Susan to use this as an additional argument, but Susan's body language remained defiant.

Martin continued, this time addressing Susan. "If we view the situation like a scientist," then to the room, "perhaps we should observe before committing to judgement."

Susan huffed again. The sight of another living human reminder her, whether she realized it or not, how alone she was. She had Elizabeth and Leonard, but she also had Martin. Now there was no one else and nowhere else in the world to separate them. Nothing made sense.

"I don't understand," she complained, "how something so catastrophic could have happened in the first place. There must be some evidence on the surface. *They* are on the surface!"

"If he returns," offered Martin, "and if he brings others, we can watch them from here," gesturing toward the television monitor on the wall, "safely."

Susan could hardly argue with the logic, but she did not like losing. "So," she said, as if they had struck some sort of bargain, "we'll decide then."

Elizabeth sighed and finished the last bite on her small plate.

Elizabeth at last voiced the anxiety that had been building in her since they had first seen the man and later came to the great room to discuss his sighting.

She looked at Martin. "There's no way anyone can get into...?"

Martin shook his head. "Four and a half feet of lead and steel. Controlled from the inside. It's built to last, and to keep bad things out."

Elizabeth collected a few dishes and moved to the kitchen sink to clean them.

Martin spoke to the room.

"You need to understand...outside, and unprotected, people are going to be ...different. We all have to be prepared for that."

Susan, still convinced they should invite the outsider down into their protected silo, asked, "Different in what way? Is it because of that protection field?"

Leonard, who had thus far been contemplative about his fears of the changes to the outside world, his doubts about their own survival in the silo, and his hopes that this man could mean a better chance of survival for all, voiced, "Because, if this protection field surrounding us is shrinking and expanding, we need to know what its power source is and control it."

Susan nodded to Elizabeth. "Yes. Maybe this silo is not as safe as we hope it is. You mapped the energy throughout the silos and found something wrong with its power source."

Elizabeth and Aaron met eyes, as he continued to play his calming music. She noted that Aaron looked as if he wanted to say something but rather than do so, he turned his gaze back to his piano keys.

Elizabeth said to Susan, "I mapped what I could find, and there appears to be a gap..."

"Exactly!" trumpeted Susan, stepping excitedly around the great room.

Elizabeth broke in, "Perhaps there is a form of energy here that we are not used to seeing, but powerful nonetheless."

Susan threw up her hands. "How can there be a power source we can't see or measure?"

Elizabeth drew in a breath to think.

Aaron simultaneously scooted to one side of the piano bench, still continuing to play.

Absently, Elizabeth wandered in his direction whispering to herself, "At some level everything is energy. Mass is energy. Movement is energy."

Susan interrupted, "Yes, there are a dozen forms of energy, but all measurable."

The music suddenly changed to dark Stravinsky-like phrases of arpeggios. Aaron's fingers and arms tossed around the keys like a mad scientist. Aaron looked up at Martin.

Martin then turned to the others, "How many notes are there?"

Susan pointed to the piano keys. "A finite number," she said commandingly.

Aaron stated, matter-of-factly, "Eighty-eight keys on a piano, but not a finite number of notes."

He struck a note and pushed one of the piano pedals, bending the note until he was soon playing the next note in the register.

"Between any two notes," he explained, "are an infinite number of notes, with differences nearly impossible to measure."

Susan shook her head. "But some notes sound better than others. They are meant to be...notes."

"Even among standard notes," Aaron continued, "some notes are more powerful."

"Harmonics," said Elizabeth.

Aaron played an arpeggio of harmonics. Martin smiled brightly.

"Harmonics," Aaron explained, returning to the calming music he had been playing before, "are like intersections of sound, that all criss-cross together, to sound like they belong from many different angles. They have a certain pleasantness in music for this reason."

Susan, meanwhile, walked to her seat at the dining table, removed her dishes, and placed them loudly in the sink.

Elizabeth scooted next to Aaron on the bench. "If all forms of energy and matter were like notes, able to reach through an infinite number of possibilities, to focus on specific intersections of energy..."

Elizabeth gaped at Aaron, beginning to understand what he was getting at and what he had tried to say in the control room.

"Those energy harmonics," she continued, "would be very powerful..."

"And," said Aaron, "unseen."

Susan lifted her eyes from the sink, about to argue the point, when Martin stood.

"We've done as much as we can tonight," he said. "I think rest will do us all good."

Martin winked at Susan, then looked toward Ask. The two both assumed the same stoic expression, then walked calmly toward the stairs. As Ask exited, Martin turned and paused, sharing a brief glance with Aaron, then he too disappeared through the stairway door.

Susan took a deep breath, and Elizabeth turned contemplatively toward Susan.

"I don't know if it is my menopause or him," said Susan cheekily, "but that man is so infuriating."

Leonard stifled a chuckle at Susan's dry humor, and smiled.

Aaron, desiring to fill the void of direct conflict with something more soothing, increased the force on the piano keys and the volume of the lyrical music from the piano. The effect was near instantaneous and relaxing.

The music caught Susan's attention, and she turned toward Aaron.

"That's beautiful Aaron," she said, taking a deep breath. "Thank you."

Leonard stood and reached a hand out to Susan. She walked from the kitchen, took his hand, and leaned her head in toward him. Together they walked toward the stairs.

As soon as they were gone, Aaron metamorphosed his song into another. This song was more upbeat, bouncy and fun sounding. Though it did maintain a similar undercurrent of romanticism. The intricate nature of the song , interestingly enough, required three hands to play. The third hand playing a single repeating note.

Elizabeth broke into a smile and leaned her back against Aaron's.

The repeating note stopped.

"Our song," said Elizabeth.

"Your song," corrected Aaron. "I wrote it for you."

She turned and wrapped her arms around him.

"*Our* song," she dubbed it, with finality.

She looked down at the keys. "But how were you able to play my part?"

He smiled and started the song again. He nodded toward the keys, and gave Elizabeth space to turn toward them. The virtuoso that she was, sat up straight and prepared herself to play.

Aaron paused at her entrance.

Elizabeth dramatically unfolded her hands, her fingers dangling over the ivories.

Then, she used one finger to play quarter notes on a single key as Aaron resumed his intricate and beautiful portions of the song.

The two laughed at Elizabeth's "virtuosity."

"You play beautifully," he said.

"You're not so bad yourself," she returned.

When it was done, Elizabeth kissed Aaron. "You wanna go to bed?"

"In the worst way," he said truthfully. "But I want to show you something first."

CHAPTER SIXTEEN

"I am not what happened to me, I am what I choose to become."

-- C. G. Jung

The Garden

Moments later, Aaron led Elizabeth into the Garden with her eyes closed, leaving the door open behind them.

"What do you see?" he asked.

"Nothing," she replied sarcastically.

"No, I mean..."

Aaron flustered, searching for the words to communicate his meaning.

"Do you remember the day we met?" he asked.

Elizabeth's playful expression faded slightly, though she still smiled. Aaron noticed her aura faded an instant then brightened and lightened.

"Remember for a moment," he said, "the feelings you had that day."

* * *

A dance studio, four years earlier.

The room was filled near to bursting with energy as Elizabeth danced silently but passionately around the floor. If her emotion had been color and the studio her canvas, every inch would have been covered in a shocking, avant-garde style all her own.

She was completely absorbed in her art.

The door to the studio had, as it turned out, a small window in it, just about head high. Occasionally, people happened by as they walked through the hall outside.

For a brief second, Aaron's was one of those faces passing by. But unlike any of the others, his returned a moment later, to stare through the window and be mesmerized.

It was not long before the door slid quietly open and he slipped in unnoticed.

Elizabeth was so engrossed in her dance, she had neither seen nor heard him. Truthfully, she was so distraught, she would not have noticed had the room flooded.

Aaron spotted the piano, however, and sat comfortably at it, studying her movements, powerful, athletic, and pain-filled, communicated with pure grace.

Her movement was so pure it was like music unto itself. Aaron was willing to watch quietly, but his fingers had a music of their own, and they desired more than anything at this moment to combine her music with his.

So, quietly at first, he allowed his fingers to play the music that she was dancing.

He never took his eyes from her, and throughout the room, her dance and his song appeared one and the same, the crescendos and quiet elegance of the music matching that of the dance.

At first, her movements were powerful and pain-filled, like someone on a ledge. But Aaron's music caught her, enticing her movements into something tender, until he brought her safely to the ground to stand on her own two feet.

Rather than completing the dance exhausted, she finished renewed. She breathed deeply, slowly regaining her awareness of the room around her, coming out of the trance of her dance, until she looked up at last at Aaron.

Neither knew what to say...she surprised by his presence, and he almost embarrassed to have intruded on her clearly private dance.

"That was beautiful," Elizabeth said at last.

Aaron relaxed slightly.

Then, to his surprise, she slowly walked toward him.

"You were beautiful," Aaron confessed back to her.

She sat on the edge of the piano bench and smiled warmly.

"We...," she began to say, but then stopped in another moment of awkward silence.

Aaron took a breath and broke the tension. "Would you like to go on a *second* date."

"Second?" asked Elizabeth.

Aaron nodded. "Well, first dates are for getting to know one another, and..." he inclined his head toward the dance floor, "I think we did pretty well just then."

"Yes," agreed Elizabeth, her warm smile broadening, "we did."

As they left the room and entered the hall, they had not looked away from each other even for a moment.

As the door closed behind them, "My name is Aaron, by the way."

* * *

Back in the tenth floor Garden, Aaron asked, "Do you remember how it felt?"

Elizabeth, her eyes still closed, smiled wryly.

"I remember having just dropped out of the dance academy, because Martin had convinced me to focus on engineering full time. And while getting the feelings out of my system, this creepy guy sneaks into the studio..."

Aaron chuckled and rested his hands on her shoulders. "No really."

She placed her hands on his.

"I remember exactly how I felt that day...more free than I had ever felt before. More connected...and I knew. I knew that even though I didn't know you, I was going to love you...and that we were going to be great together."

Now Aaron was smiling, and he could see Elizabeth's aura had changed, from the color of sunset to sunrise.

"I want you to remember that feeling," he coached. "As much as you can, no matter what you think you see, imagine that feeling is the lens through which you see the world."

Aaron began humming the tune he had played while she danced.

"Now," he continued, "look through eyes that believe what is possible."

She opened her eyes and saw Aaron smiling at her.

Slowly, however, she began looking around her. She recognized she was in the tenth floor space she had been in earlier.

But something was very different. The room had been dead and dingy. Now it was alive with color. No flowers bloomed, but the shades of greens, browns, and yellows were vibrant.

Aaron watched her expression morph into puzzlement, then wonder.

He took their hands from her shoulders and wrapped them around her waist, so together they could turn in a full circle as they looked around the room.

Elizabeth could not escape the feeling that she was trying to recognize something she should already know. All the while, Aaron hummed the song.

Aaron's song entered a refrain that, in both music and dance on the day they had met, was filled with tenderness.

Elizabeth squeezed his hands, for he had played the tune countless times in the years since. Now Aaron added new words to his song.

"Taenoril sil, da Luna Fael, Aelialtha mur..."

Elizabeth spun around and faced him. She knew these words. How had she heard them?

"...tul malia Hael," Elizabeth finished, shocked with her own recollection. "How do you know those words?" she implored Aaron.

"Had Martin taught them to you before?" he asked her.

She repeated, "Taenoril sil, da Luna Fael, Aelialtha mur, tul malia Hael."

Elizabeth did not answer Aaron, because she was already lost in thought.

* * *

She was fifteen when the worst of it happened...the worst day of her life...the day her family ended.

She had just come home from school, put her book bag in the entry hall, and walked toward the kitchen for a snack. Instantly she noticed something was wrong, as the entire entryway was filled with plants of every kind. And not all of them were in pots.

Stunned, she looked around the entryway, the stairs and her father's study for some explanation. In the study, she found it.

Her father, Martin, lying on a grass-covered desk, surrounded by a multitude of plants, smiled up at her.

Elizabeth knew her dad and mom were having problems, and she knew it was primarily because her father had been thinking and behaving differently over the past few years. He had been getting worse and had even stopped working full-time as a doctor the year before to take a sabbatical.

But after the enormous fight and all the yelling her mother had done the past weekend, she thought he was going back to work.

Work or no, though, she was worried about her father.

"I thought you were going back to work today," she said. "You promised mom."

Her father inhaled exuberantly, as if the air was filled with freshly baked apple pie or something. "Today," he announced proudly, "it was revealed to me."

"What was?"

Martin opened his eyes and turned toward Elizabeth. "All the hearts of my life."

Elizabeth did not understand, and it showed on her face.

"As we grow," he explained, "we change, and our hearts change with us. Our childhood believing heart becomes the doubting teenage heart, and finally the cynical, disbelieving adult heart."

Elizabeth was confused and still did not understand.

Martin sat up and held both of Elizabeth's hands. "My heart is fully open now, and at last I see."

He looked Elizabeth directly in the eyes. "Taenoril sil, da Luna Fael, Aelialtha mur, tul malia Hael."

Elizabeth stared at her father, confused.

"It needs me, Lizzy. I must help."

"Help? Who?"

* * *

"What does the phrase mean?" Elizabeth asked, her thoughts now back in the Garden. Whatever it meant, she felt Martin had decided it was enough for him to end their family and abandon her.

"I don't know exactly," answered Aaron honestly, "but I know that it focuses connection with Taenoril sil."

Together they repeated the words, "Taenoril sil, da Luna Fael, Aelialtha mur, tul malia Hael."

Aaron whispered, "Consider what you believe. Center your energy on what you believe is possible. Focus your belief on those you most believe in."

He resumed humming the tune as he gently coaxed Elizabeth to turn back toward the room.

Elizabeth stared into space but allowed Aaron to turn her.

As if an animator was sweeping a canvas in front of her with a paint brush, the already colorful room added multiple layers of color she had never seen before.

She held one of Aaron's hands but rapidly looked all around the room as it came alive, each shade of color bursting beyond the border of every leaf or branch.

Her hand, wrapped in Aaron's, passed over some nearby tall grasses, which leaned toward them.

Elizabeth's mouth dropped. "What?...How?"

She looked back at him. "What did you do?"

Aaron only smiled, "Just opened your eyes again."

"Do you see this?" she laughed.

Aaron nodded. "Yes, I see it."

She shook her head slightly, "Why?"

Aaron held a palm against her cheek. "Because you believe."

"What am I believing in?"

Aaron replied, "Me."

She turned around facing him, and placed a hand on his chest. "Us."

Aaron covered her hands with his. "Everyone and everything."

And in her way that Aaron loved, she leaned toward him, looking at his lips, then closed her eyes and kissed him.

The kiss was sweet. They always were.

But Aaron wanted to show her more. He gently drew away from her kiss, holding her hands, knelt, and invited her to kneel together with him, then lie down on the soft green floor.

Their heads rested at the base of the small Tree at the center of the room. Its branches bare, but its trunk beautiful mahogany.

As they cuddled with Elizabeth's head on Aaron's chest, under the base of the Tree, the gently advancing roots emanated a pale green light.

* * *

The next morning, Elizabeth's eyes opened, but she wasn't sure they had. What she was seeing now looked much as it had throughout her strange sequence of dreams during the night.

She thought for a moment about those dreams. They had seemed so real. The first, she recalled, had started with her lying with her head on Aaron's chest.

Aaron had begun whispering. 'Consider what you believe. Center your energy on what you believe is possible. Focus your belief on those you most believe in.'

Then that familiar phrase again, 'Taenoril sil, da Luna Fael, Aelialtha mur, tul malia Hael.' Elizabeth finished.

In a flash, the two of them had become one. Not their bodies, but like spirits, they hovered above themselves, intertwined with each other as some kind of ethereal self, sharing the same vision and the same thoughts.

She recalled seeing every part of the tenth floor at once, again from a vantage point outside her body. In fact, she saw her body and Aaron's, both glowing, lying in the center of what she could only now call a garden. It was so beautiful, she could not think of it as anything else.

Aaron had spoken to her then. 'I want to show you something.'

The way their perspective had changed proved to Elizabeth that she was recalling a dream, because they had moved through the silo walls, expanded their sensations, and broken out to the surface, until they were exploring the edge of a barrier that surrounded the silo complex.

There she felt, more than saw, the contrast between the living area of color and light above the silo and a vast void of destruction outside it. The area beyond the protective field had filled her with a sense of dread.

She recalled trying to extend her consciousness beyond the protected silo barrier into the unknown, but Aaron had warned her not to.

'No,' he had communicated to her.

'Why not? What is out there?'

'Nothing,' he had responded. 'A universe of nothing, and I think it wants us.'

Elizabeth did not understand his statement now anymore than when she had dreamt it, but she had, in her dream, agreed to return to the Garden.

When they had returned, Elizabeth noted the air and everything within the tenth floor space sparkled with iridescence. The trees, bushes, and grasses, as simple as they were, gleamed with their basic earthy colors as beautifully as any flower garden she had ever seen.

Now she used her own open eyes to see the same colors and plants, and was amazed to find they shimmered just as brightly as they had in her dream.

"It's not a dream," she heard next to her.

Elizabeth turned her head and looked at Aaron's shimmering face. He looked identical to how he had looked in her dream before they became spirits.

"Good morning," he said.

"Morning," she replied warmly. "I had quite a dream last night."

"That's what I was saying," Aaron said again. "It wasn't a dream." And then, without moving his lips but with as much clarity in Elizabeth's mind as if he had, she heard his voice say, 'It's not one now.'

Elizabeth's heart raced, and reflexively her fingers touched his lips. He smiled.

'It's okay,' he said telepathically.

'How do you do that?' Elizabeth wondered.

'You mean, do what you just did?' he thought playfully.

Elizabeth marveled. 'Did I? Am I?'

Aaron nodded.

Elizabeth held her hands to her head. 'But I don't know how.'

'Neither do I,' thought Aaron. 'Though I imagine it's a skill anyone can have, and perhaps humans have always had, when they believe.'

'Believing is seeing, or at least in this case, speaking,' Elizabeth smirked.

Aaron drew a wide grin. 'Believing is a lot of things.'

Something occurred to Elizabeth. 'The dream...the experience we had that I thought was a dream...we traveled, out of our bodies and outside the silo. What was that?'

'Another trait,' thought Aaron, 'though I don't know what one calls it...part of Taenoril sil I suppose.'

'That word again!' she thought excitedly.

'Yeah, it refers to the flow of belief energy,' answered Aaron. Then, off Elizabeth's puzzled expression, he added, 'but I think using it is a common trait too. I think the Garden and the words focus the energy and enhance these abilities. Martin showed me.'

"Martin!" Elizabeth said aloud.

Aaron did not answer. He did not need to. Aaron could see Elizabeth deep in thought, running through hundreds of memories, events she did not understand.

Finally, she looked at Aaron as they lay on the mossy ground in each other's arms. 'This is what Martin saw all along?'

Aaron shrugged, 'Or better.'

Elizabeth started to nod, then slowly shook her head slightly, 'Or worse.'

Elizabeth focused her eyes directly on Aaron's. He saw her concern. 'He saw this,' she said. And looking around her, he knew she was seeing the metallic walls of the silo and not the Garden it protected.

'I'm here,' Aaron thought to her. 'It's okay.'

Elizabeth returned her eyes to his and smiled reassuringly, leaning closer as she started to kiss him. But, she found she could not. She examined herself and realized she and Aaron were each covered in what appeared to be small vines.

"Uh...should I be worried about this?" she asked aloud.

Aaron shook his head, smiling.

'When the countdown jumped,' Elizabeth thought to Aaron, 'were you in here?'

Aaron nodded, 'Yup.'

'So...when you believed...the countdown...'

Aaron nodded again, 'Yup.'

A chuckle made its way up and out of Elizabeth's chest, but she caught it at her lips. She was giddy with the realization that something as beautiful as this could exist, and fascinated to find out how.

A soft colorful glow emanated from the points where tiny tendrils connected to her. The tendrils spread out from roots that extended from the small Tree and wrapped around them both. She lifted her free hand and found it separately shimmered with color, more colors than she had ever seen.

Suddenly her face lit up with understanding.

"Ultraviolet, infrared!" She exclaimed aloud to Aaron.

Aaron was puzzled.

Elizabeth excitedly continued, "When we first arrived, Martin and Ask must have been the only ones who could see..." She gestured with her free hand around the Garden. "Then you...and now me." She stared at Aaron inquisitively. "You think...?"

Aaron stammered, trying to keep up, "I think what happened... outside, happened to a world that didn't believe in each other. The bonds that held everything together were broken, and it literally fell apart."

"Now the force of that disbelief is coming down on the one place that still does," added Elizabeth, her face slipping into a neutral expression.

Aaron noted, "You have the 'I'm thinking' look again."

Elizabeth returned her attention to Aaron excitedly. "The energy differential I couldn't explain earlier...this could be it."

She shook her head as if to clear it and looked back at her hand.

"I still don't know what form of energy this is, but if it has been here all along, and we simply aren't able to measure it..."

She drifted into thought again.

"Then?" coaxed Aaron.

"Then, we find out what makes this energy grow," answered Elizabeth.

"What do you give our chances?"

She shrugged thoughtfully, "Outside forces, inside forces..."

The sound of footsteps came up the steps outside the room, and Leonard entered through the open door.

"I've been looking all over for you," he said, then froze, disgusted.

Leonard could not believe what he was seeing. Elizabeth and Aaron were both lying on a bed of decaying foliage, wrapped in rotted vines. He couldn't imagine what possessed them, and felt nauseated by the sight.

With an acidic taste in his mouth, he managed to announce, "There's something you should see, but you'd better clean all that crap off you first." He turned to leave, "Meet you in the control room."

When he had gone, Elizabeth and Aaron looked at the foliage then each other and knew that something had truly changed.

CHAPTER SEVENTEEN

"The world is very old, and soon it will be new again. I am at once rejoiced and in fear. Our future depends on the part of ourself which we present to the Darkness."

-- Mkulima wa Jua, Keeper of the African Garden

The Attack

Just how much had changed would soon become very apparent to Elizabeth and Aaron as they exited the tenth floor and descended toward the control room.

"Susan and Leonard need to see this," stated Elizabeth nodding back toward the Garden.

"Yes," agreed Aaron, adding caution. "But their belief can't be forced. Susan can't see if she doesn't believe."

"With how she feels about Martin," lamented Elizabeth, "she may never see."

* * *

Aaron and Elizabeth entered the control room to find Susan and Leonard huddled around the computer terminal where Ask had been sitting the previous day. Animatedly mumbling their thoughts and pointing at the screen, the two looked up and waived them over.

Aaron had been excited to talk to Martin about his experience with Beth, and her ability to now see the Garden, but he was not there.

"Where are Martin and Ask?" he inquired.

"Had something to do in another silo," said Leonard.

Elizabeth also wanted to talk to Martin, but what she really wanted at this moment was...data. She wasted no time and crossed directly to the computer flat screen. What she saw amazed her.

"Aaron!"

Elizabeth pointed to the corner of the computer screen, where the countdown had increased to 4 days 17 hours and 23 minutes.

"Yes," said Leonard, "we found that when we arrived earlier."

"Something's happened to give us more time," remarked Susan excitedly, not taking her eyes from her computer screen.

Elizabeth and Aaron shared a knowing look. Then, closing her eyes, Elizabeth attempted her first experiment. Aaron was puzzled, but he understood in the space of a word.

'Time,' Elizabeth communicated to him. She opened her eyes to see Aaron's brightly grinning smile.

'Time,' he repeated back to her.

Elizabeth hugged Aaron. 'We can think to each other outside the Garden!'

'Amazing!' Aaron agreed.

"Amazing," whispered Elizabeth aloud.

"But, look at this," said Susan.

Elizabeth and Aaron both turned to see Susan and Leonard were still focused on the monitor. Elizabeth stepped behind and peered over Susan's shoulder. Aaron followed.

Yet reflexively, Elizabeth's attention was drawn back to the flat top monitor and the time it showed. She knew that, assuming no other changes had occurred over the night time, the only event that had happened was Aaron's and her expedition into the Garden and their ability to see it as it truly existed. How could that...how could they... have given them more time? Was it their belief? And if so, how did their belief help to stabilize the silo against the forces from the outside?

Susan typed at the keyboard and restarted a video file.

Elizabeth's focus remained on the countdown. Her expression turned more serious, however, as she realized, 'The seconds are still ticking downward.'

Before Susan could cue and start her video, Elizabeth moved back to the table top monitor and began pinching and spreading portions of the flat screen with her fingers on the touch screen, scrolling through computer layouts and force diagrams of the silo complex.

She found the force diagram again and studied it. Like before, the diagram showed different colors inside and outside the silo, but now there was more color and brightness inside, while the dark purple outside had more volume and was much darker.

Flipping the screen back to the timer clock, 'The silo has more colorimetric stabilization,' she thought to Aaron.

He turned his head toward her as the video played.

Susan commented, nodding toward her computer monitor, "I think you're gonna want to see this. I was searching here for some other signs of human habitation..."

The monitor filled with the face of a squirrel, apparently trying to decide if the video camera was a nut and would be worth eating. Suddenly the squirrel disappeared, followed soon after by a mountain lion, as it sleeked past the camera.

It was apparent the camera was placed at the far end of the landing strip and was focused on the foliage.

Susan continued, "It's bizarre. You can see the divide between scorched land and apparently healthy forest, like before..."

She typed again on her keyboard and pointed to an overhead monitor screen. While the mountain lion slowly made its way in her video, the upper monitor was showing the same scene in real time, focused on the plant life outside. Aaron could see a clear demarcation between healthy plants and either burned or wilted plants.

"And whatever is protecting the ground over us...," added Leonard.

'Not just over us,' Aaron thought to Elizabeth.

Susan finished Leonard's statement, "...other life forms are protected as well."

Susan nodded enthusiastically toward the computer monitor. This was clearly what she and Leonard had been so excited about when they entered. The video file now showed a dirty, mangy rabbit stepping through the underbrush into the open.

"Animals which remain within the area above the silos behave normally," she pointed out. A normal appearing coyote wandered into the frame and spotted the rabbit.
Elizabeth turned to watch the animals on the computer screen.

"Those outside the silo protection," continued Susan, nodding toward the screen. "It's not just protection from singeing heat."

On the monitor, they watched as the sickly rabbit turned toward the coyote, and rather than retreating back into the underbrush, stalked after the predator. Then, in a flash, the rabbit leapt savagely at the coyote. And the two animals tumbled out of view of the camera.

Susan and Leonard turned to Elizabeth and Aaron, who were shocked by what they had just seen. The implication was unfathomable. Elizabeth was speechless.

Susan gaged Elizabeth's reaction, and asked, "You can see the problem?"

"An herbivore stalked and attacked a predator," said Elizabeth, astounded.

"Exactly," nodded Susan. "Hardly natural behavior."

Aaron shared a look with Elizabeth, then asked Susan and Leonard, "What do you think could have caused it?"

Leonard answered, "There must be some kind of toxin or pathogen."

"Could the rabbit simply have some kind of head injury?" added Aaron.

"It's possible," said Leonard.

"Is that what you believe?" asked Elizabeth.

Leonard shook his head. "No." He rewound the video file to the point where the rabbit was creeping toward the coyote. He increased magnification. "Look at the rabbit's eyes. The sclera are grey instead of white. Infection is possible, but I believe whatever affected this animal changed it fundamentally." He and Susan met eyes. "It's possible that whatever caused this is present in the environment up there."

Susan added, "Whatever it is has done more than destabilize the Earth's mantle."

Elizabeth was suddenly filled with the same sense of dread she felt when she and Aaron had been near the edge of the protective field. She closed her eyes and expanded her thoughts and senses. As she had done the night before, she felt the energy of the protective field and the darkness beyond it.

"What about that man?" asked Aaron.

Susan shrugged. "Don't know. If it's communicable, it may stay in animal populations. Though zoonotic transmission to humans is possible. We'll have to..."

Suddenly, Elizabeth no longer heard Susan as she sensed it. A wave of dark energy, the nothingness, was breaching the far end of the protective field.

Elizabeth returned her consciousness back to the control room. "Look out!" she warned.

The room jolted suddenly.

Susan's words were interrupted mid breath as the room shook violently back and forth, nearly toppling her over in her chair. Each of the others braced themselves over the control console.

Elizabeth hovered over the flat screen monitor as the room shook, but was more terrified by what she saw on the screen.

"The time!" she screamed. And everyone craned to see, the countdown clock was plummeting! Minutes scrolled downward like seconds and hours like minutes.

"What happened?" yelled Susan, as she typed on the keyboard and searched her screen.

Aaron scanned the overhead monitors, as Leonard inspected the control panel lights and dials to find anything out of range. But no alarms had fired and no sensors were awry to account for the destabilization.

Elizabeth stood up over the flat screen. She had shifted the display back to the force diagram. The purple of the forces outside the silo were intensifying. While the colors inside the silo were not changing at all.

The silo let out a fatigued, slow moan...the ominous sound of metal under extreme pressure.

"No, no, no!" panted Susan, as she typed furiously, searching from one monitor screen to another. Then, she stopped, pointed to an overhead monitor and yelled, "Look!"

Silas and Matt crouched, their hunting rifles pointed toward the cabin, as they stepped cautiously along the wooded side of the landing field clearing. Silas looked over his shoulder briefly to see Wanda, carrying the baby, and then Carl trailing close behind her, the last to cross the threshold between scorched and untouched land.

Carl, who had been watching the rear, turned toward Silas and nodded, a pistol in one hand and a bloody knife in the other.

Silas turned toward the cabin, shifting his knife and lifting his shotgun, before creeping forward. He grinned to reveal grey eyes and rows of bloody teeth.

After the last of the intruders crept passed the far runway camera toward the cabin, Elizabeth peered back at the countdown. The precipitous drop now read: 02 days 21 Hours 43 minutes, and was falling faster.

Elizabeth gripped Aaron by the arms and whispered desperately, "We have to tell them. There's no time!"

Aaron shook his head with just a slight movement and thought to Elizabeth. 'If they're not ready, it'll only make things worse.'

With the clank of boots on the metal spiral walkway outside the control room door, Martin and Ask entered and quickly moved to the flat screen.

Elizabeth looked from Martin and Ask to Aaron, down to the countdown, then back to Martin.

"A safe bet none of them believe," she pronounced, nodding up at the monitor.

Martin looked up at the monitor, then stood to study Elizabeth's face and eyes. What he saw there made him smile.

'Surprised?' she thought to him.

He gently shook his head and squeezed her hand. 'No.'

"Don't you think we should help them?" asked Susan.

"I'm not sure that's wise. You saw what happened to that animal," responded Aaron.

"They are not animals," retorted Susan, her voice raising in pitch.

"We can try," interrupted Martin, placing a gentle hand on Aaron's shoulder and giving a consoling grin to Susan. "But," he added, turning to Aaron, "we must be sure they are...healthy."

Susan shook her head. "They just survived the end of the world! Of course they're not healthy!"

"By healthy," asked Leonard, "do you mean the eyes?"

"I mean, it may already be too late," said Martin sadly.

Aaron whispered to Elizabeth, "Grey eyes...they don't believe." And then both looked at Martin.

'The darkness,' communicated Aaron to Martin, 'when it fully takes a person...their eyes turn grey?'

Martin nodded.

Susan stared at Aaron, then shifted her stare from him to Elizabeth, then over to Martin. 'What are they doing?' she thought.

She glared at Martin, her agitation building rapidly. "What have you told them, Martin?"

Leonard stepped toward her, reaching out to place a hand on her shoulder.

She shrugged it off and turned on Aaron, then Elizabeth. "You're saying the animals above us have white eyes and behave normally because they believe?"

She threw her hands out, "Believe in what, faeries?"

"Mother!" exclaimed Elizabeth disapprovingly.

Susan folded her arms, set her jaw defiantly, and turned back to the computer screen.

On the monitors overhead, the outside group had reached the cabin.

Ask slid a chair over and sat beside Susan. "May I?" he asked politely.

Susan grudgingly scooted her chair to the side, allowing Ask more room to access the keyboard. Ask typed and switched the TV monitors overhead to video feeds from several cameras in and around the cabin. One monitor showed slight movement of something stalking through the tree line outside the cabin.

Within the cabin, the intruders were searching intently through everything. The cupboards and drawers were all open, cabinet doors askew, and various items tossed about from their original position.

"No food," said one man to the tallest in the center of the cabin. The tall man held a rifle and moved things by kicking at them. He moved furniture and rugs, but found nothing hidden. Soon, he stopped searching items sitting on the floor, and scanned the ceiling instead.

Elizabeth felt chilled as the man on the screen, with piercing, cold, grey eyes, seemed to look through the camera directly at her.

He suddenly lifted his shotgun, aimed it at the camera, and fired!

The TV monitor was reduced to static.

* * *

Silas lowered his shotgun as Carl kicked at the wooden back door of the cabin, broke off the door knob, and caused the door to swing inward.

Silas and the others turned at the noise. And all gaped at the gleaming metal doors. Carl pounded on it with his fist, emitting a deep but dull thud.

'Sealed,' thought Silas.

Silas searched the ceilings again, and finding another camera, walked underneath it.

"Hey neighbor," he said, grinning to reveal a mouth of angled yellow teeth. "We're just lookin' for a little bread and honey. How's 'bout you open up here, and let us in?"

The group looked toward the metal door expectantly. When nothing happened after several moments, Silas turned back to the camera.

He nodded toward Wanda carrying the bundled baby.

"See," continued Silas nodding at Wanda, "we gotten us a baby here, and the teets dried up. Babies need food and warm places."

Wanda had never liked how Silas treated her. She had always been too afraid of him to say anything though. She knew he was mean and wasn't afraid to show it. Still, since the storm had come up, she had been feeling more and more angry and cared about Silas' meanness less and less. Now he had called her a 'cow', and she had had enough.

Wanda, who had been leaning against the wall near the front door of the cabin, placed the baby bundle on the sill to the outside window and stomped toward Silas.

277
* * *

Inside the control room, all watched the monitor as the woman screamed at the tall man. She stepped up behind him and hit his back with her fist.

With hardly a second thought or a flinch, he spun a backhand into her face, sending her sprawling toward the other side of the cabin.

Elizabeth gasped.

The baby began to cry. Though, still rolled up in its bundle, it did not move or teeter from the sill.

At that moment, another of the monitors caught Martin's eye. In the tree line, he spotted two mountain lions as they walked cautiously into the sun light.

"Stay here," Martin told the group, before disappearing out the stairwell door.

Every pair of eyes in the room shot from the stairwell door back to the monitors in search of what had caused Martin to leave so hastily. On the cabin's side camera, now clearly visible, were the two lions.

Ask adjusted other monitors for angles enabling them to see views of the lions and the window sill.

"We have to do something!" panted Susan.

"Elu is doing all that can be done," said Ask.

On the cabin monitor, the tall man returned to the screen. His grey eyes were bloodshot and venomous.

"She din't mean nothin' by that," he offered in mock conciliation. "She's good in her own way."

He spread his lips wide in another gritty grin, this time leveling his shotgun toward the elevator door.

Leonard whispered, "Grey eyes."

The tall man continued, his voice laced with malice. "Now you just open up, and we'll be all friends." And he turned toward the doors.

Susan looked at Ask uncertainly. Ask casually shook his head.

"Blast doors," he said.

The doors remain closed, and after only a few seconds, the tall man leveled his shotgun to his waist and pulled the trigger.

Buck shot ricocheted throughout the cabin, striking the man who had pounded on the door in the leg and causing the woman to whimper into a corner.

The tall man screamed at the camera. "Gon' be like that, huh! You let us in now, caus' like it or not, we comin' in! And when we do, I'll skin you for my bacon."

Aaron met eyes with Susan, who quickly looked away toward a monitor showing the mountain lions approaching the cabin. She studied their movements.

From the monitor, they could hear the baby's cries louder.

Suddenly, Ask pointed toward another of the monitors.

What appeared to be a well camouflaged hatch opened, and a moment later, Martin climbed out. He began moving quickly toward the cabin, but he was still about a hundred yards away.

Aaron held his breath and Elizabeth shook her head as the lion approached the cabin window.

"That's a female," said Susan, "and she's on the hunt."

Elizabeth turned away and looked desperately into Aaron's eyes. 'Can't watch this! It's not..."

Suddenly, both lions paused, mid-step, just at the edge of the cabin porch.

"They've stopped," marveled Susan.

Elizabeth and Aaron turned back to the monitor.

* * *

Both lions turned toward Martin. Neither pair of eyes blinked.

Martin approached the lead lion with less caution than one might think in such a situation. He calmly held a hand out under its nose.

'Please wait,' he said telepathically.

The lead lion looked into Martin's eyes. It saw a garden there, safety, and peace. Looking in the man's eyes, the lion did not feel hungry.

"The child is innocent," Martin whispered.

The lioness felt safe and sat, while Martin quietly stepped toward the window. As he knelt under the window sill, the other lion walked silently up behind the first.

* * *

"Oh my God!" gasped Elizabeth.

"No," said Susan. "It's not hunting him."

Elizabeth stabbed a hand toward the screen.

"It's right there!"

Susan shook her head. "Both lions are in pride posture, like they are among their own." Susan's expression alternated between confidence and confusion. "I don't know why, but they are not threatened by Martin. They accept him."

"Look," said Ask, pointing.

On the monitor within the cabin, showing the two uninjured intruders smashing the cabin furniture against the elevator door, a pair of hands lifted the baby from the window sill.

Inside, the moaning of the injured intruders and the smashing of the angry ones continued.

* * *

Martin stepped as quietly as he could from the cabin porch and gently pulled back the blanket. Inside he saw a cute baby with nothing but minor scratches and burns to mar his face.

The baby looked Martin in the eyes and immediately stopped crying.

To Martin's delight, the baby's sclera were a brilliant white. Martin smiled, then returned the blanket over the baby's cheek. The moment was silent and beautiful.

Suddenly, the sound and force of a blast hit him from behind. He turned and saw the tall man pointing his shotgun at him, smoke coming from the barrel.

The tall man then pointed the gun at Martin's head.

"No one takes what's mine. Even what's gonna be mine!"

No second blast came, however. Just before the tall man pulled the trigger, a blur of brown swept the intruder from Martin's view.

Martin stumbled, using his dexterity and strength to hold onto the baby. He turned to see what had happened. The lead lion had pounced and was making quick work of the tall man.

Feeling dizzy, Martin turned from the scene of carnage, back toward the hatch.

He passed the second lion, which crouched into a hunting posture and also lunged toward the cabin.

* * *

Inside the control room, the family cringed at the monitors, as screams and roars filled the control room's speakers.

Ask turned off the monitors and stood. Looking toward Elizabeth and Aaron, he smiled, 'Shall we greet our new guest?'

He stood, walked to the control room door, and exited toward the stairs.

Elizabeth gestured for Aaron to look at the table top computer screen, which read: 0 days; 11 hours; 37 minutes; 17 seconds...and count down continued.

Elizabeth locked eyes with Aaron. 'The dark force is too much!' she thought to him.

Aaron set his jaw and then shook his head.

'Come,' they both heard in their thoughts. Ask stood and looked them both in the eyes. 'We have work to do.'

Ask led the way to the stairs. The others exited. Elizabeth meanwhile wondered if anything was left that could be done.

CHAPTER EIGHTEEN

*"So do all who live to see such times. But that is not
for them to decide. All we have to decide is what to do
with the time that is given us."*

-- J.R.R. Tolkien

The Choice

Martin arrived with the child into the silo infirmary. He
placed the baby gently on a gurney, then leaned
against a bank of cabinets.

A moment later Leonard stepped in ahead of Ask,
striding directly for the baby. Expertly removing the
bundling cloth, while supporting the baby's head and
torso, Leonard began to examine the child.

"A boy," he said reflexively, followed by a random
"Hmm" or "Ahuh," as he moved step by step through
his medical examination.

"Was there anything that could have been done?"
asked Susan of Martin, nodding toward the surface.
"You know, for them?"

Martin smiled to Susan placatively, then turned to Elizabeth and Aaron. "With the protective energy gone, the Earth, and those who live upon it, revert back to chaos."

Ask added, "Lack of belief merely worsens what was already there. They were lost long ago."

Martin looked at the boy sleepily. "But he is not."

Leonard unwrapped and lifted the blanket, enabling all to see the blood on it.

"Oh my..." began Susan leaning toward the baby.

Leonard held up a hand. "The baby looks ok. I'm not sure where the blood is from."

All turned at that moment to see Ask helping Martin sit on the other gurney and place a bandage on his back.

"Martin!" said Leonard.

Leonard turned toward Martin, as Susan picked up the baby, cuddling it protectively in her arms.

Martin's breathing was labored, "I...will be...fine. Just buck shot. Not deep."

But Leonard had already gone to work examining Martin's wounds.

Martin took a slow breath and forced a grin. But his energy had become weak, and he could manage to do nothing more than close his eyes as Leonard examined him. He knew if he attempted anything else, he could not focus on the silo.

Aaron crossed to him and took a deep, slow breath. He gripped Martin's hand and saw Martin's aura fade slightly in intensity.

'There is energy in me, right?' said Aaron to Martin telepathically. 'I can help you...'

Martin's eyes flashed open, and he released his hand from Aaron's.

"No!" said Martin aloud. "Save your energy. You will need it."

Elizabeth stood beside Aaron and whispered desperately to Martin, "You're not telling us everything."

She gripped Martin's hand, and he resisted her attempt as well. But despite his attempts to free himself, she held on.

Martin's struggle weakened as he saw in her eyes a child's longing for her long absent parent. He recognized the pain and realized the need. Relenting, he said, "Let me show you something."

He offered up his other hand, and Elizabeth held it as well.

"Come with me," he whispered and closed his eyes.

As spirits in the ether, Martin and Elizabeth traveled into Martin's memory to a morning and a day she knew well. As she had recalled before, Elizabeth was fifteen again, the day her family ended.

'I had promised your mother I would return to work,' explained Martin. 'She had given me an ultimatum to choose between us or my belief. Not wanting to lose you, I had promised I would no longer believe.'

And indeed, Martin in the vision dropped Elizabeth off at school on his way to return to his practice.

But he did not return to his practice. Elizabeth watched her young self walk up the school steps, while Martin remained in his car staring at her.

'I watched you, Lizzy, and tried with all my heart to sense your energy and see your future. I tried in every way that I had learned to see it, but saw only blackness, the nothingness.'

The Martin in the vision gripped his steering wheel nervously, his inquisitiveness into Elizabeth's future escalating into a panic.

'I searched for the Garden. I reached out to the Faeleriel to allay my fear that the blackness I saw for you wasn't your death. But they, who had taught me so much about belief and a potential future, were not there.'

Martin's car turned abruptly into their home driveway. He leapt from the car and sped to the front door, grabbing potted plants on his way.

'Before I knew it,' Martin continued, 'I was back home, hauling every plant I could find into the house and around me, creating a make shift garden of my own...trying at all costs to save your future.'

After laying a final strip of grass onto his study desk, Martin laid upon it and closed his eyes. He began whispering, "Taenoril sil, da Luna Fael, Aelialth mur, tul malia Hael."

Hardly a dozen heartbeats passed when the plants he had brought into the house began to shine and glimmer. Flowers that had until then been closed, bloomed, wilted stems stood tall, and the energy of the Garden entered.

'The Faeleriel came to me then,' Martin said. 'I told them of the blackness I saw and my fear for your future, your life.'

Elizabeth recognized the appearance of the plants now, having seen the energy of the Garden herself. Then, from one of the blooming flowers, emerged a small floating ball of green light. It rose and hovered in front of Martin's face as he continued to lay on the grass-covered desk.

'They asked me then if I believed.'

Elizabeth watched Martin's body in the vision convulse suddenly, first once, then again, then in a constant stream of sobs.

'I cried, Lizzy. I saw only the choices of loosing you for the moment or loosing you forever.'

Martin nodded to the Faeleriel. 'I chose then not only to believe, but to do so no matter what happened to me.'

The Feleriel light expanded then and dissipated into a sparkling rain that covered Martin's body and soaked into his skin.

'The Faeleriel revealed everything to me the history of the Faeleriel, the world, and the Gardens. I truly understood Ask's role as Keeper of the Garden and his need to turn it over to someone within their natural lifespan. I knew I must become the Keeper and to sustain both the Garden and Ask, who would mentor me in all that was to come. I knew this, and I resolved to do this.'

Moments later, teenage Elizabeth opened the front door, placed her school book bag in the entry hall and walked toward the kitchen for the snack she never received. Elizabeth now watched her younger self notice the entire entryway crammed with plants. And again, her younger self was searching the entryway, the stairs and her father's study for an explanation why.

In the study, she found Martin lying on the grass-covered desk, surrounded by his plants, and smiling up at her.

Young Elizabeth had hoped so much that her parents' marital problems were over, that her father would behave normally...think normally. She had hoped they would be a family again.

After the fight her parents had, and the yelling her mother had done the days before, teenage Elizabeth was sure he would have gone back to work, and everything would be okay.

"I thought you were going back to work today," said Elizabeth. "You promised mom."

Her father inhaled exuberantly and announced, "Today it was revealed to me."

"What was?"

Martin opened his eyes and turned toward Elizabeth. "All the hearts of my life."

Elizabeth did not understand, and it showed on her face.

"As we grow," he explained, "we change, and our hearts change with us. Our childhood believing heart becomes the doubting teenage heart, and finally the cynical, disbelieving adult heart."

Though fifteen year-old Elizabeth was confused and still did not understand what Martin was saying, it was her mature self who now stared out those eyes, and understanding was beginning to form.

Martin sat up and held both of Elizabeth's hands. "My heart is fully open now, and at last I see."

He looked Elizabeth directly in the eyes. "Taenoril sil, da Luna Fael, Aelialtha mur, tul malia Hael."

Fifteen year-old Elizabeth studied at her father, but it was Elizabeth of today who felt the emotion and tears welling up in her eyes.

"It needs me, Lizzy. I must help."

"Help? Who?"

"One day you will believe," he said. "And you will understand that to do so, even at your own sacrifice, is belief at the highest, and that connection will bring..."

Elizabeth heard the front door open, and felt her heart sink and race at the same time. She was fifteen year-old Lizzy again and knew the next few minutes were going to be the worst ever.

"Believe wha...?" teenage Elizabeth started to ask, tears filling her eyes.

And then the shouting started.

"WHAT...the HELL...is going on?" came Susan's voice from the entryway. "MARTIN!"

In the entryway, Susan stood aghast in the center of the potted plants. Spotting Martin and Elizabeth in the study, she marched directly at him.

"Martin, you promised."

"But I found it," Martin said meekly, not letting go of Elizabeth's hands.

"No more of this soul searching crap!...We're leaving!" Susan took Elizabeth's hands and led her out of the study.

Susan guided Elizabeth to the stairs. "Pull some clothes and stuff for an overnight."

As Elizabeth slunk slowly up the stairs, Susan turned on Martin. "We'll be away tonight. Get your stuff out of here, and tomorrow you better be gone!"

The vision was over. She and Martin were returning to the silo, to the present. Elizabeth realized now that she saw what she had not seen on that terrible day so long ago.

'What else had I missed?' she wondered.

Elizabeth's consciousness was just beginning to fill her physical form, when she fully realized there was something she had missed. There was one more place she had to go back to!

'It wasn't just about the Tree! The Faeleriel...they were there in the forest when I was seventeen.'

Sensing Martin's energy return to the silo after her, she goaded, 'Weren't they?'

Elizabeth turned her energy back on his before either had opened their eyes. 'Take me there,' she insisted. 'I want to see what happened through your eyes. I want to see what you saw.'

Martin understood her need. He knew she had to see it. But he was not sure he could show her and maintain the silo for much longer.

It was a gamble though he knew he must take.

Wordlessly, Martin altered his focus, the energy around them shifted, and Elizabeth felt the rushing sensation as they once again transported into another place and time.

Elizabeth was suddenly her seventeen year-old self stomping angrily away from Martin in that Florida woodland. This time, however, she felt no anger. Instead, she spun back toward Martin.

She nodded toward him, 'Is it...you?'

Martin smiled. 'Still me, yes.'

She felt she was supposed to blame him for dragging her out to a swamp during her senior year spring break. Instead, she looked around her, amazed.

'Is this what you saw that day?' she asked, tears forming in her eyes.

But Martin did not answer. He had no need to.

Elizabeth was slowly turning, absorbing the scene that had surrounded her then, but which she was only seeing now.

The clearing was bordered by Florida pines, oaks, and occasional eucalyptus trees. All had moss, fungi and saprophytes of all kinds growing in their bark. But the bark was as brilliantly colored as any flower, and the rays of sunshine streaming through the canopy sparkled like a rainbow. Even the fungi and growths on the tree trunks gleamed.

Dozens of creatures either stood on these or hovered in the air, held aloft by wings of some type or other. The beings themselves were as varied as the forest. They stood or flew, inhabiting tiny bodies of numerous sizes and shapes, some humanoid, some insect or animal like, with wide, intelligent eyes, all watching her.

She gaped, astonished.

Elizabeth continued to turn until Martin was back once again in her field of vision. Next to him was the tiny, barren willow tree.

Only now, half full of foliage, it was not so barren. And, the willow stood only a foot shorter than Martin. From its green strands of willow leaves bloomed numerous iridescent flowers. The strands glimmered so vibrantly, Elizabeth thought they could have been crystals.

Elizabeth gasped, not out of shock, she realized, but because she had been so enraptured by the scene around her, she had not remembered to breath.

'You were right,' she told Martin. 'This is significant.'

'Do you understand why?' he asked.

Elizabeth nodded. 'It begins and ends here,' she replied. 'Belief is the beginning of all things. Its presence strengthens and unites. Its absence destroys and divides.'

Martin inclined his head positively. As he did, a figure the size of a humming bird flew toward him and hovered over his right shoulder.

But now, Elizabeth saw this was not a humming bird, but rather an intelligent being hovering under fluttering wings. 'A Faeleriel!' extolled Elizabeth.

'Not a Faeleriel,' corrected Martin, 'all are Faeleriel.'

"All?" whispered Elizabeth, scanning the forest clearing once again, looking passed any animal or insect form camouflage, to see the actual Faeleriel being underneath.

'Such beauty!' exclaimed Elizabeth. Then she focused on Martin. 'All this from my belief? Is belief the root of all energy?'

'Believing is seeing, and belief is the essence of sustaining,' he replied, smiled, and faded into mist.

For no sooner had Martin passed these words to her, she felt herself pulled from the scene and in the infirmary once again.

As they returned to the present, and their duel energies passed through a momentary singularity, Elizabeth glimpsed Martin's physical form. In that brief instant she had connected with him, she had detected something.

Opening her eyes now in the infirmary, Elizabeth gasped. She grounded herself to her own physical form, looking at Aaron, Leonard, and Susan, then back, distressingly, at Martin.

"It's not important," assured Martin aloud.

Elizabeth placed a hand over Martin's abdomen and saw his iridescence focused most intensely along his flank.

"This is why!" she shouted.

"I can...take care of it," assured Martin.

"Can you?" argued Elizabeth. "Can you do everything yourself? How 'bout having faith in us to understand..."

Elizabeth looked to Leonard, "He's bleeding internally." Then she reached out to touch Martin's left flank, but he gripped her arm and stopped her.

Martin's face now held more pain than Elizabeth had ever seen.

"No! You will need..."

Leonard had not balked. He directed his exam exactly as Elizabeth had indicated, removing the cloth over his skin and palpating for wounds.

Susan stared at Leonard and Martin and mouthed to herself in puzzled silence, 'How could she know?'

The silo rumbled again, interrupting Martin's plea for Elizabeth to save her energy. But Martin's expression was resistant and final.

Susan held onto the baby, more puzzled now than ever. "Elizabeth?"

Elizabeth continued to stand over Martin, but explained to Susan, "Aaron and I discovered the energy that protects the silo from being crushed by outside forces."

Leonard was placing the ultrasound probe over the wound and inquired, "What kind of energy?"

"Yes," agreed Susan. "How is it possible to stabilize a planet one minute but not the next?" Her frustration steadily increased and her voice intensified.

"What caused this Armageddon in the first place? How could no one know this was coming?"

Elizabeth answered, "It happened because too few believed it could."

She saw that Susan did not understand.

"And," continued Elizabeth, "someone did know it was coming."

Susan looked toward Martin, conflicted. Leonard was working to identify and dress his wounds, and yet she still could not let go of her frustration that Martin had abandoned what they had both promised would be their life together. He left his family! He abandoned them over some fantasy that he believed in! She did not know whether to cry or scream in frustration.

She held her jaw tightly closed, so much so, her head hurt. Her eyes filled with tears, and unable to see, she shook her head.

"Don't get worked up, mother," said Elizabeth. "I was frustrated too, because it didn't seem possible, based on the science we thought we knew."

Elizabeth turned from Martin and walked toward Susan. "The problem is, and has always been, that our physical laws and equations were incomplete."

The silo creaked agonizingly.

Aaron and Ask moved to a computer terminal along one counter. Ask began typing.

Elizabeth reached her hand out toward Susan. "Do you believe in me?"

Tears were streaming down Susan's face.

"Of course, but why...?" pleaded Susan.

Elizabeth said steadfastly, "Can you focus on that? On me? Can you see the world through your belief in me?"

Susan felt she would burst if her only daughter asked her to believe in faeries!

Elizabeth held her hand out in front of Susan. "Will you believe in me no matter what you see?"

Had she heard right. Susan's expression relaxed. "Believe in ...you?"

She began to lift her arm to take Elizabeth's hand, but the chance disappeared. The silo quaked violently, and Elizabeth stumbled, withdrawing her hand to balance herself.

Elizabeth looked to Aaron.

Aaron stood over the computer monitor next to Ask. They were studying the energy schematic. On it, the silo was completely surrounded by a deep indigo purple perimeter, but from underneath rose three red fingers of color.

"What are those?" called out Elizabeth.

"Magma," replied Ask.

* * *

All could see the molten rock appeared about to penetrate the complex at three points. The closest was next to one of the adjacent silos. Two others were approaching a second silo and a passageway between silos.

Elizabeth walked back to Martin, gripped his hand and closed her eyes.

Aaron reached for her, "Beth!"

Elizabeth felt Martin join her as she practically pulled his perception from the infirmary and traveled outside the silo. Aaron joined closely behind.

She felt Martin's resistance at first, but her determination to investigate what was happening would not be deterred. And he acquiesced to her and Aaron.

She could feel the energy of the protective field weakening against the onslaught of the destructive forces bearing down on them.

'How can any amount of energy repel this mass of destruction?' Elizabeth pined.

'It can be done,' assured Martin.

At the surface, the bubble had contracted to cover less than half of the airfield. A corner portion of the hangar was exposed to the space outside the field and was on fire. Areas of forest no longer within the field either shriveled or burned.

As bad as events had become inside the silo protective field, outside was devastatingly worse. The Earth had cracked and filled with rivers of lava.

Grey eyed animals from outside the bubble attempted to run into the bubble and were met by the mountain lions and other animals protecting their habitat.

'The energy to which we connect, feel, and direct is Taenoril sil. It is the life energy of all things. The measure of its strength is not in mass, but in connection. The more connected one is, the more that energy flows through us,' explained Martin.

'How then does one make the connection? I already believe.'

'There are levels of belief, Lizzy,' Martin said. 'To simply believe is the first level of connection and enables true sight, to see the world as it really is. The highest level of connection is believing, to the benefit of others, even at the cost of one's own life. Believing, in the face of benevolent sacrifice, forms a connection to Taenoril sil that is the most powerful connection a mortal being can muster.'

A geyser blasted magma just outside one portion of the protective field. Martin, Elizabeth, and Aaron traveled toward and then dove down into it, back into the black mantle alongside and below the silo.

There, three long tentacles of magma reached toward the protective bubble and the silo complex from below, as they had seen on the computer monitor. But from this sensory vantage, the situation was far worse. Lava coursed through broken mantle, but all around them, the foundation of the mantle itself was near its breaking point. If it fractured, the mantle, and everything around it would crumble and burn.

The wedges breaking apart the mantle were these three fingers of lava. If the protection field failed, they would complete the split and release the destructive forces below.

The closest finger of lava was near one of the outlying silos, silo number four. Another was farther away from silo number three. But Elizabeth feared most the lava about to breach the tunnel between the main silo and silo five.

She felt the forces around her. This, she realized, would be a crux point beginning the unstoppable cascade of destruction.

Elizabeth and the others returned their thoughts to the infirmary, and opened their eyes.

Ask pointed to the lava nearest to one of the silos. "Earlier, Martin and I were inspecting the lower levels," he said. "The forces outside are strongest outside silo number four."

Elizabeth crossed to the monitor shaking her head, "But that's not the breach that matters."

"Beth!" shouted Aaron, pointing at the screen. "The countdown!"

In the corner of the monitor screen, the countdown read: 0 days, 0 hours, 12 minutes, 43 seconds.

Elizabeth turned to Martin. "The protection field. If it's powered by connection to Taenoril sil, we can support it."

Martin's eyes filled with tears. "It was supposed to be me. I'm the Keeper."

Elizabeth told him, "Your place now is in the Garden." She inclined her head toward the monitor. "If we can do anything here, it will need you there."

Elizabeth faced Leonard. "Can you get him there?"

Leonard nodded.

Susan's eyes darted from Leonard to Martin, then back to Elizabeth. "What are you saying?"

Aaron called out, "Nine minutes, twenty-two seconds! The forces outside are too much."

"The Earth's mantle has shifted," Elizabeth announced.

"It's already happening," said Ask.

Martin warned, "Silo number four."

Elizabeth shook her head. "No! That breach will self contain. Tunnel three!" she commanded to Ask. "Take me there."

And without a look back, she, Ask, and Aaron ran to the stairs.

Less than six minutes remained.

Susan looked through tear filled eyes down at the baby and then to Leonard, tortured and conflicted. Desperately she reached out to the space Elizabeth had vacated.

Leonard stepped up behind her. She turned and painfully hugged him, taking his arm and wrapping it around the baby.

She squeezed his arm desperately, trying to convey how much she loved him, yet how terrified she was for her daughter. She looked up at him and sobbed, "I have to go."

Leonard nodded, "I know."

And with eyes that said "I love you" for the last time, they each released the other, and Susan ran to the stairs and after Elizabeth.

Leonard turned toward Martin. "What now?"

Martin gripped the arm of his friend, "Now, I need your help."

CHAPTER NINETEEN

"The mind, unfettered by the bonds of earth,
Can soar ... far above the mountains steep"

-- William E. Fein

The Darkness

In the stairwell, Elizabeth immediately noticed the change in light. Instead of being faded industrial low level light, the space around the silo was now lit with the faded green light of the Garden, sparkling as the Garden had. And the outer concrete silo wall emitted the same threatening indigo glow that the computer screen had revealed.

Elizabeth and Aaron followed Ask as he led the way quickly down the stairs.

Elizabeth had been listening to Ask's explanation of what was happening around them. "This has happened before? Like extinction of dinosaurs, Noah and the flood?"

Ask nodded as he descended. "Like that, yes."

"How many times?"

"Many," answered Aaron. Elizabeth raised an eyebrow to him and he replied with a shrug.

A clatter of stomping drew Elizabeth's attention as Ask spoke. She looked up through the stairwell metal grating and saw Susan running down the stairs.

Elizabeth sighed, then focused her attention forward toward Ask, the stairs, and the tunnel where everything could end.

Above, Susan's hands trembled, making it difficult for her to grip the stairwell railing. She was trailing far behind the others, worried that she would be too late, that something would happen to Elizabeth before she could be with her to help.

She hoped only that if all was lost and she had the opportunity to save Elizabeth instead of herself, she could.

Ahead, Elizabeth and Aaron listened to Ask as he explained.

"We do not have much time and will soon arrive at the tunnel. So let me show you the true nature of these events."

Aaron and Elizabeth both expanded their senses, felt the tingling sensation, and the rush of motion as their consciousness traveled, even as their bodies continued on their course down the stairs.

Around them, the stairwell was gone, they sensed beyond the silo to the surface above. But with Ask, they did not stop there. They were traveling beyond the protective barrier and beyond their own space and time.

They orbited primordial Earth, circling the sun covered in darkness and molten lava.

They heard Ask as he explained the visions they were seeing.

'This was our planet in its infant stage. Then as now, the natural state of our planet is not unlike Mercury...volcanic and volatile.'

From the far side of the sun, serpentine iridescent wisps of light undulated like a pride of dolphins, orbited Earth, then descended toward it.

'These are the Faeleriel. Beings of energy without physical form. They traveled through the dark energy of the universe to colonize and inhabit Earth. They have been here from the first.'

The Faeleriel flew toward the volatile planet, descended to its surface and dove down volcanoes, into the planet's depths. Seas of lava slowed into stagnant eddies, turning from molten red to solid, dark grey rock.

'Their habitation on Earth stabilized and cooled its surface, focused its volatile energy to the core, where it organized as Aelialtha, the living Earth. The surface gases then coalesced into an atmosphere.'

Clouds formed over the seas of lava and began to rain. The lava cooled into stone, and water accumulated over rock.

'All was ready, so within the early oceans, Faeleriel used their sentient energy to organize elements into molecules, molecules into tissues, and into tissues created the spark of life.'

A single-celled organism divided for the first time to form a sheet of cells, which like an iridescent jellyfish swam through water.

'Faeleriel aided the evolution from sea to land, and from species to species until one evolved with the capacity to believe. These sentient beings called themselves Thaen.'
A tiny, glowing, winged creature fluttered its wings and hovered in front of a coral colored unicorn. The Faleriel waved a hand in a wide circle, and the unicorn nodded.

'That connection to Taenoril sil,' continued Ask, 'and its bond between Faeleriel and Thaen, enabled the Thaen to understand the true nature of our world and our universe and created the entire world as a Garden.'

The unicorn stood in a vast Garden, one of many such reverent creatures and accompanied by many other strange and beautiful animals of all types.

A bird-sized, butterfly-like creature flew up from the Garden, into and over the clouds. The Earth had become a world of one enormous ocean, and one united and glimmering Garden continent.

'On the edge of the continent, however, the dark energy spurred doubt in some Thaen, and from doubt to disbelief. Through the Thaen, darkness grew,' Ask continued. 'Like fire burning through a piece of paper, the darkness spread, eating away at Taenoril sil, cutting the one Garden into many, until disbelief eliminated the many back to one. That remnant Garden then shrunk under the force of the darkness of Duadine and disappeared.'

Once again, storms raged throughout the planet, and the land was split with fire and lava.

'Over several such cycles and millions more years, life and Thaen began, receded, and began again. The one continent became three, the land cooled, new Thaen evolved to believe in Faeleriel, and color returned to the planet's surface.'

The planet cooled, and the three continents were swept over in vibrant colors.

'And so it was, through cycles of belief and disbelief ...until the dawn of Man, the Thaen of our age.'

On the surface of the Earth once again, an early human, wonder on his face, reached a hand toward a floating ball of light. The ball brightened, and the human's expression appeared intelligent. He smiled.

'Faeleriel energy, however, is not physical. They take a physical form through the connection with Taenoril sil that belief creates between Faeleriel and Thaen. Belief sustains them, enabling them to maintain their form.'

Small flying creatures, illuminated in colorful, glowing lights, flew among the humans in a lush wooded area that appeared to go on beyond the horizon.

'Over millennia, humans at first believed, then doubts and greed began. Among those who no longer believed, fighting and conquest replaced connection and understanding..."

A village was cut into the wooded area, splitting parts of a Garden apart. Within that village, one raised a clenched fist to another and struck him to the ground.

"...until they forgot their origin. Among the disbelieving, their villages became cities and cities nations. Soon one vast Garden had become many small oases. Without Taenoril sil, Faeleriel were unable to maintain the Gardens, their form, and ultimately Earth's stabilization."

A Faeleriel retreated back into the Tree of the Garden, enveloped in a flowering bud. The pedals closed and the flower shriveled into the bark of the Tree branch.

'Still, the ability to believe remains within each of us. Some experience what has been called deja vu, when a brush with Faeleriel energy causes a feeling of a memory they cannot place,' continued Ask.

Aaron thought back to the first time he heard the connecting words of the Faeleriel and now understood the familiarity.

Ask finished, 'Faeleriel hope to one day return to physical form when belief has returned to the surface.'

The ground heaved upward and lava engulfed the village.

"But without belief, the ultimate result has been and will always be ar' Ama Gedeon."

Ask, Elizabeth, and Aaron physically reached the landing at the bottom of the stairs. Ask gathered their energies and drew them back to the silo and the stairwell.

Elizabeth and Aaron gathered their individual energies and assumed their physical forms. Ask turned to them and inspected their faces. Both reached the landing, blinked, gained their bearings, and nodded to Ask.

Susan, panting heavily from running the entire way, had caught up to the group. "Thanks...for...waiting," she gasped, placing a gentle but heavy hand on Elizabeth's arm.

Elizabeth offered her an appreciative smile, but she was just as quickly distracted back to the moment.

Ask turned toward the tunnel door.

"Each ending," Ask said, "has been a new beginning."

Ask gripped the handle and looked at Elizabeth and Aaron.

"The scales of belief have again turned. Ar' Ama Gedeon...the New Beginning, is occurring. This is your Ark. Through you will come the new world."

* * *

With the baby in one arm and Martin's arm around his shoulder and neck, Leonard trudged to the stairway and spiral walkway door. Martin was breathing with difficulty and appeared nearly stuporous.

Leonard demanded, "I have to operate."

"No," refused Martin rasping. "I cannot be made unconscious. Not yet."

Martin leaned his head to touch Leonard's and whispered, "You must help me remain conscious. Talk to me. Get me to the Garden."

Leonard reluctantly looked up at his choice of path. It was six floors to the Garden floor from the infirmary. Easy for one man alone, a challenge for one holding a baby and assisting another. Hopelessly, Leonard knew he was carrying a dying man as the world imploded.

'If he passes out,' thought Leonard, '...no, when he passes out, I'll just bring him back here.' He sighed. 'Hopefully, there will be something I can do at that point.'

Thus, resigned to his and their fate, Leonard took his first steps along the spiral walkway, where if anyone should fall, he thought, the fall would not be as catastrophic as the stairs.

Allowing his mind to drift elsewhere, he searched for something to talk to Martin about. "How," Leonard asked shyly, "did you first develop the visions?"

"It was on the night of the party celebrating my twentieth year in medicine and the tenth year of the partnership," whispered Martin, speaking as he controlled his breathing.

He continued, "We had come home, tucked Lizzy into bed, but I could not sleep. We had become successful, as you know, but not happy. I asked myself, 'Why?' I stayed up all night asking, and for days and weeks more. There was something missing, but I did not know what. All I knew was that I had always wanted to do something important with my life to help others, but this did not feel like that something."

Martin grunted and the baby stirred as Leonard stopped to adjust body positions and weight distribution across his shoulders. Once done, they set out again.

"I had simply sought more meaning in my life, not spiritual, not financial. Just meaning. And one night as I lay awake contemplating what and how, a voice spoke to me saying, 'We are here.'

"I thought I was dreaming, but I was not. I thought I was going crazy, but the world was becoming clearer, more peaceful, and soon had meaning. They spoke to me in my dreams and gave me visions while awake."

"Who were they?" Asked Leonard.

"Ask's was the first voice, then later, the Faeleriel."

Martin drew in a breath and released it in a sigh.

"The 'distractions and craziness,' as Susan called my confessions and behaviors, were my attempts to understand the threat to the Faeleriel and ultimately to the Garden and all the world."

"She thought," said Leonard, "you were threatening to break up the family."

"I was working the best that I could to save it, the Garden, and our planet."

"Instead," Leonard mumbled sorrowfully, "you lost your practice and everything else dear to you."

"I'm sorry, Martin. Mine was..." Leonard's breathing heaved and his voice cracked emotionally, "one of the votes to..."

Martin interrupted, "I had voted for you to become a partner. I knew I would have to leave to complete the task ahead of me. And I wanted someone who cared, not only for the patients of our practice, but who would care for my family as well. You, my friend, did nothing wrong. You enabled me to do what was necessary.

Leonard stuttered, "You...saw..this?"

"I saw the possibilities. More importantly, it was clear our paths should cross, and that you could achieve in life what I could not."

As they shuffled along the pathway, the tenth floor landing appeared ahead.

"Everything," said Martin sleepily, "is as it should be."

Leonard nearly sobbed, "If you don't let me fix this, you're going to be unconscious now, whether you like it or not."

Leonard pleaded, "Let me help you!"

"You already have," said Martin. "You have nothing to be sorry for. Take care of Susan."

Martin nodded onward. The tenth floor landing was just ahead.

"When I am inside," said Martin, "you must go to the control room and track Elizabeth's progress. They will be in tunnel three."

* * *

In the center of the tenth floor, Leonard laid Martin down at the base of the small Tree. Something appeared different about the space from the last time he had seen it, though Leonard could not nail down what it was.

Leonard's hand lowered Martin's head gently so that he rested at the base of the small Tree's withered roots. No sooner had Leonard removed his hand, however, then a dozen of the roots branched out from the Tree, sliding over Martin's shoulders and down around his sides, until he was nearly covered with them.

As each root tendril touched Martin, it illuminated with a soft green glow. Rapidly, the series of roots and Martin enlightened one by one, until he, and the Garden were alive in light.

"I don't believe it!" Leonard exclaimed.

"You will," replied Martin, then gripping Leonard's hand desperately, Martin peered gravely into Leonard's eyes. "You must."

CHAPTER TWENTY

"We stood at the precipice, buoyed by our hope for the good in all things, and our vision of a happy world...it was that vision that the darkness craved."

-- Topper, Keeper (Ancient) of the Caeltis Garden

The Breach

Elizabeth felt the heat of the lava breach as soon as the door opened. They entered and kept low, as the tunnel was already filling with smoke and gases.

Several steps in, they all saw it. The one hundred fifty foot long tunnel had been ripped open at its center by a towering cone of magma, which boiled and spat lava, flowing both directions along the tunnel.

Ask wasted no time. He walked down the deteriorating passageway toward the volcanic spout. The family behind him was terrified, for all save Leonard had had this same fiery dream of losing each other and themselves. And none had had a dream where they could to do anything about it.

Elizabeth moved to follow Ask, but his eyes still focused on the breach, he lifted a hand to stop her.

"I am not like you are now," he said. "Do not be afraid. My time was gone long ago."

Elizabeth and Aaron inched forward despite Ask's warning.

Ask continued walking down the tunnel. The dark orange glow from the lava reflected off his face.

"I was born," he continued, "the year the first colonists arrived in North America."

Lava bubbled into the tunnel from the rent in the floor, just ahead of Ask.

"Like my tribe kin, I believed and lived long. But, over centuries, disbelief spread through the land, forcing the Faeleriel out of physical form, and diminishing the Garden. More and more, the Garden hibernated. More and more, Earth destabilized."

Ask approached the lava. He stopped with his toes at its edge.

"I was forty-one," he said, "when the Keeper before me passed his energy to the Tree and left me the last of my tribe, saying, 'Before time, there was lightness and dark. And the light came from the Aeleriel...'"

Ask lifted a foot to hover over the glowing lava, speaking the words that were the verbal history of the Faeleriel and the Gardens, passed down from Eluwallusit to Eluwallusit for countless millennia.

Susan stifled a scream, while Elizabeth and Aaron listened intently. The mantra took only a minute to recite, and during that time, Elizabeth resisted the urge to sprint out to help. For, even if she did, how was she going to help?

"Belief in a united and tranquil world had all but disappeared in the Garden country," continued Ask. "The time of the Duadine had overcome. And I could no longer sustain the Faeleriel, the Garden, or the Tree."

Ask lowered his foot onto the lava. The others behind him all held their breath. Susan shut her eyes and buried her head in her hands.

Yet his foot did not sink into the molten rock. Instead, it instantly turned to obsidian.

"Martin found me at that time. He had been searching for meaning, and had heard the Garden's call. He ventured out and found the Garden."

Ask took another step, the lava underneath his other foot turned to obsidian, and the lava between the two steps did as well.

He pauses then, ensuring the obsidian would bare his weight. It appeared to, so he walked on.

"As Keeper," Ask continued, "Martin's belief in others revitalized Taenoril sil and sustained the Garden for a short time. But we knew we only had time enough to prepare for what was to come as Taenoril sil waned."

Ask's steps turned more lava to obsidian as he walked toward the lava spout. But the amount of lava bubbling up from the rent in the cavern was too much.

Susan lifted her head and focused on Ask. Her chest heaving and breathing heavily, she forced out, "Taenoril...sil! What is it?"

Ask approached the central tower of magma that had breached the tunnel. His expression settled into resolve as he walked calmly toward the mountainous blob of fiery lava cascading from the rent.

He closed his eyes.

"Taenoril sil," he said calmly. "The energy which brings all other energies together and sustains all things. It is the conduit for life."

Ask stepped forward and reached out to embrace the lava tower.

"Through Taenoril sil, the Garden sustains me."

Susan could not believe what was about to happen, but could not hide her face again. "No!" she whimpered.

Elizabeth gripped Aaron's and Susan's hands, and squeezed her eyes closed. She whispered intently, "Believe!"

Aaron closed his own eyes and extended his energy outward.

Susan watched Ask and shook her head disbelievingly, "What is this!"

Ask responded, "Ar' Ama Gedeon. The new beginning."

The family watched as Ask's next step sunk into the mound of cascading lava. His foot disappeared into the magma, catching fire to his feet and legs.

The molten red lava cooled and solidified instantly into black, shining obsidian stone, which coursed up the mound, crystallizing, until, as Ask embraced its top with his arms and full body, the bubbling stopped.

The cavern was suddenly quiet, except for the fluttering flames.

Ask's legs were wrapped in flame, and they were spreading up his body, engulfing him.

Susan screamed, "My god!"

But within the flame, Ask showed no fear.

Ask closed his eyes a final time. "Taenoril sil."

Elizabeth opened her eyes. All around her, that which had been flowing and molten red, was now shining black, cooled stone. The fire had been extinguished.

But gone too was Ask. All that remained of his body was a column of ashes.

The smoke was thick, burning their lungs and their eyes. Susan and Aaron began to cough.

Elizabeth turned to Aaron and Susan. "Carbon monoxide! We have to go back to the stairway!"

And without a look back Aaron assisted Susan, leading the way back to the stairwell.

* * *

Aaron felt more than saw his way back to the stairwell door. The burning in his eyes and lungs was so intense at this point, he was having difficulty drawing in a breath between coughing fits. Still, he managed to keep Susan standing and moving forward.

Elizabeth paused at first to let Aaron stabilize Susan before taking her first step back down the tunnel. She had not yet taken her second step when behind her she heard a cracking sound. She turned back toward her mother and saw her and Aaron fade into the smoke and disappear.

With her mouth buried in the nook of her elbow, and blinking through her stinging eyes, she turned her head back toward the obsidian pillar and Ask's ash statue.

'Am I seeing this right?' Elizabeth asked herself as she studied the pillar's structure. Was it quavering?

She focused then on Ask's column of ashes. Yes! Something was happening. Little by little, the ashes were breaking apart and spilling downward in ashen rivulets. The obsidian trembled again and this time Elizabeth saw as well as heard the crack.

From top to bottom, a rent broke along the side of the obsidian tower. First one, then another, and with a sudden SHRAAKK, the tower shattered and blasted apart, as the pressure from the magma below pushed up and through the rent in the silo.

Elizabeth's arm muffled her scream as she saw Ask's ashes blown apart by a fresh crest of lava.

The shattered obsidian that had encased the lava flow floated away as the lava bubbled into the cavern anew.

* * *

In the control room, Leonard sat underneath the monitors at the computer terminal conflicted.

All his professional life he had lived and worked by a code that faced every obstacle based on proven methods and proven procedures. Using the standardized algorithms of his profession, he had always succeeded at either saving lives or doing everything that could have possibly been done to save a life.

Staring at the destruction at the surface and the force diagrams showing the destruction around them, he trembled uncharacteristically. There were no algorithms he knew of for these events, no scientific explanation for the events themselves, and no way for him to save lives. For the first time in his adult life, he did not know what to do.

He closed his eyes, reflexively, as the rock anthem of his early teenage years, and the one he played when he bought his first muscle car, the one he sang to himself when he landed the plane, the one he always had ready when he needed it, played in his head.

He let the driving beat sync with his pounding heart beat, and soon both seemed to be a rhythm to the same music. Assuming the roll of the virtuoso drummer, his tremor was replaced by high hat symbols action, a riff from snare to tom toms, and bass foot stomp that never failed to rock.

Leonard's mind and body relaxed as his alternate reality took over his subconscious. Since he had used this technique in trauma situations, he allowed his subconscious to now take in the environment and put the pieces together. He did so, not in an emergency room trauma bay or an operating theater, but in the control room with the monitors showing destruction and impending doom. Yet, the process was the same.

In his relaxed state, Susan and his feelings for her came to him. He had found her gregarious and lively from the start, if not overly so at times. As a coworker's wife, he would never have considered her anything else. When Martin began to miss work and Susan made excuses for Martin, his compassionate medical side gradually moved into action. After Martin's departure, Susan had been a wreck. Helping to alleviate her pain had been a natural reaction for him. Yet, the bond that later developed between them had been something entirely new.

As he slowly came out of his rock fantasy world, he thought of himself as he was with Susan, as if the world existed only of the two of them wrapped in their own bliss. His eyes opened then, and he noticed something he had not noticed before. The light in the room was changing.

It was then that he noticed the line of alarm beacons blinking an ominous red.

CHAPTER TWENTY-ONE

"We were never so afraid as when we first stepped from our home and faced our fears alone...but we were never so strong, having done so."

-- Siena and Kayla, Keepers (Present) of the Caeltis Garden

The Sacrifice

Aaron covered his mouth and eyes as he felt for the tunnel wall. He attempted to run, but he and Susan began stumbling each time he tried. Instead, he maintained a steady pace until the stairwell exit door finally came into view.

Pulling Susan up beside him, he gripped the warm stairwell door knob, twisted, and leaned his weight into it.

Both he and Susan spilled into the stairwell, and with them, a plume of noxious smoke and gas.

Caught in another coughing fit, Aaron stumbled to the intercom and pressed the talk button.

"Leonard! Leonard, are you there?"

"Yeah," came the tinny reply, "You al...?"

"Maximize the ventilation!" Aaron interrupted, yelling into the intercom. "Air...contaminated!"

Leonard's voice returned, "It's already maxed! There's only one fan. It's not enough!"

Aaron, who had bent over coughing, looked up at Susan. She was on her side next to the door sputtering for breath.

Suddenly it occurred to him, 'Elizabeth's not here!'

Aaron leapt at the door, crouched, and squinted through the smoke and darkness to spy any sign of Elizabeth. He saw none.

"What?" gasped Susan. "She's...not there?"

Aaron shook his head.

Susan rolled onto her side in panic and struggled to her feet. Reaching for the door jam, she grunted, "Beth? No!"

Aaron placed a palm on Susan's arm before she could run back down the passageway.

"No. Wait!" he said. "We don't see all she sees. We have to activate..."

"Let go of me!" she cried, pulling aware from Aaron. "She'll be burned like him."

"Don't you get it?" Aaron argued as he mentally reached out, struggling to find Elizabeth. "She is not being sustained. She sustains."

The sooty air spilled from the tunnel into the stairwell. But Susan shook her head, forced in a deep breath, and ran back into the tunnel.

Aaron closed his eyes, reaching out for Elizabeth, 'Beth...the air!'

And in that instant, her thought was there, 'Not sealed. I have to...you fix fan...love you.'

Aaron's heart pounded. He searched for her again, but felt her intensity focused elsewhere.

He knew she was right. If any of them were to survive, she had her job to do, and he had his. His expression calmed. He inhaled as deep a breath as he could. Then looking up the stairwell, he leapt up stairs two at a time.

* * *

In the tunnel, Elizabeth felt helpless watching the lava bubbling into the cavern with increasing speed and force. She had to do something.

She stepped toward the lava, having no idea what she would do when she reached it. The thought dawned on her, 'this is a one way trip.'

In that moment, Aaron's message came to her.

As she stared at the lava tower, her emotions were boiling up inside her, and her thoughts, emotions, and communication jumbled. 'Not sealed,' she was able to communicate. 'I have to!...'

And then she realized what perhaps all parents realize at some point, that at the foundation of their love is the willingness to sacrifice everything for those they care for. In fact, there was something familiar about that concept which she could not place.

She controlled her emotion and finished her thought with Aaron, not giving herself a moment more or she was sure she would be bawling.

'You fix fan...love you.' And she broke the connection. There was so much more she wished she could tell him, but now she had a job to do. Now, she had to focus.

'Belief,' she told herself. 'Sacrifice. Sacri...'

In that instant, the sensation of something familiar she had felt moments before became a memory, and the memory was crystal clear.

Martin had told her back then, back when she was fifteen and he was lying on his grass-covered desk instead of going to work, and going on about understanding what was revealed to him.

That was when he had said, "One day you will believe. And you will understand that to do so, even at your own sacrifice, is belief at the highest."

Elizabeth's expression relaxed. She was not the teenager any more. She was not a lot of things. Now, she understood.

"Belief at the highest," she said aloud. She breathed slowly and thought of Aaron. She thought of her mother and Leonard. She thought of Martin and Ask.

The barriers and fears in her mind melted away, expanding the perspective of her understanding to include, not just different visual points of view, but every thought, feeling, and energy around her.

'That is what the Faeleriel mantra was saying,' she realized.

And she spoke, "Taenoril sil, da Luna Fael, Aelialtha mur, tul malia Hael." Connect to the energy, connect to Faeleriel, from every level of Earth, to all beings who believe.

The mantle below her was fracturing. The tunnel jolted violently, and a rumbling began from deep beneath the silo. There was no time left. As she slipped her feet out of their shoes, she slipped out of the bonds of her past life, and walked on.

Since she had believed in the Garden, she had been able to see the energy in the world around her. Now that sight had intensified. Though the lava in front of her burned a fiery red, the walls, the floor, and even the air around her shimmered a sparkling white.

With thoughts of those she loved: Aaron, her mother, and even Martin, she whispered, "Sacrifice...."

She stepped to the edge of the lava and focused her energy. She did not close her eyes. She was focused as she had never been before.

"...All the hearts of my life."

Elizabeth lifted a foot over the advancing lava flow.

Susan stumbled gasping into the passageway pleading, "Baby, no!"

Elizabeth stepped back, turning her head partway to face her mother. Susan saw that, in the minutes she had been separated from Elizabeth, something dramatic had happened, for her daughter had changed. Elizabeth's pupils were dilated, the color of her irises sparkled like rays of the full moon, brilliantly light blue and white, and she appeared steadfast with resolve.

"Believe, mother," Elizabeth said.

Susan sobbed, "In what?"

"In me," Elizabeth said softly.

Elizabeth turned back to the fiery flow, but as she did, she looked upon the erupting lava with eyes that saw the cavern not just as it was, but as it could be.

She reached a hand toward the blood red lava, and her arm gleamed like sunlight off a rippling stream.

"Taenoril sil, da Luna Fael, Aelialtha mur, tul malia Hael," she said again.

Elizabeth stepped onto the lava, and though her weight began to sink into the molten stone, her body called the energy from the lava to her and around her, cooling the rock and solidifying it.

The obsidian branched out underneath Elizabeth's feet, and she could feel it supporting her.

'She's gonna die!' Susan wept to herself. 'No! No!'

Susan did not know what to think. She could only recall the things in life that she 'knew'. Martin had abandoned her and his daughter for figments of his imagination...his fanciful belief. Now Elizabeth was asking her to believe in this fantasy too. And to what end? The end to the apocalypse? Her daughters life!

Susan was caught in a battle between what she had always known was 'real' and the belief she wanted to have in Elizabeth.

Had she been able to see her own aura, she would have noted it begin to darken from purple to indigo. A coldness began to run through her. Despite the fiery stone around her, her blood began to chill and flow with Dark energy.

She watched Elizabeth take one slow step after another. But she was not sure if the smoke in the tunnel was affecting her vision or if she was succumbing to the lack of oxygen, because both Elizabeth and the tunnel were fading to grey.

Elizabeth lifted her back foot to take another step and fully set her weight on the hardened lava. Suddenly, Elizabeth's strength weakened and her balance wavered. The obsidian beneath her cracked.

She held her position and focused her energy. Now she sensed a void in the aura around her. She felt a blackness of dark energy had invaded the tunnel. Had it come through the lava siphon?

'No,' she thought. The darkness was not ahead of her, it was behind her.

Elizabeth directed her senses toward the dark energy, and to her surprise found her mother at its center.

The dark energy had begun to overtake Susan. The color of her eyes had begun to tinge grey.

Elizabeth's energy waned as she sensed the lava rumbling with vigor beneath her and beneath the silo. It called menacingly to her and threatened to bury her and them all.

Susan watched as Elizabeth faded behind a grey curtain. The coldness had been overwhelming all emotions until it at last battled her despair for Elizabeth.

But Susan's despair was still rooted in her love.

'No!' Susan demanded. 'No, I won't stop loving her!' Refusing to let whatever forces at work on her black out her feelings for Elizabeth, she focused intently on that love.

"I belief in you Elizabeth," she gasped and closed her eyes to focus on that thought over and over. "I believe." And with that dedicated thought, the chill in her veins began to warm.

Elizabeth balanced and leaned forward to take her next step, recalling the voices of those she loved and who believed in her.

'Understanding how the world works,' her memory of Martin told her, 'will save lives.'
She again slid another step over the lava, uncertain if it would support her or envelop her. Now, however, she felt the dark energy behind her dissipate. Her strength was returning, and her foot contacted the lava and turned it to obsidian.

Her memory of Aaron came to her from long ago, 'We are wonderful.'

Energy and understanding spilled out from her, and her next step turned rapidly to obsidian just before her foot touched the lava.

Susan looked at her daughter, amazed, tears welling in her eyes. "I believe in you baby." She kept her eyes open and relaxed her breathing, "I believe."

Elizabeth felt a boost of new energy. Sensing it had come from her mother's belief, she was pleased. But she breathed out slowly as she focused directly on the expanding mass of lava in front of her, extending her hand toward the magma.

The rumble from below had become a stampede, and now an avalanche. Except, this avalanche was tumbling upward, directly toward her. The Earth was about to explode.

Elizabeth thrust her hands forward. "Taenoril sil," she commanded.

At once, the sparkling of her vision and the light throughout the tunnel coalesced into her hands, bursting from her fingers directly at the molten geyser.

The geyser cast its rage simultaneously, exploding an endless spout of lava at Elizabeth. Her words and her energy struck the raging Earth's energy head on!

Susan saw the red fire and stone meet the blast of white light and had to turn her head reflexively from the pain to her eyes.

Weeping, she sobbed, "I believe in you, baby."

Steeling herself for the worst, she stood again, opened her eyes, and gaped, amazed as she saw her daughter, not encased in stone or ash, but an aura, an orb of light and iridescence that bathed the tunnel as the sun would bathe and reflect off the water.

The spout of lava was now a fountain-like tower of obsidian, solid in front of Elizabeth, but still seeping lava from its back.

Susan watched Elizabeth draw her hands back to her chest, and both heard and felt the rumbling from below build again to a deafening roar.

* * *

Aaron ran, panting, from the second floor landing into the ventilation room. He knelt beside the damaged ventilation system.

"I'm in... the vent room," he gasped to the intercom.

Leonard's voice called back, "There's not enough time! The carbon monoxide is too much. And even if you did know how to..."

"It's ok," Aaron told him. He had not been talking to Elizabeth during his run up the stairs, but he had been near her, in the way that they had now learned to do. And from that, she had given him a vision of what he needed to know. "Now I understand."

Aaron placed both hands on the fan casing, staring intently into nothing and everything at once.

His breathing quickened, and he drew on that which gave him power.

"I believe in us," Elizabeth's voice told him from his memory. And with it, his breathing calmed.

The silo walls did not, however. They began to shake and the support beams to shudder. But rather than the walls imploding, most of the creaking was coming from the fan casing as it began to move.

'Consider what you believe,' the memory from Martin instructed him. 'Center your energy on what you believe is possible. Focus your belief on those you most believe in.

The shuddering of the casing became a wrenching, and its whine a high-pitched squeal, until exhausted, the ventilation casing under Aaron's hands, settled quietly into its original position.

Placing his hands over the seam, Aaron focused and smoothed the casing metal into the rivet depressions.

Other voices and memories came to Aaron from his mind and heart. A sister's playful adoration, "I think I'll keep you, big bro."

A mother's caress, "I love you. You'll always be my baby..."

And a father's pride, "...so proud, son."

The energy in Aaron swelled, and he extended that power outward, through his hands, and into the casing. With first a jolt and then a screech, the fan spun back to life.

Within moments, the fan rumbled and clanked, gaining more and more speed. Aaron concentrated harder.

Suddenly, the vision of what Elizabeth was seeing appeared to him. He gasped and breathed deeply again, reaching his arms wide along the fan casing.

The fan shifted and balanced, and its grinding stopped, as it whirred soundlessly to life.

Aaron stumbled to the small ventilation control panel, where a gage needle inched its way back toward normal.

* * *

Elizabeth felt the energy rising long before the actual lava geyser blasted again. She extended the energy orb, which surrounded her, directly at the obsidian tower that had just solidified, shattering its pieces throughout the tunnel.

She stood over the lava funnel and gazed down into the fiery geyser. A mass of lava was rising rapidly from the crack in the mantle below.

Peering into that fiery death, she saw not just lava, but disorganized energy. It was dark, swirling and menacing.

She reached out to the expanding mass, placing one hand on the edge of the geyser tower bubbling over with a slow flow of magma, and hovered the other over the opening. With her touch channeling all of her energy, the rim of lava solidified, first obsidian black, then crystallized into clear, multifaceted gemstone.

The stone which she had touched, Elizabeth saw as a fine lattice of connected energy. The rising lava was the same energy she realized, but in chaotic disarray. But it was moldable if she could harness it.

The obsidian under Elizabeth's feet now crystallized from shining black into gleaming diamond. The lava floor opposite her, from the tower and beyond, followed and solidified.

Lava that splattered and spit from the tower itself struck Elizabeth's energy field, transformed instantly to multiple shades of gleaming stone, and from the force of their velocity, scattered around the tunnel.

The raging, rumbling, roar beneath the tunnel protested her efforts to quench its anger and force. The tunnel shook violently, building as the lava rose, faster and faster.

Susan was thrown to the ground. It was only as she brushed dirt from her arms and hands that she noticed her skin was glowing with a faintly yellow aura.

Through the deafening roar, Elizabeth breathed deeply, expanding the energy field around the geyser, and sensed the full expanse of the force assaulting her and her family. The mantle had now completely fractured beneath the silos and had joined into one enormous funnel as wide as the entire silo complex.

Racing up at her was the force and fury of a newly forming volcano.

Elizabeth focused her thoughts and her energy one more time, from her environment and her thoughts, through her body, outward as she thrust her hands into the lava just as the geyser exploded.

However, the explosion did not rage upward.

Elizabeth believed in the love of others with the power of her own sacrifice. And she had directed the full force of that power downward, crystallizing the oncoming tidal wave, directly from molten fiery magma into crystalline gemstone.

So solid was the transformation from mere rock into the hardest of stone, the mantle below had not just sealed, it had shifted back into place, more stable now than when it had formed eons earlier.

The roar had ceased. The rumbled abated. And Susan tearfully stood, stammering as she approached and reached out for Elizabeth.

Elizabeth turned toward her.

Susan gasped to see Elizabeth's brightly shimmering skin and sparkling eyes.

Elizabeth placed a hand on the crystalline wall and concentrated. The last of the rumbles and tremors in the complex ceased.

Then Elizabeth held out her hand to Susan. "Come, mother."

CHAPTER TWENTY-TWO

"It is one light which beams out of a thousand stars. It is one soul which animates all."

-- Ralph Waldo Emerson

The Seeing

Aaron stood in the elevator and relaxed his breathing.

He had not been able to connect with Elizabeth or visualize her experience. The intensity of the energy she had controlled had blocked out his ability to communicate with her. Still, he had felt the wave of stabilization burst outward to not only reinforce the protective field, but grow it by more than double.

So abundant was energy in the silo now, no count down remained, and all systems functioned in abundance.

In abundance too was his relief and thankfulness. He had communicated with Elizabeth only moments before. To know and feel that Elizabeth was alive meant everything to him.

The elevator slowed, stopped, and opened its door to the tenth floor.

* * *

Minutes later the elevator door opened again. This time, not for Aaron, but for Elizabeth and Susan.

Susan followed Elizabeth onto the tenth floor landing, where the Garden room door was now held open by a series of large vines. It appeared to Susan that the once dead Garden had now grown outward from the room, along the landing and stairwell walls.

Susan studied the Garden vines, mesmerized and perplexed.

"Where did these come from?" she asked.

Elizabeth smiled. "Come, mother," she said, guiding Susan into the Garden again.

For Susan, the past twenty minutes had been overwhelming. Her daughter had nearly been lost to a volcano, but had transformed its lava into the most stable form of carbon in existence, using her belief, and an energy form she never knew existed before.

Now inside the Garden nothing surprised Susan. Realizing and now accepting that everything she was seeing was the new reality, Susan visually surveyed the space filled with plants and growth more beautiful than any she had ever seen.

Elizabeth guided them both to the clearing at the center of the room. Aaron and Leonard knelt there, with the baby sleeping in a fresh bundle of blankets, near the small Tree.

Susan could now see that it was a tree, since it had sprouted leaves.

Elizabeth sat down next to Martin, who was lying at the base of the Tree, with its roots covering most of his body in a soft glow.

Aaron stepped around and behind Elizabeth as she placed a hand on Martin's cheek. Martin breathed softly and opened his eyes, smiling contentedly.

"I am so proud of you," he said.

Elizabeth's eyes watered. "You convinced me to study engineering to one day protect this silo?"

Martin smiled mischievously and shook his head slightly. "To one day rebuild a world."

He reached out and held her hand, squeezing it softly. "I knew the dancer, the dreamer, the believer, in you would always be there."

Tears rolled down her cheeks. "Now that I believe, I can make you better, sustain you."

Martin's eyes scanned the Garden, then to the ceiling, seeming to see to the stars.

"There is so much more for me to see, to be," he said. "You are now the Keeper. The energy of your belief is needed in the Garden."

Elizabeth's head dropped, and a tear spilled onto their joined hands.

"Place your belief there," Martin promised, "and I will always be here."

Susan sniffed as tears filled her own eyes. "What are you talking about Martin? You and your crazy ideas. You belong with us."

Martin smiled warmly to Susan. "I always will be."

He held hands with Elizabeth and Susan, as they held hands with Aaron and Leonard.

Like Elizabeth, each of their eyes now sparkled with the irises of those who believed in each other and the energy that such hope can bring.

Susan and Leonard each caught their breath as their sensation and vision expanded beyond the transformed Garden with its lush foliage and vibrant colors.

Each of them traveled with Martin, flying outside the silo complex, where the glowing protective field had expanded, stabilizing the mantle, solidifying the lava, and causing stagnant water to flow and withering plants to grow.

Their focus expanded further, far beyond their protection field, high into the atmosphere. Here, from a satellite's view, they could see the entire continent and hemisphere.

Though the majority of the land masses were still overrun with darkness and instability, in the center of the Amazon rain forest a similar protective glow was clearly growing.

As the Earth rotated beneath them, they saw additional glowing spots in central England, Eastern Africa, and southern Japan.

'Others have survived as well,' thought Elizabeth.

'Thanks to you,' replied Martin.

'Their strength was built upon yours,' he continued. 'Your energy passed through the Tree of the silo Garden to their Trees in their Gardens.'

Susan was overcome with awe at the sight and the realization they had survived. Then a wave of worry came to her.

Feeling this, Leonard asked, 'What's wrong Susan?'

'The Earth. Will it stabilize now or continue to break apart?'

'That all depends,' replied Martin, 'on what you believe.'

They returned then to Montana, the silo, and the Garden.

Martin held them in the Garden, so they could watch themselves from above, hovering overhead.

Then, with a blink of their eyes, Susan and Elizabeth were looking at one another. Elizabeth turned to Aaron, and Susan to Leonard.

They each hugged.

All then turned to Martin. He had not opened his eyes.

Elizabeth caressed and squeezed his hand.

A tear rolled down her cheek and landed on his. Like a raindrop into sand, the tear was immediately absorbed into his skin, and the glow around him intensified.

Elizabeth leaned over him and whispered. "Taenoril..."

"...siiiilll," came the last sound from Martin's body.

The glow between Martin and the roots that covered him intensified, changing from pale green to brighter and brighter white. Soon, he, the roots, and the Tree beyond him, disappeared in the brightness of the light.

"Thank you, Daddy," said Elizabeth through watery eyes.

Then the glow dimmed, faded, and was gone. Martin's body was gone with it.

Elizabeth cried, and Susan wrapped her arms around her in embrace. Tears filled both their eyes.

Aaron's voice broke through their sobs. "Look!"

All turned and saw that on an upper branch of the Tree, one of its many knobs had split open, allowing a flower bud to rise out, growing and glowing.

"What is happening?" asked Susan.

"You are believing," answered Elizabeth. "And believing is seeing."

The brilliantly colored pedals of the flower slowly opened one by one as the lone flower quickly bloomed.

Elizabeth leaned toward it.

All the pedals were now fully opened, and from within the flower stepped a small, glowing being on two legs, with wings.

EPILOGUE

Four Years Later

Omladine (the Age of Belief)

Aaron stepped to the top of a rolling grass covered hill overlooking the wooded areas below.

"Adam!" he called out.

Elizabeth, holding an infant wrapped in a silky blanket, stepped up near Aaron.

"Have you seen Adam?" Aaron asked. "It's nearly time..."

Elizabeth kissed the sleeping child on its pink forehead, then handed the child over to Aaron. She closed her eyes and inhaled softly.

Seconds later, giggling and laughing emanated from behind a cluster of bushes off to one side. From these, a boy ran chasing a floating ball of pale red light. The light hovered and bobbed above him.

A similarly sized girl and a slightly older boy followed immediately after. They too tried to reach the floating light, though all in vain.

Elizabeth and Aaron walked down the path to where the children had circled the light, attempting to coral it as they jumped toward it ineffectually.

From below, the children, Elizabeth, and Aaron were met by Leonard and Susan. Susan placed her hand on her belly and was quite pregnant.

Elizabeth and Susan both closed and opened their eyes.

The children stopped running and jumping and turned dutifully and silently toward their parents.

The floating ball of light hovered four feet off the ground. And, behind the floating light was a softball sized ball of water, suspended in mid air.

Elizabeth nodded toward the water and calmly chided, "Adam."

Adam frowned, but with a wave of his hand the water spilled to the ground, as if released by a pin.

Adam shuffled his feet, "We were just having fun."

Elizabeth regarded the ball of light. "Please forgive them, Dahlia, if their game was unkind."

The bright light glowed softly pink, then bright green. It bobbed in the air in front of them, then once over each child before floating away.

Elizabeth smiled.

"Give good thoughts, children," encouraged Elizabeth. "Leonard and I are leaving soon and may not be back for several days."

The children become animated again. The other boy, Rory, pleaded to Leonard.

"You said I could go!"

"Some day, son," consoled Leonard. "Not today."

The little girl, Kienna spread her best 'daddy please' expression across her face toward Aaron.

"But daddy, the Faeleriel are going. We want to see the colors grow."

Susan rested a calming hand on the little girl's head. "You will dears, soon enough. Life outside the Garden is still unbelieving and needs special care. For now stand by the Tree, hear its song, and when the flowers bloom, ..."

The children finish in unison, "Ar' Ama Gedeon!"

Kienna closed her eyes, pausing a moment, then touched her forehead to a budding stalk of Queen's Ann Lace.

The dozens of tiny flowers bloomed, and from each was released a tiny floating ball of light.

She smiled delightedly as they swirled around her, then scattered into the breeze.

Slowly, the water droplets on the ground next to Adam rose into the air, then suddenly coalesced back into a water ball, and splashed into the side of Adam's face.

Rory laughed and ran down a long spiraling path, chasing Dahlia. The other two children first chased after him, then distracted by a field of flowers that had bloomed and released a flutter of floating lights, danced underneath them.

The parents stood where the cabin had once been and watched their children run through the lush, brilliantly colorful Garden, extending out nearly to the horizon. Every color of the rainbow, and every iridescence of Taenoril sil shone, the colors and glimmers spilling beyond the borders of the objects or beings they decorated.

Far beyond the distant edge of the Garden, the landscape was dark.

Yet from the little hill, the family focused on the countless spiraling paths, each leading toward the enormous willow tree at the center of the Garden, in the middle of what could barely be recognized to have been an airplane runway.

Floating up the path now were a procession of Faeleriel, headed by bobbing creatures resembling winged sea horses. Behind these, fluttered and danced toward the family a myriad colorful defenders of the Garden. As they approached, the defenders parted and the Queen of the Garden gently glided forward.

The children stopped their dancing and waved excitedly toward her. The Queen smiled fondly, then turned to their parents.

'We will open the portal when you are ready,' she communicated with an internal voice that was pleasant and reassuring.

She turned to the entourage around her, and they all disappeared in a flash of light.

The children cheered and jumped back and forth.

Elizabeth slid her fingers through the fingers of one of Aaron's hands and leaned in to rub her nose against her cooing baby's nose. Then looking out across the expanse of Garden, she rested her head on Aaron's shoulder.

"I can hear the other Gardens now," she said. "The world will be new again."

Susan gently rubbed her belly and held Leonard's hand. "It already is."

THE END